earth

TOR BOOKS BY
Ben Bova

Able One

The Aftermath

Apes and Angels

As on a Darkling Plain

The Astral Mirror

Battle Station

The Best of the Nebulas (editor)

Carbide Tipped Pens (coeditor)

Challenges

Colony

Cyberbooks

Death Wave

Empire Builders

Escape Plus

Farside

Gremlins Go Home
(with Gordon R. Dickson)

The Immortality Factor

Jupiter

The Kinsman Saga

Leviathans of Jupiter

Mars Life

Mercury

The Multiple Man

New Earth

New Frontiers

Orion

Orion Among the Stars

Orion and King Arthur

Orion and the Conqueror

Orion in the Dying Time

Out of the Sun

The Peacekeepers

Power Failure

Power Play

Powersat

Power Surge

The Precipice

Privateers

Prometheans

The Return: Book IV of
Voyagers

The Rock Rats

The Sam Gunn Omnibus

Saturn

The Science Fiction Hall of
Fame, Volumes A and B (editor)

The Silent War

Star Peace: Assured Survival

The Starcrossed

Survival

Tales of the Grand Tour

Test of Fire

Titan

To Fear the Light
(with A. J. Austin)

To Save the Sun
(with A. J. Austin)

Transhuman

The Trikon Deception
(with Bill Pogue)

Triumph

Vengeance of Orion

Venus

Voyagers

Voyagers II: The Alien Within

Voyagers III: Star Brothers

The Winds of Altair

earTH

Ben Bova

TOR

A TOM DOHERTY ASSOCIATES BOOK

New York

EARTH

Copyright © 2019 by Ben Bova

A Tor Book
Published by Tom Doherty Associates
175 Fifth Avenue
New York, NY 10010

www.tor-forge.com

Tor® is a registered trademark of Macmillan Publishing Group, LLC.

The Library of Congress Cataloging-in-Publication Data is available upon request.

ISBN 978-0-7653-9719-5 (hardcover)
ISBN 978-0-7653-9721-8 (ebook)

Our books may be purchased in bulk for promotional, educational, or business use. Please contact your local bookseller or the Macmillan Corporate and Premium Sales Department at 1-800-221-7945, extension 5442, or by email at MacmillanSpecialMarkets@macmillan.com.

First Edition: July 2019

Printed in the United States of America

0 9 8 7 6 5 4 3 2 1

To every man is given the key to the gates of heaven; the same key opens the gates of hell.

—*Richard Feynman,*
citing a Buddhist proverb

bOOk OnE

+++
+++

EARTH

MESA VERDE, COLORADO

+++
+++

Para watched the young man intently as the two of them stood at the edge of the huge alcove in the cliffside, and gazed at the ancient buildings.

Outwardly, Trayvon Williamson looked like a typical young postdoc student, handsome in an earnest, eager sort of way. Actually, he was well past one thousand years old, in conventional age, but much of that time had been spent in cryonic suspension as he rode the starship *Saviour* to the Raman star system.

Para's sensors registered Trayvon at a shade over 1.8 meters tall. He was slim and lithe as a young sapling, his handsome face tanned by the sun. But there was something in his dark blue eyes that betrayed . . . what? Not fear, exactly. Not depression, nor anger.

The android's optronic brain circuits ran through the possibilities at nearly the speed of light.

Trayvon Williamson's eyes smoldered with the knowledge of death. Those eyes had seen his two thousand shipmates torn apart and burned to death in a heartbeat's span, and the memory haunted him. It was guilt that blazed in his eyes.

Why me? he was asking himself. Why did I survive while all the others were killed? Why did Felicia have to die and not me?

It took Para's delicate sensors mere nanoseconds to confirm its analysis. Trayvon's heartbeat, his breathing rate, his eyeblink tempo and even the way his fingers jittered all spoke volumes. The young man was haunted by what had happened out in space on the ill-fated mission of the starship *Saviour*.

Trayvon and Para had climbed up the steep steps carved into the cliff face thousands of years ago, and now stood in the shade of the overhanging rock. Standing side by side at the lip of the huge niche, they turned to look down at the green fields that stretched below them out to the horizon.

"How old did you say this city is?" Trayvon asked, in his clear tenor voice.

Para accessed the history records. "At least five thousand years," it replied. "This complex was already a thousand years old when the first Europeans reached this area."

"And it was abandoned."

"Yes. It had been deserted for at least several hundred years when the first Spanish explorers reached this far."

Tray nodded, then turned back and looked into the gigantic niche in the cliff's stone face. A city of two-and three-story adobe structures spread across the alcove in the rock wall for hundreds of meters: silent, empty except for the two of them—and the ghosts of the past.

"The builders created all this and then they just walked away from it," Tray said, as much to himself as to Para.

"They were driven away," his android guardian replied, "by climate shift. The natives moved down into the basin below, to better-watered lands where they could grow their crops."

"Despite their greater vulnerability to attack by hostile tribes down in the basin?"

"Apparently so," answered the android.

Para was a hair's breadth shorter than Trayvon. Completely human in appearance, the android wore a rough-looking hiking jacket of light tan and durable trousers of a slightly darker shade, much the same as Tray himself. Their boots were nearly identical, parceled out to them at the lodge at the base of the trail, far below.

Para's face was bland, its skin a shade lighter than Tray's, smooth and unwrinkled. Its hair was trimmed down to a reddish-brown fuzz, its smile mild and inoffensive. Tray was fascinated with the android's eyes: gray-green optronic visual sensors that could see far into the ultraviolet and infrared ends of the optical spectrum. They could spot a coiled rattler several hundred meters away.

"Have you seen enough?" Para asked.

Tray shook his head. "Can we go into some of the buildings?"

"There's nothing to see inside them. They were all emptied centuries ago."

"Still . . . I'd like to see what they're like inside."

Para gestured with one hand. "This way, then."

It led Tray between two of the structures and through a doorway in the side of one of them. They both had to duck slightly to get through.

"They must have been pretty short," Tray said.

"Average height among them was slightly less than one hundred and fifty centimeters."

They stepped into a roughly square room, completely empty, its floor swept clean of dust and detritus.

"Not much here," Tray admitted.

"I am curious," Para said. "Why did you want to see this complex?"

The beginnings of a smile crept across Tray's face. "I didn't think curiosity was built into you."

"It's not," Para answered easily enough. "I merely used the phrase as an introduction to my question."

Tray spread his arms as he said, "This is one of the oldest human structures in North America. Why shouldn't I want to see it?"

"*You* are curious."

"I guess I am."

"Interesting."

Tray almost laughed. "They say that curiosity killed the cat, but in my case it saved my life."

"And you feel grateful for that?"

"I feel guilty," Trayvon admitted.

Para made a very human nod. But it said, "We've spent just about as much time here as we can. We should be getting back to Denver for your meeting tomorrow with the psychotechnical staff."

a new life

While the sun slipped down toward the distant horizon, Para led Tray back down the narrow precipitous steps to the floor of the valley and the aircar they had left there.

As they climbed into the sleek, bright-skinned vehicle, Tray said, "I've always wanted to fly one of these birds."

Para shook its head. "The passengers do not operate this vehicle. It is operated by the control center, nearly a thousand kilometers away from here."

Tray nodded resignedly. "So I couldn't kill myself even if I wanted to."

"Do you want to?" Para asked, without the slightest hint of alarm.

Shaking his head, Tray replied, "Hell no. I'm not crazy."

As Para swung the car's hatch shut and pressed the button that indicated they were ready for flight, the android said, "Sometimes people who have escaped a tragedy that killed everyone they knew eventually try to commit suicide."

"Not me," said Tray.

"They feel guilty that they survived when so many others died."

"Not me," Tray repeated, more emphatically.

Para fed the young man's response into its data file and leaned back in the softly enfolding seat. Sitting beside the android, Tray leaned back too, seemingly relaxed.

The aircar buzzed to life, rose some ten meters above the grassy valley floor, then accelerated gently into a climbing curve that aimed it slightly east of due north, above the bare granite peaks of the Rockies, toward the Greater Denver complex.

Folding its hands on its lap, Para said gently, "The visual sensors in your bedroom show a good deal of REM movement in your eyes while you are sleeping. You appear to be dreaming quite a bit."

Gazing down at the bare gray-brown peaks below them, Trayvon said, "I have dreams, yes."

"Recurring dreams?"

Tray turned and looked at the android. It appeared perfectly human, relaxed, but something in those calm gray-green optronic eyes spoke silently of a purpose, a goal, a *reason* behind its bland questioning.

Almost, Trayvon smiled to himself. Para's a machine. It's doing what it's been programmed to do. Don't get angry at it.

"The dreams aren't all the same," he said calmly. "Not recurring. But they all deal with my life aboard the *Saviour*. And the ship's destruction."

"A swarm of micrometeors," Para said.

Knowing the android was pumping his memories, Tray nodded. "Micrometeors, yes. That's the most popular theory for the cause of the explosion. Supposedly they were moving so fast, and there were so many of them, that they overwhelmed the ship's shields."

"And destroyed it."

"And killed everyone aboard . . . except me."

"You weren't aboard the ship."

"I was in a pod on the other side of the star system. I was being punished."

Para fell silent.

It already knows the whole story, Tray told himself. It's just trying to get into my mind, trying to learn how I feel about it, how I'm handling the guilt.

In his mind's eye Trayvon saw once again the star Raman blazing like a blue diamond against the darkness of space. Eleven planets circled the star, the farthest of them the home of an intelligent species that was in danger of being destroyed by the wave of lethal gamma radiation hurtling outward from the core of the Milky Way galaxy at the speed of light. The starship *Saviour* had been sent from Earth to bring them shielding that would save them from the approaching Death Wave.

Trayvon was among the starship's crew, an astronomer whose assignment was to map the fields of asteroids that orbited between the system's major planets: tiny pieces of rock and ice, most as small as pebbles, a few the size of mountains.

But Trayvon had run afoul of the captain's inflexible ideas of discipline and was undergoing punishment by being assigned to a lonely one-man scoutship sent to the opposite end of the star system to map one of the asteroid swarms swinging out in the lonely darkness, far from the one world that harbored an intelligent species.

From across the diameter of the Raman system Tray saw the *Saviour* ripped apart, apparently by a swarm of micrometeors that he had not yet mapped, all its crew slaughtered.

Centuries later a new starship had returned to the Raman system and found Trayvon still aboard the scoutship, frozen in cryonic suspension by the vessel's automated systems. He was revived and returned to Earth, slightly more than a thousand years after he had originally departed.

After nearly a year of intensive psychotherapy, Trayvon was

released from clinical psychological treatment and given to the care of a therapeutic android: Para.

At last Para asked, "Why were you being punished?"

It's all in the ship's log, Tray wanted to reply. The ship's log was transmitted back Earthward on a nanosecond-by-nanosecond basis. They already knew the whole story. Resentment smoldered inside Tray. Why are they putting me through this again?

With a bitter smile, Trayvon answered, "I've always considered myself something of a musician. The captain forbade me from touching my musical instruments. I used them to compose on my own time, in my own quarters. He found out about it and punished me."

"And that's why you were at a safe distance when the *Saviour* was destroyed."

Tray was surprised to find that his voice would not work. All he could do was nod mutely.

Para smiled wisely. "So here you are, alive and well. A new life."

Tray nodded again. But he asked himself, What happens next? What am I supposed to do with my new life? Alone. A thousand years distant from my original life.

An eternity away from Felicia.

PSYCH STAFF

++

++++ ++

At precisely nine o'clock the next morning, Para rapped gently on the front door of Trayvon's apartment. Tray opened the door immediately, wearing a relaxed outfit of creaseless tan slacks and a long-sleeved pullover sweater of a slightly darker brownish hue.

Smiling brightly at the android, Tray announced cheerily, "I'm ready to have my brain picked!"

Para made a smile in return. It could see past the young man's bravado. Tray's eyes were darting nervously; there was a hint of perspiration on his forehead.

"Let's go, then," said the android.

"Let's," Tray agreed.

The medical complex's psychotechnical staff was housed on the fifty-second floor of a tower that stood a mere five minutes' stroll from Tray's apartment building. Side by side they walked along the crowded broad avenue, rode the express elevator, and entered the anteroom of Dr. Kimbal Atkins's suite, where a robotic assistant silently led them into the inner office.

The office had no desk, no conference table, no trappings of

bureaucratic power. Just a scattering of comfortable-looking armchairs with a low coffee table in their midst.

Two men and a woman rose to their feet as Tray and Para were
ushered into the office by the compactly built robot.

"Mr. Williamson," said the elder of the two men.

Tray gaped at him. Dr. Kimbal Atkins was *old*, the oldest human
being Tray had ever seen. He was no taller than Tray's shoulder,
stocky and big-bellied. His head was completely bald except for a few
wisps of dead-white hair. He wore an old-fashioned three-piece suit
of cheerless gray. His face was spiderwebbed with thin wrinkles, his
deep brown eyes were watery, but focused squarely on Tray.

Extending his slightly trembling hands, he advanced on Tray,
saying in a soft, whispery voice, "I'm so glad you could come to talk
with us."

Tray knew that an invitation from the head of the Psychotech
Department was more like a court summons than a request, but
he said nothing as Atkins led him gently to a comfortable armchair
next to the bare coffee table. Para remained by the door, seemingly
frozen into immobility.

Atkins introduced, "My colleagues: Dr. Jerome Ferguson—"

Tray shook Ferguson's extended hand. He was a handsome man,
nearly two meters tall, with a warm, disarming smile.

Para flashed a condensed biography to Tray's implanted communicator. Ferguson was a New Zealander, one of the world's leading experts in treating phobias.

"And this," Atkins continued, "is Dr. Lakshmi Ramesh."

A small, slim dark-skinned woman, Tray thought she'd look
more at home in a colorful sari than in the severely tailored russet
pants suit she was wearing.

"Hindu," Para flashed to Tray's communicator. "Nobel Prize
laureate for her work in trauma eradication."

"I'm pleased to meet you," Tray said as he took her extended hand.

"And I you," Dr. Ramesh replied, with a smile that gleamed in her dark face.

Atkins gestured for them all to sit down. As he did so, Tray saw that his chair had been placed at the focal point of the other three. Atkins was on his right, Ferguson on his left, and the attractive Dr. Ramesh sat directly in front of him.

For an instant no one spoke. Then Atkins said, "Now then, what are we to do about your condition, Mr. Williamson?"

With a smile that was only partially forced, Tray replied, "That's what I'm here to find out."

Dr. Ferguson leaned forward slightly in his capacious armchair, a friendly grin on his narrow-featured face. "We've gone over your record quite exhaustively."

"And?"

Her lovely face utterly serious, Dr. Ramesh said, "Memory erasure is indicated."

Tray felt his breath catch. "Memory erasure? Sounds serious."

Dr. Atkins reached out and patted Tray's knee. "It's nothing to be frightened of."

"It's a treatment that's been done safely for more than a century," said Dr. Ferguson, his smile somewhat dimmer than a few moments earlier.

"There is hardly any risk at all," Dr. Ramesh said.

Tray heard himself repeat "Memory erasure." He didn't like the sound of it.

"Let me explain," said Dr. Atkins, in his soft, whispery voice. Tray nodded at the old man.

"Psychological traumas are rooted in memories that are stored in the brain. Erase those memories and the trauma can be eradicated."

"Eradicated," Tray echoed.

"Quite completely," said Dr. Ramesh.

"And what gets eradicated with the trauma?"

MEMORY WIPE

+++
++++ +++

"Practically nothing!" Dr. Ferguson replied.

Tray stared at the man. He looked honest enough, eager to convince Tray there was nothing dangerous about the procedure. Which was what he believed, obviously.

But Tray wasn't convinced.

Atkins understood Tray's reluctance. "Back in the old days," he explained, "when we had to depend on chemical injections to inhibit memories, there were more than a few cases of overdoses, near-fatal memory loss."

"But that was before we met the Predecessors," Ferguson interrupted.

Out of the corner of his eye Tray saw Para—still standing by the door—lift its chin a notch. The Predecessors were the race of intelligent machines that had first warned humankind of the approaching Death Wave.

"The Predecessors," Tray repeated.

Dr. Ramesh explained, "They shared with us their development of positronic brain probes."

"Which they had developed when they decided to create the humanoids that eventually made contact with us," Ferguson finished for her.

Tray shook his head. "This is getting deep."

Smiling benignly, Dr. Atkins took control of the explanation. "The salient point is that we learned about positronic brain probes from the Predecessors and developed the technology to perfect our memory erasure technique."

"And it works fine," Ferguson said firmly. "No worries."

No worries, Tray thought. It's not *his* brain they want to invade.

"So there you are," Atkins said, with a spread of his liver-spotted hands. "We probe your brain, remove the memories associated with Felicia Cantore, and you're free of the inhibitory trauma that's crippling your personality."

"Remove all my memories of Felicia?"

"Yes. Total eradication. It will be as if you'd never known her."

"But I don't want to have my memories of Felicia erased!"

"It's for your own good," Dr. Ramesh said, earnestly.

"I want to remember her!" Tray insisted. "I think of her every day. Every night."

"And that's crippling your emotional development," snapped Dr. Ferguson.

"I don't care!" Tray half-shouted. "I won't give up my memories of Felicia!"

Ferguson stared at him for a disappointed moment, then turned to Dr. Atkins. Dr. Ramesh look as if she wanted to say something, but instead turned her head and also looked toward Atkins.

The chief of the Psychotech Department shook his head like a sadly disappointed grandfather, then said gently, "I'm afraid that decision is not entirely yours to make. We are required to make our own recommendation to the medical division's board of governors. You will probably be required to submit to the memory erasure procedure."

Tray stared at the old man, too stunned and angry to reply. But he was thinking, Like hell I will!

invitation

++++++++++++++++++++++++++++++,+++++++++++++++++++++++
+++

with para at his side, tray left the meeting and—
fuming—went down the elevator and out onto the
sunny, busy boulevard.

For hours they strode in silence through the crowds of pedes-
trians, Tray telling himself he should cool down, drown his anger.
But he muttered irritably, "Nobody's going to erase *my* memories."

Para did not respond. It merely walked at Tray's side, in silence.

Para never argues with me, Tray realized. It just goes along until
I've calmed down, and then tries to reason with me. With an inner
grumble, Tray told himself, Well, this is one time reasoning isn't
going to work. I don't want to forget Felicia, and that's that!

Finally they stood before the building that housed Tray's apartment. They went up an elevator, then along a moving carpeted
hallway to Tray's quarters.

"I will wait here in the corridor while you change into a fresh
outfit," said Para.

"No," Tray countered. "Come in with me. Keep me company."

"Are you certain . . . ?"

"I'm not angry with you, Para. It's Atkins and his knuckleheaded
assistants that I'm sore with."

Para was incapable of sighing, but the android gave every

appearance of being distressed. "Dr. Atkins has the authority to command you to undergo a memory erasure procedure."

Grimly, Tray replied, "He can command it. But can he make me obey his command?"

"Let's hope it doesn't come to a confrontation," said Para.

Tray opened the door to his apartment. Para hesitated.

With a ghost of a smile, Tray said, "You're the closest thing I have to a friend, Para. Come in with me, please."

Para knew that Trayvon had been introduced to a small army of people his own age: medical personnel, human relations experts, other patients. He had been polite with them, even social. He had attended parties with them, joined them in outings beyond the medical facility's grounds, spent long evenings in earnest discussions with small, intimate groups. But he had formed no lasting relationships, made no real friends, had no sexual encounters.

It was as if Trayvon Williamson was himself an android: human in appearance and behavior, but incapable of truly human interactions.

Para stepped into the three-room apartment's sitting room. Tray headed for the bedroom to shower and change for dinner. The android had been in the room many times before. It was neatly decorated with comfortable furniture and electronic wall hangings that could be changed by voice command. At present they showed views of great architecture: the Pyramids, the Great Wall of China, the Survivors' Plinth in drowned Manhattan, the Geodesic Dome that protected Florence.

All unchanged since the day Trayvon had first stepped into this apartment, Para saw.

One corner of the sitting room was filled with Tray's musical assembly, noisemakers of various pitches and timbres, covered with a thin coating of dust. Untouched for weeks on end, obviously.

As it listened to the sounds of rushing water from the bathroom shower, Para wondered how it could break through the iron barrier Tray had built around himself. The android had hoped that the visit to Mesa Verde might have begun to open Tray's barricaded personality. Apparently not. The young man remained behind the protective walls he had built, alone with his feelings of guilt.

Is memory erasure the only way to help him? Para wondered.

At last Tray came in from his bedroom, dressed in a crisp new outfit of silver jacket, slacks, and a collarless shirt of glittering blue, nearly the color of his eyes.

"Where shall we have dinner?" he asked, almost eagerly. "I'm tired of the restaurants here in the center. Let's go into town for something interesting."

Para imitated a human reaction: It nodded. "You have been invited to a reception at the World Council regional center—"

Tray felt his face twist with distaste. "A diplomatic reception? One of those stuffed-shirt affairs? Why in the world—"

"It's being given to honor Jordan Kell. It's his birthday."

"Jordan Kell?" Tray blinked with disbelief. "I thought he was dead. Or at least retired."

Para replied, "Retired, not dead."

"He must be a million years old."

"Approaching three thousand," Para said. "Of course, most of that time had been spent in cryonic suspension."

"He's gone on several star missions," Tray acknowledged.

"He led the first one, to Sirius. The one where we first met the Predecessors."

"And learned about the Death Wave."

"He married one of the women he met at Sirius," Para added.

Tray nodded. "A human, created by the Predecessors from tissue samples that they took while visiting Earth. Secretly."

"It's a very romantic story."

Tray stared at his android guardian for a silent moment, his mind obviously considering the possibilities.

"If we go to this reception . . ." he hesitated for a heartbeat, then went on, "do you think we'd actually get to meet Jordan Kell?"

Para realized that this was the first real enthusiasm it had seen in its charge. "I believe it might be possible to arrange a meeting," it said, straightfaced.

Trayvon overlooked the equivocation. "Then let's go meet him!"

As it recorded the spark of interest in Tray's behavior for later study, Para ordered an air taxi.

JORDAN KELL

++
+++

Tray ducked out of the taxi's door and gaped at the regional headquarters of the world council.

It was a massive, imposing building, blazing with lights. Among Denver's soaring, earthquake-proof mega-towers, the World Council building was a magnificent structure, only a few stories high but sprawling across more than a thousand hectares.

"Versailles," Para said as it and Tray stood at the curb gaping at its splendor. "Copied from the French palace near Paris. The original was built by Louis XIV and opened in 1682. It contained 2,300 rooms in a space of 63,154 square meters."

"It's . . ." Tray fumbled for a word. ". . . big."

Para's lips curled slightly. "Its purpose was to overawe the nobility and completely humble the peasantry."

"I guess it did that."

"Yes. But it didn't prevent the French Revolution. Louis's grandson, Louis XVI, was executed in 1793, together with his wife. Thousands were guillotined during the Reign of Terror."

Tray nodded, remembering his childhood history lessons. He and Para started up a curving walkway toward the palace.

It stood in the middle of a graceful green park. Tray saw bison munching contentedly on prairie grasses off to one side. Delicate columns flanked the building's entrance. A handful of people—the men in dark suits, many of them bearing colorful ribbons on their chests, the gowned women glittering with jewelry—were mounting the stone steps of the entrance, attended by robotic servants.

"We're late," Tray said.

"Not really," Para reassured him. "Kell himself hasn't arrived yet."

Tray started to ask the android how he knew that, then realized that Para's internal communications equipment linked him intimately with data systems around the world and even out in space.

Side by side they walked up the steps to the building's entrance. A single person stood at the open doors, tall and stately, wearing a modern suit of black that reflected the lights from inside the big double doorway. He smiled and nodded at the arriving guests. Tray guessed that it was an android, but it was impossible to be sure, it looked completely human although it wore the dark-jacketed attire of a servant.

"Trayvon Williamson and Para," said the greeter, with a fixed smile. Tray realized his guess was correct: It was an android. It had scanned them as they came up the stairs. "Welcome, gentlemen." It gestured them through the doorway.

They stepped into a crowded foyer, buzzing with dozens of conversations. Tray knew none of the people there. It was impossible to tell their ages or their backgrounds. They all looked youthful, in the prime of life. Tray felt out of place and badly underdressed in his silver jacket and open-necked shirt.

"I'm not in the right uniform," he whispered to Para.

"It's perfectly all right," said the android, its eyes pointing to another young man; this one in a hunter green outfit. "Formal dress is optional."

Tray realized that Para had checked the requirements for this dinner before they'd left his apartment. He felt better, but still out of place. Try to relax, he told himself. Nobody cares what you're wearing. But still he felt uncomfortable.

The young man in the green jacket and slacks came up to him, a beautiful dark-haired young woman on his arm.

With a beaming smile, he said, "It's good to see someone else who isn't wearing a monkey suit."

Tray forced a smile. "I didn't realize we were coming here until the last minute."

"Doesn't matter," the man said, with a shake of his well-coiffed light brown hair.

"You look fine," said his companion, smiling beautifully. She was the most magnificent woman Tray had ever seen: tall, graceful, utterly lovely. Midnight dark hair tumbling to her bare shoulders. Eyes the color of sapphires.

"And you look beautiful," Tray blurted.

"Thank you, kind sir," she said, dimpling into a smile.

The man introduced himself and his companion. "I'm Mance Bricknell, and this is Loris De Mayne. We're with the Geophysics Department at the university."

Tray couldn't take his eyes off Loris De Mayne. She was nearly his height, clad in a sparkling strapless gown, stunning.

"And you are . . ." she prompted.

"Trayvon Williamson," Tray gulped. Turning slightly, "And this is Para, my mentor."

"Mentor?" Loris De Mayne's beautiful face contorted slightly into a puzzled frown.

"I'm a patient at the hospital," Tray said, feeling foolish, awkward.

Bricknell's eyes widened slightly. "You're the survivor from that starship that blew up!" he realized.

"Yes," Tray admitted. "That's me."

"You've been on a starship mission," Loris said, as if it were important.

"The only survivor," said Bricknell, almost like an accusation.

Tray didn't know what to say, what to do. He wanted the floor to open up beneath his feet and swallow him.

Para saved the awkwardness by nodding toward the foyer's entrance. "I believe the guest of honor has just arrived."

Everyone was turning toward the entrance as a man of medium stature, clad in a handsome suit of pearl gray, stepped into the crowded foyer. His face was thin: sharp cheekbones, an almost-hawkish aquiline nose, a slim mustache over a smile that looked to Tray to be almost shy, apologetic.

"Jordan Kell," said Bricknell, in a whisper that was close to adoring.

"It's him," Tray heard himself say.

"Yes," said Para, at his side.

Kell was not imposing physically, nearly a head shorter than Tray, elegantly slender and lithe. Yet he seemed to radiate confidence, authority. He stood smiling at the doorway as the evening's guests arranged themselves into a reception line to greet him.

"Come on." Bricknell tugged at Loris De Mayne's slim, graceful wrist. "Let's greet the guest of honor."

Tray followed the two of them, with Para at his side.

"I thought Kell was married to that woman from New Earth," he said as they stepped into the reception line.

"She died," Para half-whispered. "He's been alone for many years."

"He hasn't remarried?"

"No."

Conversations along the reception line dwindled to hurried whispers as Kell slowly made his way among the guests, smiling, nodding, having a few words with each person before moving along.

At last he reached Tray.

As Tray extended his hand, Kell's smile faded into a serious expression. "You're Trayvon Williamson, aren't you?" he asked.

"Yes, sir," Tray replied.

"It's good to meet you, young man. We have a lot to talk about."

Feeling surprised, stunned, Tray gulped, "We do?"

"Oh, yes indeed," said Kell. Grasping Tray's hand firmly, he said, "Later, when these formalities are over."

Tray nodded and repeated, "Later."

Kell stepped to Para, shook the android's hand and muttered a few words, then proceeded down the long reception line, smiling and nodding, continuing his brief conversations with each guest.

Tray followed Kell with his eyes until Loris De Mayne caught his attention with, "Shall we head for the bar?"

Before Tray could think of a response, Para said, "Roberts's rules of procedure state that a motion to head for the bar is always in order."

Bricknell laughed, took Loris by her braceleted arm, and led the way through the crowd from the foyer to the dining room, where a small squad of android bartenders was busily serving drinks to the guests.

SPEECHES

+++
+++

The dinner seemed tedious to Tray.

He and Para were seated at a table for six, near the dining area's rear, far from the head table, next to the sliding door that apparently led to the kitchen. Robotic waiters rolled through the doorway, carrying the various dinner courses to the tables arranged across the dining area's vast floor.

The room was enormous. Tray thought that half the population of Denver could be seated in it with room to spare. Magnificent draperies hung at the three-story-high windows that lined the side walls. Chandeliers dripping with flickering candle-like lights hung from the high, shadowed ceiling.

Bricknell and Loris De Mayne had been seated at one of the tables up front, near the long, raised head table where Jordon Kell and the other notables sat.

Tray picked at the salad and then at the meager slice of unidentifiable roast meat that the robots served. Para ate nothing, of course, but sat looking attentively at the head table as speaker after speaker droned on endlessly. Kell sat in the guest-of-honor's chair, apparently listening thoughtfully to each of the speeches.

Most of the speakers were men, each of them congratulating themselves on how they had helped the human race survive the

Death Wave of lethal gamma radiation that had swept through the Milky Way galaxy.

"We have survived," one of the speakers blared triumphantly. "We have faced the worst that nature can throw at us and survived."

The audience applauded politely.

"And more than that," the speaker thundered on. "We have helped other intelligent species to survive the Death Wave. We have triumphed over death itself!"

That brought most of the substantial audience to their feet, clapping lustily.

Once they settled down again, the speaker half-turned toward Kell, seated beside him.

With a huge, satisfied grin, the speaker announced, "And now it is my privilege and honor to introduce a man who needs no introduction, the man who has led the human race through the emergency to triumph, the former president of the Interplanetary Council—Mr. Jordan Kell!"

The entire audience rose to its feet as a single creature and rocked the mammoth room with applause. Tray found himself standing, banging his hands together lustily, just as mesmerized by the moment as all the others. Until he noticed that Para, on his feet beside him, was clapping only perfunctorily.

Once they sat down again, Tray leaned toward the android and asked, "You aren't impressed with emotional oration?"

Para made the beginnings of a smile. "I'm afraid that such a reaction is not within my range of capabilities."

Tray nodded, then turned his attention to Kell, now standing at the speaker's podium.

"I fear that I don't have much to add to Senator Stover's oration. We have survived the Death Wave, thanks to the help of the Predecessors. We have indeed helped other intelligent species to survive that lethal danger. We have suffered losses in this quest and we grieve for them."

Tray saw that Kell was speaking without notes, without a prepared text. Or, he wondered, does the man have his speech recorded somehow in his brain? With microimaging, that was possible, he realized.

Kell was going on, "We have taken on a deep responsibility. We have contacted sixty-three intelligent races among the stars within a two-thousand-light-year radius. Most of them are not as developed as we are. Most of them had no inkling that a wave of lethal gamma radiation was approaching their worlds. Most of them would have been wiped out if we hadn't protected their worlds with the proper shielding.

"Now the question is, where do we go from here? Do we abandon those worlds and leave them to develop on their own? Or do we try to help them, guide them, lead them to a richer, fuller existence?

"The choice is ours. We cannot avoid it."

The capacious room fell absolutely still. Tray felt as if all the people at their tables had been frozen into silence.

Kell looked out at his vast audience for a long, silent moment. Then he nodded once and said, "Thank you."

argument

The dinner broke up quickly after Kell's brief speech. Most of the guests streamed toward the doors at the rear of the hall, although a few dozen men and women gravitated toward Kell, still at the head table.

Tray saw that Bricknell took Loris by the hand and headed for the crowd clustered around Kell while he stood uncertainly by his emptying dinner table.

Gesturing toward the head table, Para said, "Councilman Kell said he was looking forward to speaking with you."

"Yes," Tray said uncertainly.

With a barely detectable nod, Para confirmed, "You should go up there and speak with him."

Tray nodded uncertainly, but started forward, Para at his side.

By the time they made their way to the front of the hall, the crowd around Kell had diminished somewhat. Tray saw that Loris was still standing beside Mance Bricknell, her eyes focused on Kell, as if there was no one else in the cavernous room.

Standing beside Kell was a tall, broad-shouldered man with thick dark hair and an intent look in his deeply brown almost-black eyes.

Jabbing an extended forefinger toward Kell's chest, he was saying, "You're right, as usual, Jordan. We have a tremendous opportunity before us."

"A tremendous *responsibility*, Harold," said Kell mildly.

The man broke into a deep, toothy chuckle. "Responsibility, opportunity . . . it's all the same thing in the final analysis, isn't it?"

"Not quite, I'm afraid."

Still grinning, the man countered, "Don't split hairs, Jordan. The human race is on the threshold of a new era. An interstellar community! We're going to be the leader of an interstellar community."

Smiling uneasily, Kell turned slightly toward Trayvon and beckoned him to come stand beside him. "Harold, I'd like you to meet the sole survivor of the *Saviour* disaster."

The big man's face flashed puzzlement for an instant, then his hearty smile returned. He put out his meaty hand. As Tray reached for it, Kell made the introduction:

"Trayvon Williamson, this is Harold Balsam, currently president of the Interplanetary Council."

Balsam's grip engulfed Tray's hand, powerful, smothering.

"How do you do, Trayvon Williamson?" he said.

"It's good to meet you, sir," said Tray.

Still smiling brightly, Balsam turned back to Kell and said, "The *Saviour* was the only ship we lost. You know that."

With a curt nod, Kell replied, "You're forgetting the *Mishima* mutiny."

Balsam's smile winked out. "The court ruled it wasn't a mutiny."

"But people were killed."

For a moment, Balsam looked exasperated. But he put on his smile again and said, "Even with that, we've had an excellent record in our star missions. Excellent record."

Kell made a brusque nod. "I can't deny that."

Bricknell jumped into the confrontation. "I've volunteered for a star mission."

"Have you?" Balsam said, his smile widening. "Good for you, young man."

"This is Mance Bricknell," Kell introduced. Gesturing toward Loris, "And Loris De Mayne. Both geophysicists."

Balsam focused on Loris. "And are you going to the stars also?"

Before she could reply, Bricknell said, "I'm trying to convince her that she should."

Looking slightly flustered, Loris said, "I have . . . obligations . . . responsibilities, here on Earth."

"Our future is among the stars," Balsam said. "It's inevitable."

Kell said, "I quite agree."

"You do?" Balsam said, with exaggerated astonishment. "Then what are we arguing about?"

With a tight smile, Kell replied, "I wasn't aware that we were arguing, Harold."

Balsam laughed and patted Kell's shoulder. "You're right, Jordan. We're both on the same team, despite minor differences."

"I suppose so," said Kell.

"Good," said Balsam. "Good." Turning toward Tray and the others still clustered around the speaker's podium, Balsam raised his voice to say, "I'm afraid I must bid you all good night. I still have miles to go before I sleep."

Kell's thin lips arched into a smile. "The woods are lovely, dark and deep," he murmured.

Balsam looked puzzled briefly. "What's that . . . oh, another part of the poem." He grinned at Kell. "Good for you, Jordan. Quick on your feet, as usual."

With that Balsam turned and headed toward the doors at the rear of the hall. But not without a long glance at Loris De Mayne. Tray thought the man came close to leering at her. It made him feel annoyed.

Jordan Kell said softly, "Mr. Williamson."

Suddenly feeling red-faced with embarrassment, Tray pulled his attention away from Loris. "Yes, sir?"

"I'd like to talk with you about your time on the *Saviour*."

"Of course," Tray replied. "What would you like to know?"

"Not here," Kell said, his face looking almost amused at Tray's eagerness. "Could you come to my office sometime tomorrow?"

"Certainly," said Tray. "What time would be good for you, sir?"

Kell pursed his lips slightly, then answered, "Why don't we have lunch together? Could you come by my office around noonish?"

"Certainly! Of course."

"Fine." Turning to Para, Kell said, "I presume you can find my office."

"Of course," said Para.

"Excellent. I'll see the two of you around noon tomorrow, then."

Para made a slight bow of acknowledgment. So did Tray.

Kell said farewell to Bricknell and De Mayne, then left the table. Tray noticed that a pair of husky-looking young men fell in step behind him. Bodyguards? Tray wondered. Why would he need bodyguards?

Mance Bricknell let out a soft whistle. "Jordan Kell wants to talk with you in private," he said, his voice edged with wonder. "That's an opportunity."

"Opportunity?" Tray questioned.

"I mean," Bricknell said, almost stammering, "Kell is one of the most important people in the solar system. And he wants to talk with you! In private, no less!"

Tray glanced at Loris De Mayne, who was staring at him. "I suppose he wants a firsthand description of the . . . the . . ."

"Disaster," Para finished for him.

Tray nodded. He found it difficult to get more words past his constricting throat.

"It must have been awful for you," said Loris, her voice low, sympathetic.

Tray saw that the big dining hall was nearly empty now. Robotic waiters were clearing the tables like a procession of ants marching back and forth from their nest.

The three of them—even Para—were waiting for him to say something. In his mind's eye Tray saw the starship's explosion from across the diameter of the Raman system. A sudden glare of light. Then nothing. Tray remembered how he had fumbled with his capsule's telescope controls. Nothing to be seen but scraps of twisted metal hurtling outward from the explosion. Nothing recognizable as a human body.

He realized that his hands were shaking again. He pulled in a deep breath and struggled to command his body.

"I . . . I was the only one to survive the explosion," he said, his voice faint, weak with memories. "The capsule's automated systems tranquilized me. The next thing I knew, the medical team from the rescue mission had reawakened me. Three hundred and seventy years had passed."

"And you were unconscious all that time," Loris said, her voice as muted as Tray's own.

"Cryonic suspension," Tray said. "Deep sleep. It's as close to death as a human body can come."

"For three hundred and seventy years," Bricknell murmured.

Para spoke up. "But that was all in the past. Trayvon is here with us now, alive, ready to take up his life once again."

Tray nodded, but fought down the urge to ask, "What life?"

LUNCHEON

+++

+++

Tray was surprised to see Harold Balsam in Jordan Kell's office. At dinner the previous night he'd caught a strong impression of competition, rivalry, between the two men. But there was Balsam sitting before Kell's efficient little desk, imposingly large, relaxed, and smiling.

Kell got up from his high-backed padded chair and came around his desk as Tray and Para entered the office. It was a sizable room, thickly carpeted, with a round conference table in one corner and a ceiling-high credenza opposite. Low bookshelves and cabinets lined the other walls; artworks from across the solar system hung everywhere. On the other side of the room a handsome wide floor-length window looked out on the complex of buildings that made up the headquarters of the Interplanetary Council.

Tray stared out at the bewildering mix of building styles. He recognized a replica of the Parthenon from Athens, another columned temple that looked vaguely Aztec, and a beautifully graceful structure that must have been copied from Angkor Wat in Cambodia; in the center of the sprawling hodgepodge of styles a soaring skyscraper dominated the entire mixture.

As Tray stepped uncertainly into the office Balsam half-turned in his handsomely striped armchair, a wide smile on his beefy face.

"Trayvon," said Kell, extending both his arms toward him, "I'm so glad you could come."

Tray shook Kell's hand and nodded toward Balsam. Para stopped just inside the door while Kell gestured Tray to the luxurious chair next to Balsam's. Feeling a bit uneasy, out of place, Tray sat down next to the Council's president.

As Kell retook his handsome desk chair he gestured toward Balsam and said, "Harold here has invited me on a trip to Jupiter."

Smiling broadly, Balsam said, "I was surprised—shocked, really—to learn that Jordan's never seen the Leviathans."

"I've seen the videos and the data files," Kell said, almost defensively. "I've reviewed all the pertinent information about them."

With a shake of his head, Balsam said, "But that's not the same as seeing them for real. Creatures as big as cities, swimming in Jupiter's endless ocean! You owe it to yourself to see them with your own eyes."

"Perhaps you're right," Kell admitted.

Balsam reached out and jabbed Tray's shoulder. "Now that's a typical politician's answer. Perhaps I'm right." With a deep-throated chuckled, he added, "What he's really saying is 'Go away, Harold. Stop bothering me.'"

"Not at all!" Kell protested.

"I've outfitted a ship and a deep-diving vessel," Balsam went on. "Completely at my own expense. Won't cost your beloved taxpayers a centavo. All expenses paid. Out to Jupiter, dive into the ocean, see the Leviathans firsthand."

Kell glanced at the ceiling, as if seeking heavenly guidance, Tray thought. Then he focused on Balsam once again.

"Harold, you're making it very hard for me to say no."

"Then you'll do it? When?"

Breaking into a happy grin, Kell said, "How long will the trip take?"

"Three weeks, maximum. We'll jet out to the Jupiter system at one-gee, spend the maximum time in the ocean with the big beasties."

"Three weeks." Kell's smile diminished somewhat. "All right. When do we start?"

Balsam muttered, "Let me check . . ." He closed his eyes briefly, and Tray realized he was contacting an aide through an inbuilt communicator. "Two weeks from today. How's that fit your schedule, Jordan?"

Kell turned to the screen at one side of his desk. "Looks doable."

"Great!" Balsam heaved himself up from the chair and stuck his arm across Kell's desk. "My people will send you all the details."

Rising to his feet, Kell said, "Fine." He glanced at Tray and added, "I'd like Mr. Williamson to come with me, if that's all right with you, Trayvon."

Tray gasped, "Me?"

"You. Are you game?"

Tray gulped once, then answered, "Certainly!"

"The two of you, then," Balsam said cheerfully. "And that young man we were talking to last night. What's his name? Bracknell?"

"Bricknell," Kell corrected. "Mance Bricknell."

"And his girlfriend. Loris something-or-other."

"I'll see if they're willing to go," Kell said.

"They will be," Balsam said firmly. "It's the chance of a lifetime. To see those big whale things up close and personal."

He nodded once, as if convincing himself that he was right. Then, "Well, I've got to run. Lots of details to attend to."

And he hurried out of Jordan Kell's office, leaving Tray feeling astonished. Even Para, standing by the door, seemed puzzled.

Blinking, Tray said to Kell, who was still on his feet behind his desk, "That man moves like a lightning bolt."

His eyes still on the partially open door, Kell nodded warily. "Yes, he does, doesn't he?"

Luncheon was served at the big round table in the corner of Kell's office by a pair of robots—salad, delicate sandwiches of meat and cheese, and a light creamy dessert.

Kell asked questions about the *Saviour* disaster, gently probing Tray's memory. To his own surprise, Tray found himself speaking quite easily. It was as if once he started recalling the tragedy he couldn't stop talking about it.

The two men sat with the littered remains of their luncheon scattered across the table, while Tray talked nonstop and Para sat inertly beside him. Tray knew the android was recording every word he said and sending it all to the psychotechnicians back at the hospital, but it didn't matter to him. Once he began to speak it all came out in a steady, suffering stream.

"There wasn't anything I could do," Tray said, his voice low, steady, unflinching. "I was orbiting more than twelve billion kilometers from the *Saviour*. One moment it was there sending out its regular homing beacon and the next it was a flash of light. Nothing left. Nobody left. They were all gone."

His face totally serious, Kell asked, "That's when the capsule's automated medical systems put you into cryosleep?"

Tray nodded hesitantly. "I suppose so. It all got kind of confused. I guess it was too much for my mind to accept."

"But you seem to have gotten it down in good order now," Kell observed.

"I've had more than a year to sort it out," Tray said. Then he added, "And a lot of psychological help."

"Indeed," said Kell, with a curt nod. "Well, it's all behind you now."

Tray nodded back at him, but he was thinking, No, it's not behind me. It's in my dreams. It's in my thoughts. Felicia will never be behind me.

Kell abruptly changed the subject. "Did I push you too far by inviting you on this Jupiter flight?"

Feeling relieved to get away from his haunted memories, Tray honestly replied, "I was surprised, but . . . no, it's a wonderful opportunity. I'd love to see the Leviathans close up. Maybe I can compose a musical piece about them."

Kell's face lit up. "That's right. You're a musician, aren't you?"

"Amateur," said Tray.

"Maybe this trip to Jupiter will make a professional musician out of you."

"Maybe it will," Tray replied. "That would be good."

JOVE'S MESSENGER

Tray stood on the observation platform, flanked on either side by Kell and Para, as he goggled at the huge curving bulk of *Jove's messenger.* The spaceship hung weightlessly in its orbital docking berth, a bright silvery globe that dwarfed the trim metal structure of the platform.

The platform itself was part of the elevator system that rose from a mountaintop in Ecuador up to the nearly 40,000-kilometer altitude of the twenty-four-hour geosynchronous orbit and beyond. It was encased in clear Plastiglas, so that onlookers could stand in shirt-sleeved comfort while a team of human and robotic workers serviced the huge ship.

Beyond the curving rim of the spacecraft Tray could see the enormous bulk of Earth, dazzling blue and white, incredibly beautiful.

The home of humankind, he thought. The nursery in which a race of large-brained hominids created a civilization that now reaches outward to the stars. A trace of a musical passage twined through his brain, but it was too placid, too calm to represent such an awesome theme.

I'll have to come up with something better, he told himself. Something grander.

"It's impressive, isn't it?" asked Jordan Kell, his eyes fixed on the gigantic spacecraft.

"It certainly is," replied Tray. His voice climbing almost a full octave, he asked, "President Balsam owns this spaceship?"

Nodding, Kell answered, "Indeed he does. He's an incredibly wealthy man. Half the metals and minerals that the rock rats pry out of the Asteroid Belt are part of his wealth."

"Wow."

Para spoke up. "I can give you his exact monetary worth as of this moment, if you like."

Kell shook his head. "No, thank you. It's quite considerable, I'm sure."

"Indeed," said Para.

Kell turned away from the spacecraft and started toward the elevator that would bring them back to Earth's surface.

"He's awfully generous," Tray said as he followed Kell. "This spacecraft must cost hundreds of millions."

"Many hundreds," Kell acknowledged. "Probably more like a billion or two."

Tray shook his head, goggling at the idea of such wealth.

"And he's—"

Kell laid a hand on Tray's shoulder, silencing him. With a grim smile he said softly, "Wait 'til we're back in my office."

Tray blinked, puzzled, but went silent.

They reached the elevator doors, which slid open as they approached. The cab resembled a comfortable sitting room, with cushioned benches lining its walls. A man-tall refrigerator stood in one corner, with a small service bar next to it.

Para went straight to the service bar. "Can I offer you some refreshment?" it asked.

Tray tried not to frown. Para had become his constant companion over the past months, yet its inherent instinct was to act as a servant, automatically.

"Sit down here with us, Para," he said, patting the bench. The android obeyed instantly.

Kell smiled. "You find it just as hard as I do to accept the android's inbuilt reflexes," he said.

"Para's an equal, not a servant," Tray said tightly.

Kell sighed. "We've had robotic helpers for more than a millennium, yet the average human still thinks of them as servants."

"I don't," Tray snapped.

"You're not average," Kell said, tapping Tray's thigh with a forefinger.

Eventually they raided the refrigerator for a brief snack as the elevator plunged back toward Earth. Orbital towers studded the planet's equator, reaching upward from the ground (or ocean-anchored bases) to the altitude of geosynchronous orbit, nearly 40,000 kilometers high, and beyond. They reduced the cost of going into space enormously.

Once on the ground, the three of them boarded a shuttle flight that took them back to Denver and the capital of the Interplanetary Council.

As they entered Kell's office, Tray asked the question he'd been thinking about since they'd been in orbit.

"Why did you stop me from asking about President Balsam's generosity, when we were looking at his ship?"

Kell stood by his desk and shrugged. "I'm just a little superstitious, I suppose."

"Superstitious?"

"No, not really that," Kell replied. "It's just an ancient piece of advice that's wedged itself in my mind."

"Advice?" Tray asked.

"About Balsam's generosity."

"What about it?"

Kell hesitated, then quoted, "Beware of Greeks bearing gifts."

dark age

Tray stared at Jordan Kell, who sank down in his dark desk chair and leaned back tiredly. The chair seemed to enfold him protectively.

"You don't trust President Balsam?" Tray asked.

"Not completely, no," Kell replied. With a smile that had a bitter tinge, he added, "In politics, it's difficult to give your complete trust to anyone."

Tray thought that over for a silent moment. Then he asked, "You don't completely trust me, then?"

Kell's face eased into an almost fatherly smile. "Let me put it this way, Trayvon: I trust you more than Harold Balsam."

And who do I trust? Tray asked himself silently. Who can I trust?

The answer came to him immediately: Para, of course. Tray trusted the android implicitly. But humans? He looked at Jordan Kell, sitting behind his desk. Yes, I think I can trust Mr. Kell, Tray told himself. I'm sure I can. Almost.

As if he understood the turmoil in Tray's mind, Kell gestured toward the room's single, sweeping window.

"Look out at this city we've built, Trayvon. Look out at our global civilization . . . our interplanetary civilization. What do you see?"

Frowning with puzzlement, Tray replied, "As you say, we've built an interplanetary civilization. We've reached out to more than two dozen other star systems. We've helped other civilizations to survive the Death Wave."

"A magnificent achievement," said Kell.

"It certainly is."

"And where do we go from here?"

Tray saw an intensity in Kell's eyes, an eagerness to hear the answer he wanted to hear.

"I . . . I don't really know," he replied. "I suppose that's for the Council to decide."

Kell sank farther into his enfolding chair. "The Council. Led by President Harold Balsam."

"I guess so."

"Half the Council thinks we've done enough for our neighboring brethren. They think we should leave them alone and enjoy our survival of the Death Wave. We've labored long enough, they claim; now we should relax and enjoy the fruits of our victory."

Tray started to reply, but realized that Kell wasn't finished.

"The other half of the Council," Kell went on, "wants us to go out to the civilizations we've found and help them, develop their resources, teach them our technology, lead them to our level of refinement. They're already talking about an interstellar civilization, led by Earth."

"Is that possible?"

Grimly, Kell answered, "It's been done before, in our own history. The Roman Empire. The Chinese Empire. The European conquest of the Aztecs and Incas and other Native American civilizations. The Japanese co-prosperity sphere. The North Atlantic Treaty Organization. The Pan-Asian federation."

"That's all ancient history," Tray objected.

"And history doesn't repeat itself, eh?" Kell smiled bitterly. "But as some American observer once noted, history doesn't repeat it-self, but it rhymes."

"Rhymes?"

"We're in danger of entering a new Dark Age, Trayvon. That's what I fear. The human race is on the edge of settling into an inter-stellar empire, a huge re-run of the Roman and other empires of the past, where one group of intelligent creatures—us—lords it over groups of lesser developed intelligences—the peoples of the star systems we helped to survive the Death Wave."

Tray blinked with confusion. "An empire?"

"Oh, they won't call it that. They'll give it some peaceful, cheer-ful name. But it will be an empire nonetheless, with humankind at the top and all the races we've discovered serving us."

"That . . ." Tray hesitated, trying to pull his thoughts together. "That doesn't sound right."

"It's not right," Kell said, his voice suddenly iron-hard. "It's a system that leads inevitably to revolt, to war and destruction. That's what Balsam and his followers are heading for, and that's what we must prevent them from achieving."

"An interstellar empire."

"A recipe for disaster."

Masters and Slaves

"Prevent them?" Tray asked. "How?"

Kell shrugged his slim shoulders. "If I knew I'd tell you. The only real tool we have is history: the record of our own past. The only technique I can see is jawboning: trying to convince Balsam and his allies through patient, logical argument."

Tray sank into one of the capacious chairs in front of Kell's desk. "Jawboning."

"In private conversations with Balsam and his allies. On the floor of the Council meetings. Speeches, meetings . . . as Jesus said, wherever two or three are gathered."

"Will that work?"

"I wonder," said Kell. "Balsam can offer the Council a rosy picture of enormous gains for the people of Earth. The wealth of an interstellar empire could be ours—for a while."

"That sounds impressive."

"Of course it does. But the costs! The human race would become the overlords of all the intelligent civilizations we've encountered— for a while. Inevitably, though, those other peoples would gain strength, gain knowledge. Inevitably they would demand their fair share of the empire's wealth. Inevitably conflict would arise. Perhaps even war."

"An interstellar war?"

"That's what I fear. Sooner or later."

Tray felt his brows knitting in perplexity. "How soon?"

Again Kell's slim shoulders lifted in a frustrated shrug. "I'm not sure. A hundred years? A thousand?"

Tray's breath whistled from between his lips. "You're worried about the possibility of an interstellar war a thousand years in the future?"

"Maybe more. More likely less."

"It's hard to get anyone worked up over something so far in the future. And it might not even happen at all."

Kell shook his head. "It will happen. I've gone down every pathway our future analysts have forecast. They all end up in conflict. War. Destruction."

"But . . . if it's not going to happen for a thousand years, it'll be just about impossible to get anyone concerned about it now. People just don't think in such long time spans."

"Tell me about that!" Kell burst out. "I haven't been able to get anyone to listen to me—starting with Balsam. He's all aglow with visions of an interstellar empire, with himself at its head."

Tray sank back in the luxurious chair. "I can see why you're worried. It's like someone trying to warn the Roman emperor Tiberius that the Huns will sweep across Europe in a few hundred years."

"Worse," said Kell gloomily. "Balsam and his followers think that the human race will always keep a technological superiority over the other races scattered among the stars. Yet our own technology isn't developing much at all."

His expression hardening, Kell went on, "We were handed the technology for interstellar flight by the Predecessors. Our own scientific studies have dwindled to repetitions of work done centuries ago. There are actually so-called scientific leaders who claim we've reached a peak of development and there's not much more we can learn about the universe."

Tray saw anguish on Kell's face.

Gesturing toward the room's sweeping window, the older man said with some heat, "Look at our city out there! Most of the buildings are copies of older monuments. Our so-called leaders are looking more toward the past than the future.

"We're not making progress anymore! Professors are telling their students that we've reached a plateau of knowledge where the best we can hope for is to add a few decimal places here and there to what we already know! It's a recipe for disaster."

"But that's all far in the future, isn't it?"

"The future starts now!" Kell insisted. "What we do now, *today*, shapes what we can accomplish tomorrow."

Tray tensed in his plushly comfortable chair, his mind spinning.

"What we're heading for," Kell went on, "is an interstellar empire where the human race will have to work very hard to prevent those other races from developing their own civilizations. Masters and slaves, that's what they're heading for."

"Masters and slaves," Tray repeated, in a whisper.

Wearily, Kell uttered, "It's a recipe for disaster. A formula that leads to ultimate collapse."

"What can we do about it?"

Kell smiled bitterly. "Trayvon, my lad, if I knew I would happily tell you."

LORIS DE MAYNE

++

++

utterly depressed, Tray left Kell's office—accompanied by Para, of course. On the street the android summoned an automated cab that took them back toward Tray's quarters at the medical center.

Once they were settled on the cab's comfortable rear seats, Para announced, "You have received a message from Loris De Mayne."

Tray felt his eyebrows shoot up. "From Loris De Mayne? Really?"

Flatly, emotionlessly, Para replied, "Really."

"What did she say?"

Para focused on the cab's front seat and Loris De Mayne's beautiful image took shape there—several sizes smaller than life, but stunning nonetheless.

"Trayvon, this is Loris. I wonder if you could come to my apartment this evening? I'm having a few friends here for dinner, and they'd all love to meet you."

Tray blinked at the young woman's image. They'd love to meet me, he thought. Meet the sole survivor of the *Saviour* disaster, he realized. I'm an object of curiosity because I'm still alive and all the others are all dead.

Yet even while his mind ran those bitter thoughts past his consciousness, he heard his mouth saying, "Yes, thank you! I'd love to meet your friends!"

It was a lie and he knew it.

"Trayvon! Welcome!" With a sweeping gesture of her slim arm, Loris De Mayne ushered Tray into her apartment. She was wearing a sleek floor-length gown of dazzling white, decked with glittering asteroidal jewels at her throat, wrists, and earlobes; her lovely arms bare, the slim skirt slit to her hip, her midnight hair tumbling to her bare shoulders and sparkling with metallic chips.

"I'm delighted you could come," she said as she led Tray through her foyer and into a sizable living room already crowded with glittering young women also in jewels and long evening dresses and equally young men in dark, formal suits. Tray felt instantly shabby, out of place, in his comfortable slacks and nubby sports coat.

He stammered, "I . . . I didn't realize it would be . . . formal . . . dress-up."

Loris De Mayne smiled glitteringly at him. "Oh, don't worry about that. We tend to dress up too much. You're a breath of fresh air."

Feeling more like a beggar who'd somehow fallen in among the cream of society, Tray let Loris introduce him to a dozen or so couples, all of them impeccably gowned and suited. He wished Para had come with him; the android would remember each and every name, and even look up their biographies if Tray asked it to.

Tray forgot the names of the people almost as soon as Loris introduced them to him. Sensory overload, he thought. Too much information piled on too quickly.

Then he realized that he could quietly contact Para through the communicator that had been implanted in his brain. Tray felt somewhat better for that: He wasn't alone among this pack of elegant strangers.

Loris herself was completely at ease among these people. They were her friends; she had probably known them since childhood. Tray felt totally out of place, a stranger in a strange land. His attention focused on Loris herself, smiling, exchanging pleasantries with her friends. The most beautiful and vivacious woman in the room.

She led Tray to the bar that had been set up in a corner of the big, crowded room. People moved aside to allow them to reach the curving dark faux wood structure. A humanform robot stood behind the bar, its expressionless face focused on them.

"I'll have a Martian Blitz," Loris told the robotic bartender. "What about you, Tray?"

He saw that her sapphire eyes were radiant, like softly glowing jewels. And also that he didn't have the faintest idea of what he should ask for.

"*Ginger beer,*" Para's voice whispered in his mind.

Gratefully, Tray repeated, "Ginger beer."

The robot nodded once and repeated, "Ginger beer, coming right up, sir."

With their drinks in their hands, Tray and Loris edged their way toward the sweeping windows that looked out on the city. Music thrummed through the air, a few couples had begun to dance.

Standing beside a potted young tree, Loris asked, "Tray, do you like to dance?"

He coughed down his mouthful of tart ginger beer and looked at the dancers gyrating athletically in the middle of the room. "Uh . . . I've been in cryosleep for nearly four hundred years, you know . . ."

Loris's eyes went wide. "Of course! Oh, Tray, I'm so sorry. I didn't mean to embarrass you."

"It's okay," he said. "Not your fault." Grinning, he added, "It's a real honor to have the best-looking woman in the room ask me to dance with her."

Loris smiled at him. Through lowered lashes she murmured, "Flatterer."

Tray shook his head. "Not flattery. Look around. Nobody here looks half as beautiful as you do."

For a long moment they stared at each other, neither one of them certain of what to say next.

"There you are!"

Tray looked up and saw a bulky young man standing before Loris and himself with his fists on his hips and a stern look on his face.

"You invite us to meet the lone survivor of the *Saviour* disaster, Loris, and then you monopolize him for yourself," the stranger said in a mock-accusing tone.

Completely unfazed, Loris replied, "The night is young, Rige."

"And you're so beautiful," the fellow quickly replied. Turning to Tray, he went on, "That line is from an ancient American popular song. It's one of my hobbies, ancient popular music."

Tray started to tell him that he himself was an amateur musician, but stopped himself before uttering a word.

Without a shred of enthusiasm, Loris made the introduction: "Tray, this is Rigel Charpentier. Rige, Trayvon Williamson."

"Our guest of honor," said Charpentier as he put out his right hand.

Tray shook the proffered hand. "Pleased to meet you."

"And I you," Charpentier said. He looked pleasant enough, Tray thought. Roundish moon of a face, soft and clean-shaven. Light brown hair. Bulky figure. Eats too much and doesn't exercise enough, Tray thought. His dinner jacket looked expensive; it glittered with tiny flecks of jewels.

"Rige is an astronomer," Loris said.

"Astrophysicist," Charpentier corrected.

Her voice dripping acid, Loris said, "Of sorts."

"Of sorts?" Rige put on a hurt expression. "Is it my fault that we live in an era where all the big astronomical questions have either been answered or lie beyond the capabilities of our instruments?"

"That's hard to believe," Tray blurted.

That launched a long exposition by Rigel Charpentier. He spoke nonstop about the human race's level of understanding of the universe, the capabilities of modern astronomical technology, the completeness of current astronomical theories.

Obviously bored, Loris left the two men and disappeared into the crowd. Tray could easily follow what Charpentier was rattling on about, and he felt glad that the big fellow was so eager to talk about his work. His self-important monologue meant Tray didn't have to say a word.

Gradually a small group of people began to gather around them, listening to Charpentier's nonstop sermonizing.

But all too soon the astrophysicist said, "Enough about my work. What happened to the *Saviour*? How did you survive the catastrophe?"

SURVIVAL

"I wasn't on the *saviour* when it exploded," Tray answered. "I was on a scoutship on the other side of the planetary system."

"Lucky you," said one of the women.

Lucky, Tray thought. Lucky to be alive, when all the others of the crew are dead. All of them, including Felicia Cantore. She and Tray had decided to ask Captain Uhlenbeck to marry them once Tray returned to the *Saviour*.

"All gone," Tray murmured. "I was the only one to survive."

"What caused the explosion?" asked one of the stylishly dressed young men.

Tray shook his head. "Unknown. There wasn't enough of the ship left to determine."

"I heard it was a swarm of miniature asteroids," someone said.

"Maybe," Tray half-agreed. "That's the leading theory."

"More than two thousand people," said one of the young men. "Wiped out like *that*." He snapped his fingers.

"What a shame."

"A tragedy."

Tray saw that Loris had rejoined the group. She stood toward the rear of the gathering, her luminous blue eyes focused on him, her face etched with concern.

"What happened to the primitive natives that the *Saviour* was supposed to protect from the Death Wave?"

A surge of guilt engulfed Tray. "They all died, too. By the time the rescue ship reached the Raman star system, the Death Wave had swept past. It killed everything on the planet."

"But you survived," someone said. Tray heard a tone almost of accusation in his voice.

"The ship's systems put me into cryosleep and activated the screening that protected me from the Death Wave," he told them. "The rescue ship revived me, once it arrived."

"Four hundred years later."

"Not quite four," Tray corrected automatically.

"You were damned lucky."

"I guess I was." But Tray thought, Lucky to be alive when all the others died. Felicia and all the others. All dead. In the blink of an eye.

As if she sensed Tray's inner anguish, Loris pushed to the front of the little crowd, saying, "That's enough. Let's change the subject."

The crowd began to disperse. Loris grasped Tray's arm. "Are you all right?"

He nodded dumbly.

"I'm sorry," Loris said. "I didn't realize how powerful those memories are for you."

Forcing himself to stand straighter, Tray muttered, "It's okay. I'm all right."

She led Tray through the crowded room and out onto the balcony. In the clear air of the Colorado evening the stars glittered like jewels scattered across the sky. The Moon had just climbed above the rolling flatland of the Great Prairie, casting a soft radiance on the sawtoothed horizon of the Rockies, to the west.

Tray said, "It's pretty, isn't it?"

Loris smiled at him. "Wouldn't feel so pretty if this balcony wasn't heated."

Tray extended his hand. "It's not glassed in."

"Energy screen. Keeps the cold air out."

He nodded. Another gift from the Predecessors, not a discovery by human scientists.

In a low voice, Loris said, "I'm sorry."

"For what?"

"For letting them gang up on you like that. I didn't realize . . . I mean, I just found out that your fiancée died in the ship's explosion."

Tray blinked at her. "You were looking up my history?"

Biting her lip, Loris nodded. "I should have checked it out before I let those vultures loose on you."

With what he hoped was a careless shrug, Tray replied, "It's okay. They were curious. Curiosity is the foundation of knowledge."

"It can be painful, though."

"Sometimes," Tray agreed.

She stood there on the balcony with him, close enough to touch. Close enough to kiss.

"So this is where you are!"

Turning abruptly, Tray saw Mance Bricknell stepping through the doorway from the room full of partygoers.

With an almost accusing look, Bricknell said to Tray, "Are you trying to make time with my girl?"

Before Tray could think of an answer, Loris snapped, "You don't own me, Mance."

He stepped up beside her and slid an arm around her waist. Tray saw that Loris stiffened and carefully stepped out of his grasp.

"I think I'd better be going," Tray said.

"It's early," Loris countered. "Dinner won't be ready for an hour."

Thinking of how painful another hour with this crowd would be, Tray temporized, "Early for you. I haven't been up this late for a long time." It was a lie, but he hoped it would work.

It did. Loris, with Bricknell at her side, walked Tray to the apartment's foyer, where he said good night to them both.

But as he rode the elevator down to the street level, Tray couldn't help grinning to himself. The most beautiful woman at the party spent enough time with me to make her boyfriend jealous. Not bad.

invitation

++
++

The following morning, Tray was plowing through a debriefing questionnaire, with Para sitting across the dining table from him, when the phone implanted in his skull thrummed.

"Loris De Mayne," said Para.

Tray felt his pulse quicken. He nodded to the android and Loris's form took shape in the middle of the apartment's sitting room. She was wearing a formfitting athletic suit, her arms and long legs bare, her dark hair tied up atop her head. Her bare skin glistened with beads of perspiration.

"Good morning!" she said cheerfully. "I hope I'm not calling too early."

Shaking his head, Tray replied, "Para and I have been up for hours."

Loris smiled at the android; to Tray it looked forced, not natural: a formality, a ritual. Para inclined its chin once, almost solemnly.

"Am I calling at an inconvenient time?" she asked. "Did I interrupt something important?"

Tray started to reply that he was merely going through a debriefing about last night's party, but hesitated. Instead he answered,

"Nothing that can't be interrupted. How are you? How long did the party last?"

Loris hiked her eyebrows and said, "Oh, it went on for hours after you left. Most of the people were disappointed that you didn't stay longer, though."

"I'm sorry," Tray said. "I . . . well, I just felt sort of . . . uncomfortable, out of place. All those people asking me questions, like I was some sort of exhibit."

Her lovely face looked stricken. "Oh! I didn't realize! How stupid of me! Unfeeling!"

Tray instantly tied to soothe her. "Oh no! It's not your fault! It's just that . . . this is all new to me. I've been jumped more than a thousand years into the future of the time when I was born. I'm trying to get accustomed to it, to fit in somehow."

"Of course you are," Loris replied. "I should have understood that right away. I'm sorry, Tray."

"There's nothing to be sorry about."

"Can you forgive me?"

"There's nothing to forgive."

Loris hesitated a moment, then said, "Look, Mance is dying to show you the work he's been doing. Would you like to come to his studio? It'll be just the three of us. No crowds."

Thinking he'd prefer it to be just the two of them, Tray heard himself reply, "Sure, I'd be happy to."

"Wonderful!"

"What kind of work is he doing?"

Loris's smile lit up the room. "He's a historical architect. He studies the past . . . ancient civilizations, that sort of thing."

Tray nodded to her. "Sounds interesting."

"I'll pick you up this afternoon," Loris said, beaming with satisfaction.

With a glance at Para, who nodded approval, Tray asked, "Two o'clock?"

"Perfect."

"Para can beam directions to your car."

"Wonderful," she repeated.

At ten minutes before two Tray and Para left the luncheon cafeteria on the top floor of the medical building where he lived and went down to its entrance. Outside, it was a warm, sunlit afternoon with just a hint of chill sliding down from the distant mountains.

"A historical architect," Tray said to his mentor. "That must be interesting."

Para nodded minimally. "I can show you some of his work, if you'd like to see it."

Realizing he was far more interested in seeing Loris than architecture, Tray temporized, "Uh, no. No thanks. I'd rather let him show his work to me the way he wants to present it."

Para nodded, but Tray couldn't help feeling that the android was suppressing an urge to laugh at him.

He heard himself ask, "Do you ever laugh, Para?"

"Yes, if the occasion calls for such a response."

Tray thought about that for a moment. "Same as I do."

"We try to be as human as possible."

Before Tray could formulate a response to that, a long, low-slung vehicle pulled up almost silently to the curb in front of them and settled on its barely visible tires. A door swung upward and Loris De Mayne climbed out of the car's shadowy interior.

"Hello, Tray!" she called as she stepped toward him.

She was wearing a formfitting white outfit, bare arms and legs, her hair coiled up atop her head. In his hospital-issued tan sports coat and darker slacks, Tray felt only slightly shabby.

For an awkward moment Tray didn't know if he should shake her hand, kiss her cheek, or wrap his arms around her in a loving embrace.

Loris solved his problem by placing both her hands on his shoulders and giving him a peck on the lips.

"Right on time," she said cheerfully. "Punctuality: the pride of princes."

Tray gaped at her, awkward and confused.

Turning slightly toward Para, Loris said, "I'm afraid there's only room for two in my car. You'll have to follow us in a cab."

Tray pulled his wits together. "That's all right. Para can stay here and monitor me remotely. Right, Para?"

"Of course," said the android.

"Fine," Loris said happily. She gestured Tray into the low-slung car, slid in next to him, pulled the door down, and ordered the vehicle to take off. It rose a few centimeters off the pavement, its tires folding inward, and flew off toward the highway in almost absolute silence.

Para stood on the sidewalk alone and watched the car disappear in the distance.

hi5+OriCaL arChi+eC+ure

"This car can scoot along at nearly five hundred klicks per hour," Loris said happily.

Sitting beside her in the tight two-seated compartment, Tray wondered why the machine was built for such speed. Here along the aerial guideway traffic was automated, controlled by the citywide guidance system. They were zooming along at considerable speed, he saw, but while all the cars on the guideway were moving equally fast, they all kept their places: no one was allowed to maneuver past or around the other cars.

His eyes on the traffic surrounding them, Tray asked, "Have you driven that fast?"

"Now and then," Loris replied. "On race tracks, where there's no imposed speed limit and you can drive the beast manually."

"Do you enjoy that?"

She bobbed her dark-haired head up and down. "It's a blast. You're in control of the car and the devil take the hindmost!"

"Aren't there accidents?"

"Now and then. Nobody gets hurt, though. The automated safety systems protect the drivers."

"So there's no risk."

"Not much. But a lot of excitement, fun."

Tray sat back, with the protective seat curling around him. Excitement, he thought. Fun. It's all make-believe, really.

"Mance really mangled up his car last year. They had to pry him out with the big tongs, but he didn't have anything worse than a few bruises."

"Lucky for him."

Loris giggled delightedly. "He showed off those bruises for a week or more. Wherever he went, he'd roll up his sleeve and display his badges of honor."

Tray nodded wordlessly.

They reached the university campus and parked the car at the entrance of a multistory garage. Tray watched with interest as the garage's automated systems hoisted the car to a parking space overhead. Then they walked for less than five minutes in the warm afternoon sunshine to the building that housed Bricknell's—his what? Tray wondered. Laboratory? Workshop? Studio?

It was none of those. Loris led Tray to a third-floor office with Bricknell's name outlined on the door's electronic nameplate. She rapped once and opened the door without waiting for an answer.

Bricknell was seated at a wide, sweeping desk near the office's ceiling-high window. The walls seemed to be viewscreens, glowing faintly. No laboratory apparatus, no workbenches, just a pair of comfortable-looking armchairs in front of the dark faux-wood desk.

Bricknell popped up from his desk chair as Loris and Tray stepped in.

"Hello," he said, with a pleased smile. He started to come around the desk, saw that Loris quickly seated herself, and hesitated. His smile fading, he said to Tray, "Welcome to my command center."

"Thank you," said Tray. He shook Bricknell's proffered hand, then sat down beside Loris.

There was an awkward silence until Loris said, "I thought Tray would be interested in your historical analyses."

Bricknell nodded earnestly. "The study of history is important. You can't know where you're heading unless you understand where you've been."

Tray nodded back. "That sounds about right."

Warming slightly, Bricknell said, "Very well, then. Where have we been?" He reached out a hand and momentarily held it over his desktop keyboard. The office's lights dimmed, the window went dark, and the wall screens began to glow more intently.

human history

+++
+++

In the darkened office, Bricknell asked Tray, "You do have an implanted communicator, don't you?"

Tray nodded as he replied, "Yes. They put it into my skull the day I arrived here. I'm still not completely accustomed to it, though. Sometimes the images seem—"

"That's perfectly all right," Bricknell interrupted with an airy wave of his hand. "Your communicator can pick up the signals I'll broadcast."

With a slightly nervous glance at Loris, who looked totally at ease, Tray said, "That's good."

"Better than good," said Bricknell. "The communicator will allow you to *experience* human history."

"Experience it? I don't understand."

"You'll see."

Bricknell danced his fingers above the symbols etched into the top of his desk while Tray sat tensely in the softly yielding armchair. The room seemed to grow darker. Tray could barely make out Loris, sitting next to him.

He heard Bricknell murmur, "The projection depends on sensory manipulation, sort of like hypnosis."

Hypnosis? Tray wondered.

The office melted away. Tray blinked as Loris, Bricknell, everything in the office faded from his sight. For an instant he was in total darkness, then suddenly the world lit up all around him.

He was on a city street, crowded with strangers carried along narrow moving lanes of slidewalks. The sky was clear blue. The weather was pleasantly warm, with golden sunshine pouring down on everyone.

Suddenly someone on the slidewalk pointed skyward. "What's that?" she asked, in a loud, frightened voice.

In his mind, Tray heard a voice saying, "The war began with an unprovoked nuclear strike on cities all across the Northern Hemisphere . . ."

The world exploded. The people, the crowd, the city transformed into a hellish glare of heat and agony. Tray felt his flesh melting, bubbling, flayed from his crumbling bones.

But there was no pain. Suddenly he seemed to be high above the Earth, staring down at a blackened, smoking wasteland that stretched as far as he could see. A whole continent, reduced to smoldering ashes.

"The final war," said a calm, deep voice in Tray's mind, "reduced Earth's population to a scant few survivors, lucky enough to be in deep underground shelters when the nuclear bombs were unleashed."

Horrified, fascinated, Tray watched wordlessly as humankind's off-world societies came to the rescue of the original home of humanity. Relief missions from the Moon, from Mars, from the scattered bases of the rock rats strewn across the Asteroid Belt, from the research centers orbiting Jupiter and Saturn streamed Earthward, carrying medicines, food, building supplies, hope.

With dizzying speed, Tray saw Earth's civilization rebuilt, the survivors of the nuclear holocaust and their off-world brethren working together to build a new world, without war, without immense disparities between rich and poor, without hunger and disease and pain.

Out of nuclear devastation rose a new civilization, uniting the societies on the Moon, Mars, the other planets, and the far-flung worldlets of the Asteroid Belt. A human society, wiser and kinder, flayed with the memory of war and devastation.

Outward the new society moved. Out toward the stars. On the planet circling the major star of the Sirius system they encountered a completely human race. Only gradually did they learn that these humans had been created by the Predecessors, a race of machine intelligences that had spread through much of the Milky Way Galaxy.

The Predecessors told the visitors from Earth that all life in the Milky Way was imperiled by a Death Wave that had erupted in the galaxy's core, some thirty thousand light-years away. This wave of incredibly energetic gamma radiation was surging through the galaxy, killing every living thing it touched.

The Death Wave would reach Earth's vicinity in two thousand years. The Predecessors had the technology to shield Earth and the rest of the solar system from the gamma radiation's deadly effects. In return for that shielding, the Predecessors asked humankind to help them in their mission, assist them in their quest to reach out to other intelligent species scattered among the stars and aid them to survive the Death Wave.

Humankind rose to the challenge. With the help of the Predecessors' greatly advanced technology, human expeditions went to the stars and saved fledgling civilizations from annihilation.

Tray's eyes misted over as he saw one of those missions of mercy, the starship *Saviour*, destroyed by a swarm of asteroids that shredded the ship and killed everyone aboard it.

Everyone except for one young man: Trayvon Alexander Williamson.

Tray was blubbering unashamedly as the history display ended and Mance Bricknell's office lit up again. Through tear-filled eyes he saw that it was now evening outside. The sun had set. Streetlights illuminated the campus complex.

Loris reach out and gently touched his arm. "Are you all right?" she asked, her voice low, concerned.

Tray nodded and pulled in a deep, steadying breath. "It's a lot to take in, all at once."

"Yes, I imagine it is," she said, turning a glare toward Bricknell.

The historian sat back in his cushioned desk chair and touched his fingertips together. "Perhaps I shouldn't have given you the entire scenario in one shot," he said.

Pawing at his eyes, Tray admitted, "It's . . . it's pretty powerful."

"It's the history of our species," Bricknell said, almost defensively, "as accurately as I could put it together."

Her sapphire eyes turned accusingly on Bricknell, Loris snapped, "You didn't have to pour it over him in one continuous blast."

"Maybe I shouldn't have," Bricknell conceded.

"No," said Tray, regaining his self-control. "It's better this way. Get it all out on the table."

"That's what I thought," Bricknell said.

"It was cruel," Loris insisted. "Sadistic."

Tray shook his head. "No. It's all right. I'm sorry I broke down like that. I should be able to control myself better."

Bricknell almost smiled. "In a way, I guess your reaction is an honor to my presentation's power."

Tray didn't trust himself to do more than nod.

Loris studied his face for a moment. "Are you sure you're all right?"

"I'm fine," Tray choked out.

"Good," said Bricknell.

Loris still looked unconvinced.

"The question now," Tray heard himself say, "is where do we go from here?"

Bricknell broke into a wide grin. Gesturing to the deepening shadows of evening outside his office window, he answered, "I'd say the first place we should go to is dinner." Peering at Tray, he added, "If you feel up to it, of course."

Tray glanced at Loris, then said, "I'm fine. Dinner's a good idea."

Bricknell silently made a reservation as Loris studied Tray's face.

"Are you sure you're all right?" she asked once more.

With a confidence he didn't really feel, Tray replied, "I'm all right. It was kind of overwhelming, though."

Bricknell took it as a compliment. "It's a powerful presentation, true enough."

As the three of them got to their feet Bricknell said, "I've ordered an aircar. We're going to my favorite restaurant, the Mile High. Dinner's on me."

Loris shot him a skeptical glance. "On you? Or on your department?"

Bricknell's grin dimmed slightly. "Well, I do have an expense account. One of the privileges of my rank."

Loris smiled back at him. "Good. Then we can order whatever we want."

*   *   *

The Mile High Restaurant revolved slowly atop a slim silver tower that rose above all the other buildings in Denver. Tray could see the bare rock peaks of the Rockies rising in the west and the seemingly endless expanse of the Midwestern prairie to the east, a careful green and yellow gridwork of food crops.

Tray, Loris, and Bricknell were seated by a robot waiter at the outer rim of the rotating restaurant, next to the tall windows that circled the establishment. Tray found himself mentally counting how long it took to revolve all the way around and see the rising Moon again.

"Your presentation," Loris asked Bricknell, "is it finished? Completed?"

From his chair beside Loris and across the table from Tray, Bricknell said, "It will never be completed. I add new information to it every day."

"Really?"

Bricknell jabbed a forkful of salad as he replied, "Oh, it's in good enough shape to show it to interested individuals. The Council's education division wants to use it in their history classes, of course. And several Council members have asked for private showings."

Tray looked up from his own salad. "It's a powerful presentation. I'm sure it will have quite an impact on whoever sees it."

Bricknell looked pleased. "That's because it directly impacts the brain's receptor centers. You didn't merely see and hear a presentation. The central reception areas of your brain were directly stimulated."

"That's why it has such an emotional effect," Loris guessed.

"Exactly," said Bricknell. Leaning closer and lowering his voice, he added, "President Balsam has asked me to prepare briefing sessions for key members of the Council. President Balsam! Himself!

He called me to his office and asked me to work up sessions for key Council members."

Tray heard himself ask, "Won't that be going too far? Sort of like brainwashing?"

Bricknell's face twisted into an angry frown. "What do you mean, 'brainwashing'? I'll be showing them history, not propaganda!"

"History that you've selected. You'll be showing them what you've decided they should see."

With a shake of his head, Bricknell retorted, "My presentation has been reviewed by the university's History Department and the whole board of deans. They've approved it."

"Without any objections?" Tray probed. "Without any requests for changes, additions, deletions?"

Hotly, Bricknell snapped, "They voted to accept the presentation as I showed it to them."

"No objections at all?" Tray asked again.

"Oh, there were a few nitpicks, but they got voted down."

Tray nodded. After a glance at Loris, he admitted, "Well, it certainly is a powerful presentation."

"Thank you," said Bricknell. Without a trace of appreciation in his voice.

recipe for disaster

++

Para was waiting for Tray when he returned to his apartment in the medical complex.

"Would you like a refreshment?" the android asked as Tray closed the door behind him.

"No thanks," said Tray. He went to the sofa and sank into it. "I had a big dinner."

"Perhaps an after-dinner libation?"

Tray simply shook his head.

Standing by the bar that separated the apartment's living room from its kitchen, Para said, "You had quite an experience with Dr. Bricknell's presentation."

Tray stared up at the android's humanform face and realized, If I didn't know it was a machine, I could easily mistake it for a real human being.

"It was powerful," he agreed. "Like being put through a wringer."

Para hesitated a split-second, then asked, "A device for ringing bells?"

Tray laughed and shook his head. "No, no, no. A device for squeezing the water out of wet clothes."

"Ah," the android said. "Now I understand."

More seriously, Tray asked, "Did you see Bricknell's presentation?"

"I received it from your implanted communicator."

"What did you think of it?"

For a moment, Para didn't answer. But before Tray could repeat his question, the android replied, "It is a very clever condensation of a crucial period in human history: the transition from nation-states to a single, unified interplanetary political structure."

"Yes," Tray agreed slowly, realizing that the emotional impact that brought him to tears had no emotional effect whatsoever on the android.

Without moving from where it stood, Para asked, "I wonder if Councilman Kell has seen Dr. Bricknell's presentation."

"I doubt it."

"Perhaps you should tell him about it. It might be helpful for you to get his reaction to it."

Tray stared up at Para for a long moment. At last he said, "You might be right."

Jordan Kell's tightly sculpted face looked quite serious, concerned, as Tray told him of his experience with Bricknell's history presentation.

Kell appeared to be sitting at his desk in the middle of Tray's living room, although actually he was halfway across the city, in his own office.

"I've heard rumbles about Dr. Bricknell's history," Kell muttered. "He's shown it to quite a few people at the university."

"But not to you?" Tray asked, from his chair by the window of his apartment.

"Not to me," Kell replied.

"Isn't that . . ." Tray fumbled for a word. "Curious?" he finally said. "I mean, he's apparently shown it to President Balsam and several other Council members."

Kell broke into an icy smile. "I'm not one of Balsam's pets. I'm the leader of the opposition."

"Oh. I didn't know."

"The Interplanetary Council isn't a band of sweetly harmonious individuals, Trayvon," Kell said. "There are differences of opinion, sometimes rather sharp differences."

"I didn't realize . . ."

Kell's smile turned warmer. "No reason why you should. We do try to keep our differences among ourselves. Everything is very civil. Very polite. If I want to call a fellow Council member an underhanded, sneaking thief, I state it in the politest form possible."

"Really?"

His smile widening even more, Kell went on, "Fortunately, it very rarely gets to that point. Still, there are differences of opinion among the Council members. Quite natural, of course. But some of them are troubling."

"Troubling?"

Kell hesitated a long moment. At last he said, "The basic difference between President Balsam's outlook and my own are over where we should be heading in the immediate future."

Tray nodded.

"Balsam and his cohorts," Kell went on, "feel that we've survived the Death Wave, and we've helped other intelligent species to survive. Now, they feel, we should relax and enjoy the fruits of our labors."

"The fruits of our labors?"

"We should take control of the intelligent species we've saved from the Death Wave. We should establish an interstellar empire, with Earth at the top of the ladder."

Tray blinked with surprise. "An interstellar empire? Among star systems that are hundreds, even thousands of light-years apart? That's ridiculous!"

"Not as ridiculous as you might think," said Kell. "The Predecessors have shown us how to communicate at superluminal speeds. Physical objects can't move faster than light, but information can."

"But . . ."

"That means," Kell went on, "that we could send orders to dozens of star systems almost instantaneously. We could establish commerce, trade, build industries, create an empire. That's what Balsam and his party want to do."

"But the physical goods," Tray objected, "the trade materials, the products, the *people*—they'd still be limited to the speed of light."

"Exactly," said Kell. "What they're really proposing is a network of civilizations linked to Earth, but quite free of direct control from Earth. We could order a planetary system to do this or that, and the order would be received faster than light, almost instantaneously. But the materials involved, the goods and the people, would still be restricted to the speed of light."

"It sounds stupid," Tray said.

"No," Kell corrected. "It's subtle. And pernicious. It means that human overseers can settle on those planetary systems and rule like kings, beyond the control of Earth's Interplanetary Council. It means that the so-called empire they want to create will really be a hodgepodge of star systems where a handful of humans can live like emperors and the indigenous civilizations will be ruled like slaves."

Tray felt shocked. "Slaves?"

"That might be too strong a term," Kell admitted. "But the humans would definitely be at the top of the ladder and the natives beneath them."

"Like the old Roman Empire."

Kell's lips curved slightly into a bitter smile. "As I've quoted before, although history doesn't actually repeat itself, it rhymes."

"Rhymes," Tray echoed.

Suddenly Kell pushed his desk chair back and got to his feet. "Look at where we stand," he said, stepping around his desk. "Balsam and his people claim we've reached a plateau in our history, a place where human advancement levels off. We've faced the Death Wave and survived. We've helped other intelligent species to survive. Now we can lean back and take it easy, enjoy the fruits of our victory over extinction."

"It sounds good," Tray admitted. "Lean back and enjoy the fruits of our victory."

"Yes," said Kell. "It sounds wonderful. Until you realize that what they're actually saying is that we should make ourselves masters of an interstellar empire and lord it over the other intelligent races that we've met."

"Lord it over them?"

"Keep them poor and ignorant, while we take their wealth for ourselves."

Tray felt his body tensing as he sat and looked up at Kell, on his feet.

"It's a recipe for conflict," Kell said bitterly. "It's a recipe for ultimate disaster."

moral 'suasion

+ +

+ +

Feeling more than a little perplexed, Tray asked, "what can we do about it?"

Kell hunched his shoulders in a brief shrug. "I've tried jawboning, but I'm afraid that the shining vision of an interstellar empire with us at its pinnacle has dazzled too many of the Council members for jawboning to have much effect."

"Then what . . . ?"

Smiling minimally, Kell said, "That's why I accepted Balsam's invitation for this Jupiter excursion. It will give me a few days to talk with him, man to man, with no interruptions."

Tray considered the possibilities for a few moments. "Do you think that's why he invited you to go?"

"I think it's possible. Balsam can't be completely indifferent to the slippery slope we're heading for. Maybe a few days alone, just the two of us talking freely, without interruption, is what he's really after."

Tray fought an instinct to shake his head. Balsam didn't seem like the kind of person who could be willingly talked away from a goal he wanted to achieve.

* * *

"What do you think I should do, Para?"

Tray and the android were on the rooftop of the building that housed Tray's apartment. The wind sweeping down from the Rockies felt chill, a real bite to it, despite the bright sunshine that drenched the city's myriad towers.

Para's facial expressions were limited, Tray knew. The people who had designed and built the android had deliberately limited its ability to show emotions, since the machine was not designed to experience them. Yet Tray felt that Para was not truly the impassive, totally detached logical machine that it appeared to be. Para *cared* about him, Tray felt.

But then he remembered that the android's behavior was designed to resemble human manners as much as possible. It's a machine, Tray reminded himself. Don't anthropomorphize it.

Still, Para stood beside him, looking and acting almost completely human. Almost.

With as much of a smile as it was capable of showing, Para said mildly, "Your range of options is somewhat limited. Councilman Kell has invited you to accompany him on this journey to Jupiter. You could refuse—as politely as possible—and remain here."

"But then I wouldn't see the Leviathans," Tray countered. To himself he added, Or be with Loris.

"If that is important to you, then you should accompany Councilman Kell."

Tray thought it over for several silent moments. Then, "Why did he invite me to go with him? I don't understand that. I'm nothing to him—"

Para interrupted. "You are his surrogate son."

"Son?"

"Of course."

"That's crazy," said Tray.

"No, it is well within the human suite of behaviors. Councilman Kell has no family. Both his first and second wives are dead. He has no children of his own. He has spent virtually his entire life in civil service. He is alone, as far as family is concerned. You have become his surrogate son."

The knowledge rocked Tray. Jordan Kell, one of the most important men on Earth, feels that I'm his son? He realized that he himself had no real family of his own, no one but Para. Perhaps I need a surrogate father as much as Kell needs a son, Tray thought.

He bounced these thoughts in his mind while they left the rooftop and returned to his apartment. As they entered the pleasantly warm sitting room Para said, "A phone call for you . . ."

"From who?"

"Whom," Para corrected.

Tray felt his brows knitting. "Who's calling?"

"Dr. Atkins's assistant."

"I don't want to talk to him."

"It," said Para.

"Take a message," Tray snapped. Then he added, "Please."

The robot's form took shape in the middle of the sitting room. Unlike Para, the robot looked obviously mechanical, its face covered with aluminum alloy, its mouth nothing more than a speaking grill. Its body was humanform, but smaller than an average human being, unclothed, sheathed in brightly polished alloy.

In a voice that was obviously mechanical, the robot said, "Dr. Atkins has scheduled your first exploratory interview for next Monday at oh nine hundred hours, in the conference room next to his office. Please confirm at your earliest convenience."

Tray swung his focus from the robot to Para. And blinked. Para looked almost completely human. Even though the range of emotions it could display was limited, compared to the robot Para was more like a companion, almost a brother.

"I won't be able to make that appointment," Tray heard himself say.

Without a moment's hesitation the robot responded, "Please tell Dr. Atkins what date and time would be convenient for you."

"I'll call him."

"When?"

Tray equivocated, "Tomorrow, sometime tomorrow."

"Thank you," said the robot. Its projection winked off.

Para said, "You have no intention of calling him, do you?"

"That's right," Tray admitted.

"You realize, of course, that Dr. Atkins could use the power of the law to compel you to submit to the memory erasure procedure."

Grimly, Tray nodded. But he said, "They'll have to catch me first."

LP Chalet

\+++
\++

"You mean there's no way I can refuse Atkins's decision to tinker with my mind?"

It was bright morning outside the apartment's windows. Brilliant sunshine drenched the buildings, the walkways, the roads that carried an unending swarm of vehicular traffic.

Para was standing beside one of the windows, yet the android was focused not on the scenery outside the apartment, but on Tray, sitting tensely on the plush sofa. Like Tray, Para was wearing light brown slacks and a cheerful bright short-sleeved shirt.

But its response to Tray's question was far from cheerful.

"I have spent the night going through the legalities of your situation," said the android. "Apparently Dr. Atkins has the authority to force you to submit to the procedure."

"That can't be true," Tray objected.

"I believe it is. You can check the legal records for yourself, of course, if you wish."

Tray shook his head. "I wouldn't find anything that you couldn't."

"Then the legal situation is clear. You must obey Dr. Atkins's directives."

"I don't want my brain sliced up!"

Para shook its head minimally. "There is no slicing involved. The procedure uses positronic beams to erase specific memories."

"I don't want it," Tray repeated.

"The decision is not in your hands. Dr. Atkins and his team have the authority—"

"I don't want it!" Tray shouted.

Para went silent, but kept its green optronic eyes focused on Tray. Tray pushed himself up from the sofa and paced across the sitting room, once, twice . . .

"You could appeal to the director of the medical staff," Para suggested.

Tray stopped his pacing and turned to face the android. "Fat lot of good that would do," he grumbled.

"I agree," said Para. "The decision has been made. I don't think there's anything you can do to avoid the erasure."

"Not legally."

Neither Para's facial expression nor the tone of its voice could express surprise, but Tray felt the shock in the android's response.

"You are thinking of an illegal act?"

"Extralegal," Tray replied tightly. "I'm not going to steal anything. I just want to stop *them* from stealing my memories."

"How?"

"I don't know," Tray admitted. "But I'm not going to stay here and let them tinker with my memories."

"Your memories of Felicia."

Tray nodded. "I don't want to lose her."

For several moments Para was silent. Tray and the android stood facing each other in absolute stillness. Tray's mind was racing: memories of Felicia, of the *Saviour*'s destruction, of Atkins and his determination to slice Tray's memories out of his brain. He thinks he's doing the right thing, Tray realized. He thinks he'll be helping me.

Para broke the silence. "I can find only one recourse open to you."

"What is it?"

"Appeal to Councilman Kell. He is still a member of the Interplanetary Council. Perhaps he can help you."

Tray nodded. "Kell. Yes. If he can't help me, nobody can."

They met for dinner that evening. Para thought it would be better if Tray met Kell alone, without his android chaperone, so it stayed in Tray's apartment. But it remained linked electronically to Tray's communicator, recording everything he and Kell said.

At Kell's suggestion they met at a continental restaurant named Le Chalet. It was far from downtown Denver, in a quiet ex-urban neighborhood on the shore of a man-made lake: small, quiet, decorated to resemble an old Swiss ski lodge.

But Tray barely noticed the bare wooden beams holding up the ceiling, nor the electronic "windows" that displayed scenes of the Alps as they had been before global warming melted all their snow away.

Kell was already seated at a table for two, off in a quiet corner of the restaurant. He got to his feet as the restaurant's human proprietor showed Tray to the table.

"Good of you to come out all this way," Kell said graciously as they sat down. "I live in this neighborhood and this way I don't have to travel downtown."

Tray glanced around the restaurant. "It looks like a nice place."

"Good food, no frills, no entertainment—except on Friday nights, when the proprietor's son plays the accordion." Lowering his voice a notch, Kell added, "I wouldn't recommend this place on Friday nights."

Tray laughed politely. They made their selections from the electronic menus built into the tabletop. Tray picked almost at random. The menu choices made no difference to him; he didn't feel hungry at all.

Then Kell asked, "So what's your trouble with the medics?"

Feeling relieved to get at the problem, Tray swiftly outlined the situation. Kell nodded silently until he finished.

Guardedly, Kell said, "Memory editing is a well-accepted therapeutic procedure. And Dr. Atkins is one of the top men in the field."

"I don't want my memory edited," said Tray.

The robotic waiter arrived with their salads. Once it left, Kell asked, "There's something you want to remember?"

"Some*one* I want to remember."

"Ah."

"I don't want to lose my memories of her."

Kell hesitated, then said, "And you're willing to fight the medical establishment to keep your memories of her?"

"Yes."

"Despite the fact that they're convinced the erasure would remove the block that's hindering your recovery?"

"They're convinced," Tray said. "I'm not."

Kell looked at Tray for a long, silent moment. Then, "I'm not sure there's anything I can do to reverse their decision. If Atkins and his people want to, they can have the police bring you in for the procedure."

Tray felt his entire body tensing.

"It's within their prerogative," Kell said.

"Damn!"

"But it doesn't have to come to that. I'll do all that I can to help you."

Tray nodded tightly. "Thank you, Mr. Kell."

"Jordan."

With the beginnings of a smile, Tray replied, "Thank you . . . Jordan."

memories

That night Tray's dreams were haunted with memories of the *saviour* mission. And of Felicia.

He dreamt that the two of them were walking slowly along one of the long passageways that ran the length of the starship. People passed them by: couples, crew members hurrying on their missions, officers chatting amiably among themselves. But they were all shadow figures, hardly real. Felicia walked beside him, her hand solidly in his.

Tray couldn't quite make out what they were talking about: wedding plans, preliminary scans of the intelligent creatures they were going to save from the Death Wave, something, nothing. The only thing that mattered was that they were together and they loved each other.

Felicia's face was something of a blur to Tray. He tried to concentrate on her eyes, her lips, her smile. But it was all maddeningly out of focus, as if he were looking through a misty, fogged window.

Suddenly Captain Uhlenbeck stood between them: stern, frowning, his face splotchy red with anger.

"I told you not to touch those noisemakers of yours," the captain said, his voice heavy with menace. He was a short, squat, ugly man with thick lips and a short temper.

Tray argued, "In the privacy of my own quarters—"

"Privacy?" Uhlenbeck snapped. "Privacy? There is no privacy aboard this ship. You will obey my orders! No exceptions!"

And Tray found himself in the lonely scoutship, on the other side of the Raman star system. He watched, helpless, as the *Saviour* was ripped apart by the meteor swarm. All aboard were killed. Felicia. Dead. Snuffed out in an instant. Killed.

Killed by a meteor swarm that I could have mapped out, warned them, saved them from—if I hadn't been exiled to the other side of the star system. Anger welled up within him. Rage. *I* didn't kill Felicia, he told himself. Fat-headed Uhlenbeck did!

Tray's eyes snapped open. He was lying in his bed, in his apartment in the medical center on Earth. Felicia's mutilated body was spinning through space hundreds of light-years away. Dead. Killed.

Because of me, Tray realized all over again. Not Captain Uhlenbeck. Because I didn't recognize the danger that the meteor swarms posed. Because I didn't detect the swarm that killed her. My fault. All my fault.

He lay there safe in his bed and told himself that he couldn't detect the meteor swarm, couldn't warn Felicia and the others. He was twelve billion kilometers from the ship, alone, exiled.

Still, he cried. He lay there in the safe warm bed and sobbed until he ran out of tears.

He lay there twisted in the sheets until morning sunlight brightened his bedroom. He got up slowly and showered, dressed. Precisely at nine a.m. Para knocked gently at his front door as the android did every morning. Tray went through the motions of going down to the building's nearest cafeteria for breakfast with the android. Para ate nothing, of course. Tray left most of his breakfast untouched.

"You have no appetite this morning," the android observed.

"I dreamt about Felicia."

"Again."

"Again."   .

Para hesitated, then spoke up. "Are you sure that avoiding the memory erasure procedure is your best course of action?"

"Yes!" Tray snapped. "I don't want to lose Felicia."

Another hesitation. Then, "She is dead, Trayvon."

"Not to me." Tray tapped his temple. "I've got her in here and I'm not going to let them take her away from me."

Para blinked slowly, as if digesting the information. At last it said, "Then you will need a place to hide."

"Hide?"

"Dr. Atkins can ask the police to take you by force and bring you to the clinic where the procedure is to be performed. You will need a place to hide from the police, sooner or later."

Tray fell silent, absorbing the idea.

Para began, "Perhaps Councilman Kell—"

"No," Tray interrupted. "I don't want to get Jordan in trouble with the Powers That Be."

"Who, then?"

Without an instant's hesitation, Tray replied, "Loris. She can help me."

"Loris De Mayne?" For the first time since he'd known the android, Tray felt that Para was surprised. No . . . it was shocked.

"Loris De Mayne," Tray repeated. "She can help me. If she wants to."

CONSPIRACY

"Hide you?" Loris's beautiful eyes went wide with surprise.

She and Tray were walking along a bustling sidewalk on the edge of the medical center. Loris had driven there to meet him.

Tray studied her lovely, sculpted face. Her eyes were bright blue, sparkling in the sunshine. He thought of Para's deep green eyes. The android's eyes were the green of optronic technology, while Loris's eyes were warm, living, enticing.

She focused on Tray as she asked, "Why do you need to hide?"

Tray realized once again that she was almost his own height: tall, athletically slim, beautiful. Her face showed a mixture of curiosity and concern.

He began to answer. "The medical staff has decided that they want to erase my brain of certain . . . certain memories from the *Saviour* mission."

They walked through the crowd for several steps before Loris asked, "Certain memories?"

Tray suddenly wished he hadn't asked for Loris's help. He looked at the crowd around them, walking, chatting, laughing as though they hadn't a care in the world.

At last he replied to her, "The doctors think that some of my memories are blocking my full recovery. They think that if they erase those memories I can be cured."

"Cured of what?" Loris asked. "You seem perfectly normal to me."

Tray spotted an empty bench in the mini-park they were passing. He grasped Loris's hand and led her across the grass to it. They sat, side by side, while the rest of the world paraded along the walkway, ignoring them.

He sat there in the afternoon sunshine and explained, "We were going to get married. But she was killed along with everybody else—except me."

Loris stared at Tray for a long silent moment. Then, "You were going to get married?"

With a solemn nod, Tray replied, "Her name was Felicia Cantore. I loved her and she's dead, killed by the meteor swarm that I failed to detect."

"And you feel guilty."

"I don't want them to cut my memories of her out of my head," Tray said, in a low urgent whisper. "Those memories are all I have left of her."

"But the medical staff . . ."

"They've decided that those memories are blocking my recovery. My feelings of guilt." With the heat of resentment rising inside him, Tray went on, "They want to scrub my brain and make me a happy citizen. A brain-dead happy citizen."

"You must have loved her very much," Loris said, in a near whisper.

"I still do."

She nodded. Tray found that he couldn't face her stare. He turned and looked out at the crowded walkway, at the people passing by endlessly.

At last Loris broke their silence. "So you need to hide from the police—assuming that the doctors send the police to bring you in for their treatment."

"Yes," said Tray, grasping at the hope. "Just for a week or so, until *Jove's Messenger* leaves for Jupiter."

"You plan to go on the expedition."

"To see the Leviathans. Of course."

Loris fell silent again. But Tray could see from her facial expression that now she was thinking, considering, planning.

At last she said, "The best place to hide is where they'd never look for you."

"I suppose that's right."

"And where would they never look for you?" she asked, smiling satisfiedly.

Tray shook his head. "I don't know."

"I do."

"Where?"

"Aboard the ship that's going to Jupiter!"

"*Jove's Messenger?*"

"Of course," Loris said, smiling brilliantly. "They'd never think of looking for you there. It's the perfect hiding place."

Feeling his brows knitting, Tray asked, "But how can I get aboard the ship before the other passengers?"

"You leave that to me," said Loris. "I'll get Uncle Harold to take you on as the ship's astronomer. He'll do that for me."

"Uncle Harold? You mean Harold Balsam, the Council president?"

Loris bobbed her head in happy acknowledgment.

"He's your uncle?"

"Almost. An old friend of the family. He's been after me for months."

"After you?"

Her smile dimming only slightly, Loris said, "He finds me attractive."

"Attractive? You mean . . . sexually?"

"What else?"

Tray sank back on the park bench, his mind spinning.

Loris was saying, "I'm sure he'd sneak you on board the ship if I went to bed with him."

"No!" Tray snapped.

Loris blinked at him. "No?"

"I can't have you prostitute yourself for me."

"Prostitute . . . ?" Loris's expression went from delight to shocked surprise. She stared at Tray for a long, silent moment.

Feeling miserable, Tray tried to explain, "I know you want to help me, and I thank you for it, but I can't let you—"

Loris's smile returned, but this time it was sympathetic. "I forgot that you were born nearly a thousand years ago."

"That's got nothing to do with it."

"Of course it does," she said, not unkindly. "Your attitudes about sex are terribly out of date, Tray."

"Out of date?"

"Tray, we were taught in school that sex is for pleasure, not for procreation. We have chromosomal selection centers and remote insemination labs. Artificial wombs where babies are brought to term. Women don't get pregnant now. Who wants to bloat out like a balloon and take all those risks?"

"I . . . I didn't know," Tray stammered. "Nobody at the medical center discussed that."

With a careless wave of her hand, Loris went on, "Oh, there are primitive cults here and there, religious communities, even ordinary women who want to experience pregnancy and natural childbirth. Ugh!"

"But sex," Tray asked, "that's still normal?"

"As normal as sunshine and apple pie," Loris said happily.

Tray heard himself ask, "And Mance? What about him?"

"He wants me to go to Jupiter, of course. He'd love to have me all to himself for a few weeks."

Tray felt his cheeks warming. "You two . . ." He couldn't finish the sentence.

Her smile fading, Loris said, "There's nothing serious between Mance and me. We have sex together now and then, but that doesn't mean anything."

"It doesn't?"

She shrugged. "Not as much as it did in the old days. We're a lot more free and happy. Sexual tensions and all the troubles they produced are almost a thing of the past."

Tray stared at her, red-faced with embarrassment.

PASSAGE

++
++++ +++

Loris was smiling at him as if what she had just proposed to do was no more important than asking a friend for a favor.

Loris's words repeated themselves in his brain: *Sex is for pleasure, not for procreation.* But that takes away all the responsibility, he told himself. And the guilt. And the furtive satisfaction.

Oh brave new world, he quoted silently, that has such people in it.

But something deeper in his mind rose to confront him. I can't let her do this, he told himself. It might mean nothing to her, but it means a lot to me.

With a sad shake of his head, Tray said, "I can't let you go to bed with Harold Balsam just to help me. Or with anybody else, either. It's not right."

Loris's smile turned pitying. "You're a prisoner of ancient myths, Tray. We've outgrown those old ways."

"I can't let you do it," he said, feeling miserable. "I just can't."

Loris stared at him. At last she murmured, "You're locked in ancient superstitions."

"I guess I am," he admitted.

"Like someone from an old story book: a man of honor."

With a dismal nod, Tray replied, "I just can't do it, Loris. I can't agree to let you . . . allow you . . ."

Loris reached out and clasped his hand. "All right, Tray. All right. Let me see if I can get Uncle Harold to let you onto his ship without going to bed with him. Will that be all right?"

"Could you do that?"

"I could try."

He clutched her hand in both of his. "That would be fine. Wonderful."

"We'll see," said Loris.

For two days Tray waited for word from Loris. Para watched him pacing anxiously across the apartment's sitting room, endlessly rubbing his hands together, as if washing them.

Atkins's robot assistant had called each day to ask when Tray would be available to begin the memory erasure procedure. Tray had neither answered nor returned the calls. Para had warned that sooner or later the police would call on him.

"You are a prisoner of outdated attitudes," the android said. "I never realized what complications such an antique sexual mind-set can produce."

Tray stopped pacing. Staring at Para, he responded, "Maybe Atkins and his team should remove my attitudes about sex."

Para shook its head. "I doubt that they could. Such attitudes must be ingrained in so many parts of the brain that—"

Tray heard the brief tone that announced a phone message.

"A call for you," the android announced. "From Loris De Mayne."

"Yes?" Tray fairly shouted.

Loris's familiar figure appeared in the middle of the sitting room. She was on her feet, wearing a simple knee-length dress of light blue that complemented her eyes beautifully.

Smiling, she announced, "Tray, you can board *Jove's Messenger* tomorrow, any time after nine a.m. You are listed on the ship's manifest as resident astronomer."

"You did it!" Tray called out.

"Yes. Everything is set."

Suddenly embarrassed, Tray heard himself flounder, "You didn't have to . . . you know . . . he didn't make you . . ."

Loris's smile widened. "No, Uncle Harold was a perfectly sweet gentleman. I didn't have to use my feminine wiles on him."

Tray felt weak-kneed. "Thank you, Loris. Thank you so much."

"I'll see you on the ship when I come aboard, in two days."

"You're coming to Jupiter, too?" Tray's voice shot half an octave higher than normal.

"Yes," said Loris. "I've decided to go with you and Mance."

Tray's elation vanished like a puff of smoke. She's coming aboard with Mance Bricknell, he realized.

EVASION

+++
+++

"One of the many advantages of a global government," Para was saying, "is that human beings are no longer divided into separate nations."

The android and Tray were sitting side by side in a sleek, swept-wing commercial rocketplane, heading for Quito, Ecuador, and the space elevator that rose to orbital altitude and beyond, based a few kilometers outside the city.

Tray had felt nervous as they filed past the customs examiner at the Denver spaceport, but the robot passed them with only the briefest hesitation as it scanned the identification information on its desktop screen.

"The purpose of your trip?" the robot had asked.

"Vacation," Tray had lied.

And that was it. The two of them followed the line of passengers to the debarkation gate and into the airliner.

The rocketplane took off like a normal aircraft, but once at altitude its nose lifted and its rocket engines ignited with enough thrust to force Tray deep into his cushioned seat.

Turning to Para, Tray said over the muted growl of the rockets, "Next stop, Quito!"

Para nodded once, completely calm. Tray's pulse was thumping.

Customs inspection at the Quito airport was slightly more

exacting than it had been in Denver. The inspector, a uniformed human woman, checked Tray's identification on her viewscreen, then asked him where in Quito he would be staying.

Before Tray could think of an answer Para replied, "We haven't decided that yet. This trip is a rather spur-of-the-moment decision."

The woman eyed the android with some distaste.

Tray found his tongue. "I've always wanted to see Quito," he lied. "I understand it's a very beautiful city."

The inspector broke into a pleasant smile. "It is indeed a very beautiful city. Especially the central square. My brother manages the finest hotel in the city there. It's called El Paradiso."

"El Paradiso," Tray repeated. "We'll look for it."

With that, the woman waved them through customs.

A dead-black car was waiting for them at the curb outside the terminal, with a rake-thin young man in a dark suit leaning against its fender, holding up a tablet-sized screen that proclaimed *Trayvon Williamson*.

Tray shook hands with the youngster, who opened the car's rear door and took his and Para's meager travel bags.

With a purr of power the car pulled out into the moderate traffic. "To the star tower!" the driver called happily over his shoulder as they reached the lane where the car lifted off the ground and took to the air.

"That was easy," Tray said to Para. "No problem."

The android nodded minimally. "I expect that we'll be subjected to deeper scrutiny at the elevator."

Tray said, "I guess so." Then he turned and watched the city of Quito passing below them.

* * *

Once they landed at the foot of the space elevator, Tray offered the driver a generous tip. Which the young man refused, with a wave of his hand. "Señor Balsam's people have already paid me very well. *Vayan con Dios, señores.*"

As Tray and Para walked along the beautiful flowered shrubbery that lined both sides of the curving walkway, Tray craned his neck at the space elevator, rising from a set of foundation mountings that gripped the earth solidly and soaring up beyond the clouds.

"It's magnificent, isn't it?" he breathed.

Para said, "Splendid indeed." Then the android nodded toward the trio of uniformed policeman standing in front of the entrance to the elevator's housing.

As they approached the waiting policemen, Tray rehearsed the story they had invented. *We're here to check out the astronomical equipment aboard the ship. We were invited by Council president Balsam himself.*

But the sergeant in charge of the trio, portly, with a thick dark mustache, grinned widely at them. "Señor Williamson, welcome! Council president Balsam has personally instructed us to help you in any way you require."

Surprised and relieved, Tray thanked the sergeant. Turning slightly toward Para, he introduced, "This is Para, my—"

"Your servant, of course," said the sergeant. "Come! This way to the elevator. It has been reserved specifically for you."

The two other policemen took the bags that Tray and Para had been carrying and the five of them marched calmly to the waiting elevator.

The elevator doors slid open, revealing a luxurious room lined with comfortable cushioned benches with a fully-stocked refrigerator and drink dispenser in one corner.

"It will take more than two hours to reach the level where your spacecraft is orbiting," said the sergeant, still smiling. "Have a pleasant ride!"

Then he and his men stepped out of the elevator, the doors slid shut, and Tray and Para sat side by side on one of the luxurious benches.

Before either of them could speak a word, the elevator began to rise smoothly, silently, and they left Earth behind them.

book two

JUPITER

JOVE'S MESSENGER

Tray felt a tendril of anxiety as he and Para walked along the Glassteel-covered passageway that led from the space elevator's Low Earth orbit level to Council president Balsam's spacecraft, looming huge and bulbous in front of them.

Glancing backward over his shoulder, Tray saw that the elevator's intricate structure soared far beyond this level, past the geosynchronous orbit's altitude, more than 40,000 kilometers high.

It's magnificent, he said to himself. A tower that reaches toward the stars.

Yet he couldn't escape the tendril of fear that roiled deep within him. There's nothing between us and the vacuum of space except this frail covering of Glassteel. The cold and emptiness of space is hardly more than an arm's length away from us.

Para brought his attention back to the here and now. Nodding toward the oversized hatch at the end of the walkway, the android said calmly, "A welcoming committee of one is waiting for us."

Tray looked along the passageway and saw a single smartly dressed young woman waiting in front of the hatch.

"Welcome aboard, gentlemen," she called as Tray and Para neared her.

Tray smiled at her. In this age of virtually perpetual youth it was impossible to guess her age, but she looked bright, vigorous, smiling, with the cool blue eyes and short-cropped golden hair of a Viking princess.

"Thank you," he said as he came close enough to extend his hand. She took it in a firm, warm grasp.

"I am Rihanna," she said.

Tray's implanted communicator flashed that her name, in Scandinavia, translated as "nymph." She looked too buxomly solid for a nymph, he thought. Pretty, though, with a welcoming smile that dimpled her cheeks.

"I'm one of Captain Tsavo's aides," she said to Tray, ignoring Para, standing at his side. "He's asked me to show you around the ship, get you familiarized with everything."

Tray smiled and nodded. Para said nothing.

Rihanna led Tray, with Para beside him, through a maze of passageways that led to his quarters, a sparse bedroom only slightly larger than a closet.

"We don't have accommodations for your android," she explained cheerily. "You can let it stand in a corner at night, I suppose."

Tray felt his brows knit slightly, but Para said, "I can stand out in the passageway. It makes no difference to me."

Rihanna grinned at the android. "Like a faithful hound, protecting its master's sleep."

"I'm not Para's master," Tray snapped, immediately regretting his impulse. He tried to explain, "Para is my friend, my companion."

Rihanna's grin morphed into surprised puzzlement.

"Your companion?" she asked, clearly unable to believe Tray's words. "Your friend? A machine?"

"An *intelligent* machine," said Tray.

The young woman gawked at Para for an uncomfortable moment, then shrugged her slim shoulders. "Have it your way," she said.

grand tour

Tray's orientation took several days. Rihanna seemed determined to show Tray every aspect of the huge ship's facilities, from its command center to its power plant, from the food processing equipment to the life support systems. She showed up at his door precisely at 0900 hours each day, and led Tray and Para to a different section of the huge ship.

Tray trudged along dutifully, with Para beside him, as the young officer rattled off prepackaged descriptions of the various sets of equipment and introduced Tray to the crew personnel at each station. Tray nodded and said what he hoped were the proper things while Para patiently recorded each word.

After several days of mind-numbing orientation lectures, Rihanna led them along a short, blank-walled passageway. Her perpetual smile seemed to grow even larger than it had been over the previous days.

"Now we get to the interesting part," she said, as if what she'd already shown them had been ordinary, humdrum.

She stopped in front of an oval hatch marked EXCURSION MODULE: AUTHORIZED PERSONNEL ONLY.

"This is the entrance to the excursion module," said Rihanna.

Tray nodded, thinking, That's what the sign says.

"Once we're down near the surface of the Jovian ocean," she went on, her voice betraying just a hint of excitement, "you and your party will board this module and go out into the ocean, down to the depths where the Leviathans swim."

"How deep will that be?" Tray asked.

Rihanna blinked once, and Tray suddenly realized that she might be an android, like Para, and not human at all.

"The Leviathans swim at a level that's at least several hundred klicks below the surface of the ocean."

"Then we'll have to go that deep," said Tray.

"And deeper, most likely."

Tray stared at her. She certainly looked human enough, he thought. But there was something about her, something that seemed . . . *programmed* instead of spontaneous.

Unfazed by Tray's staring, or perhaps not noticing it, Rihanna was reciting, "The Leviathans cruise through Jupiter's planet-wide ocean in gigantic family groups. They are intelligent, sort of, but their intelligence has very few points in contact with our own. We live in such a different environment from theirs. Our scientists have managed to establish some contact with them, but it's rather rudimentary. The differences between our two levels of intelligence are sizable."

Para spoke up. "Humans have a much wider range of experiences than the Leviathans."

"That's true enough," Rihanna responded. After a heartbeat's pause, she added, "Of course, the Leviathans must deal with the Darters, the predators that attack them—especially their young."

Tray asked, "The Leviathans communicate among themselves, don't they?"

"Visually," said Rihanna, with a very human nod. "They flash pictures on the flanks of their enormous bodies. You'll see, when we get down among them."

She's human, Tray thought. It's just the prepackaged lectures that she delivers that makes her seem almost like a machine.

Dimpling into a smile, Rihanna asked, "Are you ready to enter the Excursion Module?"

"Yes!" Tray answered eagerly.

It turned out to be a big disappointment. Rihanna gave a spoken order and the heavy oval hatch swung outward, revealing a long narrow passageway. With Para behind him and Rihanna up front, Tray stepped carefully over the hatch's coaming and followed the young woman along the tight metal-walled corridor.

"This is no ordinary submersible. The module is spherical," Rihanna was explaining, falling back into her lecture mode of speech. "It consists of seven layers of spheres, one within another, which compress in reaction to the enormous pressure of the Jovian ocean at depth."

"May I ask," said Para, "what the pressure will be at the level where we'll be cruising?"

Rihanna hesitated before answering, "I don't have the exact numbers at my fingertips . . ."

Tray realized she was human, after all.

". . . but it's enormous," Rihanna went on. "More than a million times the pressure at the deepest level of any ocean on Earth. Megapascals, enough to crush an ordinary submersible like an eggshell."

"And that's where we'll be cruising," said Tray.

Rihanna nodded. Tray could see her shoulder-length blond hair bobbing up and down.

"That's where you'll be cruising," she agreed.

The long passageway ended in a circular deck. Tray saw what was obviously a control center, rows of dials and gauges curving around a deeply padded chair.

Rihanna pointed toward hatches along the curving bulkhead. "Privacy stations for six people, with complete sanitary systems."

Moving to the unoccupied central chair, she pointed to the large viewscreens studding the forward bulkhead. "These will give you a complete, three-hundred-sixty-degree view of your outer surroundings. With luck, you'll cruise among the Leviathans and even communicate with them—within the limits of their understanding, of course."

"Of course," said Tray, but he was thinking that limits of understanding apply to both sides of a conversation.

Rihanna went on to explain that their submersible's crew would consist of only one person.

"This vessel's systems are highly automated, of course. Your crewman will be actually a human backup to the ship's inbuilt systems."

"Only one person," Tray echoed. "Is that wise?"

"Of course it is!" Rihanna snapped. "Captain Tsavo knows what he's doing."

"I didn't mean to imply that he didn't."

"Once you go down into the ocean you'll be cut off from contact with *Jove's Messenger*. You'll be on your own. The responsibilities of your captain will be enormous."

Too much for one person? Tray asked himself. But he didn't say it aloud.

Family Gathering

The three of them spent most of the day in the excursion module. Rihanna talked them through the control system and, more important to Tray, the sensors that would show them the Leviathans in their natural habitat.

For the first time, Tray realized that they would be seeing what the sensors showed, not directly viewing the Leviathans as they swam through Jupiter's all-encompassing ocean. He felt disappointed, but realized that this was the best that modern technology could offer.

It was late afternoon by the time they returned to Tray's coffin-sized quarters. Rihanna bid them a cheery good-bye with a reminder, "Dinner's at nineteen hundred hours, sharp. Captain Tsavo won't wait for you if you're late."

"Where's the galley?" Tray asked.

Her pleasant expression dimming only slightly, Rihanna answered, "Where I showed you yesterday: one deck above this one, turn right, end of the passageway."

Nodding, Tray said, "Oh yes, I remember now. We've seen so much the past few days, it's all kind of a jumble."

Rihanna's smile returned to full wattage. "You'll figure it all out in a day or so. Anyway, I'm sure your android can show you the way."

Para said nothing. Rihanna left the tiny chamber and Tray closed the hatch behind her.

Turning to Para, Tray said, "That was kind of exhausting."

"Would you care to take a nap?" Para asked. "I can wake you when Councilman Kell and the others arrive."

"That's right, they're coming aboard today," Tray recalled. He thought it over for an eyeblink and decided, "Thanks. I think I will stretch out for a little bit."

He went to the narrow bunk that took up most of the cabin's space.

"Wake me when Mr. Kell and the others arrive," he said to Para. Then he added, "Please."

"Of course," said the android.

The others, Tray thought as he stretched out on the bunk. That includes Loris. Smiling to himself, he turned over on his side and closed his eyes.

Tray fought his way out of the dream. He was aboard the scoutship in the Raman system again, watching the flash of light and the expanding sphere of debris that had been the *Saviour* moments earlier.

Para was gently shaking his shoulder. Tray opened his eyes. "Wha . . . ?"

"President Balsam has arrived," Para said gently. "Together with Councilman Kell, Dr. Bricknell, and Lady De Mayne."

Tray pushed himself up to a sitting position, blinking the sleep away. Then he asked, "*Lady* De Mayne?"

"Her father is a hereditary nobleman."

"Hereditary nobleman? In this day and age?"

"The family is Norman. They keep their ancient traditions."

"Lady De Mayne," Tray muttered as he got up from the bunk.

Leaving Para standing by the narrow bunk, Tray washed, dressed, and hurried to the ship's galley. Up one level and to the right.

By the time he got there, Balsam, Kell, Bricknell, and Loris were already in the galley, which was a cramped self-service cafeteria with a single long table that could seat ten people. Harold Balsam stood nearly a full head taller than the others, dominating the scene, speaking in an overly loud voice.

"This ship is the finest that money can buy," he was saying, jabbing a forefinger against Jordan Kell's chest. "The European Consortium of Universities oversaw its design. You can't get better than the CoU."

Kell, smaller, leaner, much more elegant than Balsam, nodded patiently. Mance Bricknell stood next to him, with Loris De Mayne at his other side.

Loris.

She was wearing a simple one-piece jumpsuit, dark gray, but it clung to her slim figure like a famished lover. Tray had to try three times before he could say hello to her.

"Hello yourself," she replied with a smile.

He grinned back at her. It was difficult to say much because Balsam was rambling along.

"In the old days," the council president was declaiming, "people had to immerse themselves in perfluorocarbon liquid or some such to equalize the pressure. Sank themselves into the gunk, filled their lungs with it, and actually breathed it. That was the only way to withstand the pressures of deep dives into the ocean."

Kell nodded minimally. "But we don't need to do that anymore."

"That's right, Jordan. Modern technology has solved the problems of high-pressure survival."

Smiling tightly, Kell murmured, "Most of the problems."

Balsam looked puzzled for a moment, then recovered and broke into a toothy grin. He wrapped a beefy arm around Kell's shoulders and with his free hand gestured to the dining table. "Come on, let's eat."

"You're not waiting for Captain Tsavo?"

"He'll be along, sooner or later," Balsam said.

The five of them lined up at the dispensers, Tray at the end, directly behind Loris.

"I'm glad you decided to come along," he said to her, keeping his voice low.

Half-turning toward him, she replied, "I am, too. I'm looking forward to seeing the Leviathans."

Bricknell, standing ahead of Loris, spoke up. "They live so deep in the ocean that we can't observe them normally. We have to send submarines down to their level."

"It's their ocean, after all," Loris said.

"They don't *own* it," snapped Bricknell.

Tray heard himself reply, "Don't they?"

"Not legally."

From the front of their impromptu line, second only to Balsam, Jordan Kell said, "The Council has ruled that the natives of an ecosphere have first rights of ownership to their domain."

"Oh, that's just political babble," Bricknell countered. "Those Leviathans don't *use* their ocean for anything."

"They live in it," Kell said mildly.

"But they don't use it," Bricknell insisted. "They don't develop the resources."

Loris spoke up, "Like the way we're mining Jupiter's upper atmosphere for fusion fuels."

"Exactly," said Bricknell.

"Without asking the Leviathans' permission," Kell pointed out.

Shaking his head, Bricknell countered, "They wouldn't know what we're talking about. They have no concept of anything except the ocean they live in."

Tray wanted to argue with Bricknell, but realized he really didn't have anything to say. Keep your mouth shut, he told himself. He remembered an old aphorism: Better to be silent and thought a fool than to open your mouth and prove it.

But the budding debate was suddenly ended by Captain Tsavo's entrance into the dining room.

Captain Tsavo

"Sorry I'm late," came a booming basso profundo voice from the galley's entrance.

Tray and the others turned. Captain Tsavo stood framed in the hatchway, a half-dozen centimeters taller than its curved frame. A bright smile in his dark face, he ducked through the hatch and strode to Tray's side, picking up a serving tray with a smooth easy motion.

"I had to resolve a slight difference of opinion between my first mate and the chief engineer," Tsavo explained. With a sigh, he went on, "The duties of command come before dinner, I'm afraid."

Tray had to crane his neck to look into the captain's face. Tsavo's skin was a smooth unglossy black, the darkest complexion Tray had ever seen on anyone. More than two meters tall, Tsavo was sleekly slender, with long slim arms and legs. He was in uniform, an impeccably spotless light blue outfit that accentuated his height and lean physique.

Kell stepped out of line and came up to the captain. Barely as tall as Tsavo's shoulder, he put out his hand.

"It's a pleasure to meet you, sir."

Tsavo's smile could have lit up a whole village. "And I am very pleased to meet you, at last, Councilman Kell."

Balsam put down his tray and also hustled to be at Tsavo's side.

With a wide grin he grabbed the captain's hand and said, "It's good to see you again, sir."

His own grin still in place, Tsavo pumped Balsam's hand. "How do you like your ship?" he asked.

"Haven't had a chance to go through it all yet," Balsam answered, "but what I've seen of the crew looks top rate."

"They're all good people," said Tsavo. "The cream of the crop."

His beefy face grinning, Balsam said, "For what I'm paying, I expected nothing less."

mission plan

+ +

+ +

The six of them sat at the galley's lone table and listened to Tsavo explaining the fundamentals of the ship's systems while they ate.

"*Jove's Messenger* is built to take you down to within five hundred kilometers of the surface of Jupiter's ocean," the captain told them. "There we'll detach the excursion module and you will enter the sea."

"Who'll be piloting the module?" Kell asked.

"One of my brightest young officers," said Tsavo. "Gyele Sheshardi. From Australia. Very competent. Cool head, heart of gold."

"I've met him," Balsam said, from across the table. "Isn't he kind of young to be in command?"

"It's his first command opportunity, true enough," Tsavo replied. "I'm fully satisfied that he can handle the task of commanding the excursion module. Does that give you an idea of what I think of him?"

"Well, yes, I suppose so . . ."

"I trust young Gyele implicitly," said the captain. "He'll be fine."

An awkward silence settled on the diners. Until Loris spoke up.

"The excursion module needs a name," she said. "I don't think we should go into the ocean in a vessel that hasn't a name of its own."

"By god, you're right," said Balsam.

"A name," Bricknell agreed.

"How about one of Jupiter's children?" Balsam suggested.

With an ironic smile, Kell pointed out, "Jove had hundreds of children, if you accept all the old myths."

"Why do we have to name it after a figure from mythology?" Loris asked. "Why not an actual person, out of real history?"

"Like who?" Bricknell asked.

"A great scientist, like Hawking."

"English," Bricknell sneered.

"Da Vinci?" Kell suggested.

"How about Edison?" asked Balsam. "Or . . . what's his name, the one who invented the first submarine."

"Fulton?"

"No, Bushnell," Kell replied.

"Never heard of him," Balsam said, shaking his head.

Kell shrugged and reached for his coffee cup.

"Why not Juno, then?" Loris suggested.

"Jupiter's wife?"

"Queen of the heavens," said Loris.

"I thought you wanted to get away from mythology," Balsam objected.

"Not necessarily," Loris replied.

Tray spoke up. "What about the greatest explorer of ancient mythology: Odysseus."

"Ulysses?" Balsam asked.

Before anyone else at the table could speak, Loris asked, "How about the goddess who protected and guided him?"

"Athena?"

"Athena," said Loris.

Putting down his coffee cup, Kell said, "Athena was originally a warrior goddess. But over time she became a goddess of wisdom, protectress of the city named after her, Athens."

"And of the craft of war," Loris added, "not just bloodthirsty bashing."

"You can look at Athena as a record of humankind's evolving from savagery to civilization," Kell went on.

"Athena," Tray repeated. "A good choice for a protectress."

"Any objections?"

Tray looked around the dining table. Bricknell seemed to want to say something, but he held his tongue. Balsam didn't look too pleased either, but he too kept silent.

"Athena it is, then," said Kell. "By unanimous vote."

Tray smiled inwardly at how Kell had taken command of the debate. He's a leader, Tray said to himself. No wonder Balsam worries about him.

Once nothing was left of their dinner except crumbs and empty cups and glasses, Captain Tsavo raised his voice: "I think this would be a good time for you to meet Gyele Sheshardi."

"Our lone crewman," Balsam said, in a half whisper.

Tsavo got up from his chair as the hatch to the galley opened and a young man stepped in.

The galley fell absolutely silent.

Standing in the open hatchway was a young man, little more than a meter and a half tall. His skin was dead gray, his body stocky but his arms and legs childishly thin. His brows seemed slightly heavier than normal and his face showed his Negroid heritage. Like Tsavo, he wore a light blue uniform, but Tray thought he looked almost like a child playing make-believe.

An Aboriginal, Tray realized. An Australian Aboriginal.

"Meet Lieutenant Gyele Sheshardi," said Captain Tsavo, in his deep, rumbling voice. He began to introduce the others, starting with Balsam.

Sheshardi's smile seemed forced, Tray thought, as he went around the table shaking hands with the others. From the rigid rictus of his smile and the stiffness of his body language, Tray figured that the young man would rather be on the edge of hell than here among them. When he came to Tray his extended hand was trembling noticeably.

The introductions finished, Tsavo told Sheshardi to sit next to Tray.

"Have you had your dinner, Gyele?" the captain asked, his voice booming across the narrow galley.

Sheshardi's baby-sized face bobbed up and down. "Oh, yes, sir. Hours ago."

"Have some dessert with us, then."

With a shy smile, Sheshardi answered, "Thank you, no. I am quite content."

"Good," said Tsavo. "Now tell us what they need to know about the excursion module."

The Aboriginal visibly relaxed as he began to explain about the module's various systems. He's at home now, Tray realized. His size, his heritage, his fears and hopes for the future don't matter now. He's talking about the technology, and he knows his stuff.

Sheshardi went into exquisite detail about the excursion module's sensors, its control system, the features of its privacy quarters and the individual entertainment systems that had been installed in each of them.

Turning to Tray, Sheshardi said, "Your billet has been equipped with a hand-sized recorder that can produce a full range of musical instrumentation, Mr. Williamson."

Tray nodded his acknowledgment.

Balsam interrupted, "I'll need to be able to receive messages from the Interplanetary Council's staff, of course. There's no time off for me, not even in Jupiter's ocean."

Sheshardi shook his head. "I'm afraid that will be impossible, sir. Once we are immersed in the ocean, all communications will be cut off."

Balsam's brows knit into a frown. "I didn't realize . . . that is, no one told me that I'd be isolated . . ."

"The ocean blocks electromagnetic signals very effectively," Sheshardi explained. "Captain Tsavo, of course, will receive any messages that come in for you and have them waiting for you when you return, naturally."

"Naturally," Balsam huffed.

"Messages can be sent to the module in specialized capsules, can't they?" Kell asked.

"If they are deemed important enough," Sheshardi replied. "Of course, on occasion the capsules have been lost."

"Important messages," Loris murmured, "wandering through Jupiter's boundless ocean."

Tsavo changed the subject. To Sheshardi he revealed, "We have given the module its own name: *Athena*."

Sheshardi's dark face lit up. "The ancient Greek goddess of wisdom! An excellent choice."

"Have it inscribed on the module's hull, Gyele," Tsavo said.

"Yes, sir. Right away." The Abo fell silent for a moment. Transmitting the order, Tray comprehended.

Tsavo's bloodshot eyes swept the table. "Any questions?" he asked.

Tray saw uncertainty in their eyes. A memory of his school days flashed in his mind: No one wants to be the first to speak.

Then Loris raised her hand slightly and asked, "How long will we be in the ocean?"

Tsavo turned to Sheshardi and nodded benignly. The youth replied, "That depends on the Leviathans, to a considerable extent. If they don't mind our presence among them, we are equipped to stay in the ocean for fifty hours."

Tray heard himself ask, "What happens if they *do* mind our presence?"

With a tight smile, Sheshardi answered, "Usually, they merely run away. It's quite a sight, these monstrously huge creatures accelerating to top speed. They could leave our module quite alone and speed off."

"Do they ever get aggressive?" Bricknell asked.

The Aborigine shook his head. "In all the years we have been observing and interacting with the Leviathans, there has not been one recorded incident of their behaving aggressively. They are very gentle giants."

"But they have run away from us," Kell said.

"Yes. Now and then. They can move away quite quickly. Much faster than we can follow."

"Why do they run away?" Bricknell asked.

Sheshardi hunched his shoulder in a puzzled shrug. "Who knows? Our scientists have tried for many years to understand their behavior."

Kell asked, "The predators—the Darters—how big do they get?"

"Small, compared to the Leviathans. If the Leviathans can be compared to a fair-sized city in size, the Darters are no larger than a city hall."

"But dangerous."

"Extremely. They have battered our observation submersibles now and then. Sunk them."

"Crewed submersibles?" Kell asked.

"Unfortunately, yes."

Loris asked, "And what happened to their crews?"

"All lost."

A gloomy silence fell across the table.

Then Balsam put on a grin and asked, "And you, Lieutenant Sheshardi, how many times have you gone down there among the Leviathans?"

Sheshardi glanced at Captain Tsavo before answering, "Oh, this is my first time. I've never been in the ocean before."

Final Preparations

Tray awoke the next morning with vague memories of a dream drifting through his mind. He was on the *saviour* again, with Felicia, standing in an observation blister, looking out at the splendor of the stars. But it wasn't Felicia, he realized. The woman was Loris: tall, slim, coolly elegant.

As he got up from the narrow bunk he tried to remember more of his dream. But he could recall nothing except that the two of them—himself and Loris—were holding hands as they gazed out at the magnificent panorama of blazing stars and swirling clouds of glowing dust.

And he kissed her.

"You need a cold shower," he grumbled to himself.

He was halfway finished dressing when Para quietly opened the door from the passageway outside.

Brightly, the android asked, "Did you have a pleasant sleep?"

Grinning self-consciously as he tugged on his shoes, Tray answered, "Yes. Very pleasant."

"We are required to bring our clothing and effects into the module—"

"The *Athena*," Tray corrected.

Hardly missing a beat, Para went on, "The *Athena* module this morning. Have you packed what you want to bring aboard?"

"Just a couple of changes of clothes and some toiletries," Tray replied. Then he added, "And my camera."

"*Athena*'s automated sensors will record everything we observe."

With a hardly visible grin, Tray said, "But not the passengers. The module's system will record the Leviathans." Picking up his palm-sized camera from the bedside table, he went on, "I want to record the people we're riding with."

Para was unable to register surprise, but the android asked, "Why would you want to do that?"

Tray hesitated as he thought up a cover story. "The music I want to write should include the human reactions to the Leviathans, don't you think?"

Para blinked once, twice. Then, "I hadn't thought of that."

Tray suddenly felt sorry for the machine. "You've got a lot to learn about human desires, Para. Maybe I can help you, teach you."

"I would welcome that."

Tray nodded, but he kept to himself his real reason for bringing the camera. He wanted to film Loris.

Tray and Para got to the *Athena* module ahead of everyone else. No one was there; the module seemed empty, cold, and lifeless.

Tray made his way to the door with his name on it. Para stood close behind him, carrying Tray's modest travel bag. The privacy module was cramped, not a centimeter larger than it needed to be. It was in perfect order, bunk neatly made up, slim closet empty, awaiting Tray's clothes, bathroom alcove of toilet and mini-shower gleaming under the ceiling lights.

Tray went straight to the electronics handset resting on the bedside stand. He picked it up, scanned its screen, and selected Beethovan's "Moonlight Sonata." The piano music filled the narrow compartment, slow, measured, filled with unrealized dreams.

Turning to Para as he switched off the handset, Tray grinned tightly and said, "This ought to be able to record whatever I want to put down."

"It seems very capable," Para answered. Tray couldn't help feeling that the android was proud of its fellow machine.

Para lay the travel bag on the bunk, unzipped it, and began hanging Tray's modest set of clothes in the minuscule closet while Tray took his toiletries kit to the phone booth–sized lavatory.

Tray stepped back to the bedside. Spreading his arms, he said, "Well, this is going to be home for the next couple of days."

"Rather tight," said Para. "I suppose I should stay out in the control center overnight."

Tray nodded absently.

He heard voices from out in the control center. Opening his cubicle's door, he saw Loris and Bricknell standing amidst the module's control and command equipment, glancing around a bit apprehensively. They both carried travel bags hanging limply over their arms.

"Welcome aboard," Tray said, smiling, as he stepped out of his own compartment.

Bricknell nodded uncertainly, while Loris smiled back at him.

"It's not much, is it?" Bricknell sniffed.

"It's only for a couple of days," said Loris. She spotted her name on the door next to Tray's. "Excuse me; I've got to unpack."

With a dispirited pout, Bricknell said, "That should take all of a minute."

"At least two," Loris countered as she entered her cubicle.

Bricknell looked around the control center. "Where do we eat?" he asked no one in particular. "There's no chairs, no table."

Pointing to a ceiling-high gleaming steel door, Para replied, "According to the module's schematic, our food is stored in the refrigerator there, and we can sit on the pull-out chairs that line the rear bulkhead."

Bricknell looked where Para pointed, his doubtful expression easing only slightly. "Not all that comfortable, is it?"

Tray said firmly, "We're here to see the Leviathans, not for creature comforts."

Bricknell nodded once. "You can say that again."

debarkation

Tray felt his pulse thumping along his veins as the five passengers stood in *Athena*'s compact control center. No, he thought, not five of us: six. Para's with me. Tray thought of the android as a person, not a machine.

Jordan Kell and Martin Balsam had arrived together, like old friends starting out on a pleasure jaunt. Balsam loomed over Kell's trim figure: Tray thought of an overfed gorilla standing next to a sleek jaguar. But the gorilla's expression worried Tray; it looked . . . sly, crafty.

Tray's palms felt warm, sweaty. Then he noticed that Balsam was perspiring visibly and Loris and Bricknell both looked tense. Only Jordan Kell seemed relaxed as he stood directly behind Gyele Sheshardi, who was sitting in the command chair. From the little he could see of their young skipper, Tray thought Sheshardi looked like a child playing grown-up.

But the Abo was going through the departure checklist very professionally, quietly scrutinizing the readouts of each system and mechanism of *Athena*'s myriad equipment with cool intelligence.

Suddenly the communications screen started flashing a red URGENT. INCOMING MESSAGE FOR PRESIDENT BALSAM. URGENT. Sheshardi twisted 'round in his oversized chair and looked up questioningly at Balsam.

The Council president frowned slightly and muttered, "No rest for the weary."

"Do you wish to see the message?" Sheshardi asked.

Looking and sounding exasperated, Balsam answered, "I guess I'll have to. Put it on-screen, please."

A sleekly attractive redheaded woman's face appeared on the communications screen.

"This message is for Council president Harold Balsam," she said, in a flat, emotionless voice. "The Council has scheduled an emergency session tomorrow at nine hundred thirty hours GMT to consider Australia's motion to accept the Aborigine appeal to deny access for the construction of the Macdonnel Ranges power complex. Your presence is urgently required. Please reply immediately. Message ends."

Balsam's jaw sagged open. Kell turned to him and said, "I thought that issue was settled."

Shaking his head wearily, Balsam said, "Apparently the Abos aren't satisfied."

Nine thirty tomorrow morning, Tray thought. Balsam can't possibly get back to Earth by then.

But the Council president was already saying, "I can attend the meeting remotely, with an FTL communications link."

"But not from here," Sheshardi pointed out. "This vessel is not equipped with FTL transmission equipment."

"Damn!"

Kell asked, "There's no similar message for me?"

Sheshardi shook his head. "Only for President Balsam."

"They want you to preside over the meeting, Harold," Kell said. "They don't need me there. My people will vote in their usual bloc."

"Damn, damn, damn," Balsam repeated. "Of all the times to schedule an emergency session."

Loris asked, "What are you going to do?"

Heaving a heavy sigh, Balsam replied, "I'll have to go back to *Jove's Messenger* and set up an FTL link with Earth for tomorrow's meeting."

"We can delay our departure, can't we?" Tray asked.

Sheshardi shook his head. "*Jove's Messenger* is not equipped to stay two extra days or more. We would have to restock the ship's stores and plan an entirely new trajectory into Jupiter's atmosphere."

"Damn!" Balsam repeated.

"To come all this way . . ." Bricknell groused.

Balsam drew himself up taller. "You go ahead without me. I'll chair their damned meeting and you people go down to see the Leviathans."

"That doesn't seem fair," Loris said.

"No, no," Balsam countered. "You go, as scheduled. I can see the Leviathans some other time."

Kell started to say, "Harold, I don't think—"

Balsam stopped him by placing a heavy hand on Kell's shoulder. "Go on without me, Jordan." Forcing a grin, he added, "It's my ship, isn't it? I can see the damned fish any time I want to."

"Are you sure?" Kell asked.

Balsam nodded heavily. "You've been Council president, Jordan. You know that duty comes before pleasure."

Sadly, reluctantly, Kell replied, "I'm afraid you're right, Harold."

Balsam grudgingly left the *Athena* module. As the hatch closed behind him, Tray turned to Kell and said, "That was perfect timing, wasn't it?"

Kell stared at the closed hatch. "Yes, I suppose it was."

Gyele Sheshardi peered over the back of his command chair and said, "You should all be seated and strapped in."

Excitement bubbling through him, Tray pulled down one of the folding chairs and, instead of sitting on it himself, gestured for Loris to sit on it.

With a smile she murmured, "Thank you, kind sir."

Bricknell pulled down the seat on Loris's other side and plopped himself down on it without a word. But his face showed clear displeasure.

Tray sat at Loris's other side, Kell beside Bricknell.

Para said, "I can remain standing."

But Sheshardi cautioned, "Flying through the cloud decks can be quite violent, you know."

Para glanced at Tray, who nodded, then sat beside him and began buckling the shoulder and lap belts. Sheshardi turned his attention back to the instruments. Tray fought the urged to grasp Loris's hand. She was close enough for him to pick up the scent of the perfume she was wearing. It reminded him of Felicia.

"It's a shame Harold has to miss this," Kell muttered.

Bricknell said, "It's his responsibility as Council president."

"Yes, but just the same . . ."

"He can see the big beasts whenever he wants to. This is his ship, isn't it?"

Kell nodded. Unhappily, Tray thought.

Sheshardi asked, "Is everyone ready for departure?"

The four passengers nodded.

Sheshardi said, "Aloud, please. For the ship's log."

One by one, each of them, including Para, announced they were ready to go.

Tray couldn't see Sheshardi's face: from where he was sitting the command chair hid his childlike figure entirely. But he heard a satisfied lilt to the Aborigine's voice as he reported to Captain Tsavo, "*Athena* ready for debarkation."

Tsavo's face was visible on the main viewscreen. He dipped his chin once as he said, "Departure in ten seconds."

The master clock on Sheshardi's control panel began counting down, "Nine . . . eight . . ."

Tray felt his innards tightening. Turning his head toward Loris, he saw that she was staring at the screen that showed the clock, its second hand ticking away. On her other side Bricknell licked his lips nervously. Even Kell looked tense, expectant.

". . . two . . . one . . . *launch!*"

Tray felt a gentle push against his back. The clock disappeared from the screen, replaced by a view of Jupiter's multihued clouds streaming across the giant planet's face.

"We're on our way," Sheshardi announced, his voice quavering slightly.

"Into the clouds," said Bricknell, almost breathless.

Loris added, "And then down into Jupiter's boundless ocean."

As Tray sat tensely, strapped into his chair along the command center's rear bulkhead, he remembered a line from a book he had read as a child: "Flying is long hours of boredom punctuated by moments of sheer terror."

Well, we've got the boredom, he thought. *Athena* had bounced and jittered for hours as it dove through Jupiter's massive, turbulent cloud deck, but now that they were finally beneath the clouds the flight had smoothed into a monotonous constancy.

The air was clear—and empty. No birds, no creatures of any sort were visible. Just the immense, endless ocean far, far below them, flat and seemingly calm. Their ship was cutting through Jupiter's hydrogen-rich atmosphere at nearly the speed of sound, but as far as Tray could see in the viewscreens, they were hanging motionless, suspended above a boundless ocean in air that was empty of life.

But then, "Look!" Loris shouted.

She pointed at the control console's central viewscreen, where an object was floating in midair, so far away that it appeared to be little more than a dark-colored dot against the underside of the clouds that roiled above them.

"A blimp," said Sheshardi.

"Blimp?"

"That's what they're called. The scientific name for them is *Medusa Jovianus* or something like that."

"Can we get closer to it?" Kell asked.

"Not without ruining our flight plan," Sheshardi answered. "But we can magnify the image . . ."

The blob in the viewscreen seemed to hurtle toward them, taking form as they watched.

It was a massive fat sausage shape, floating in the atmosphere, trailing a cluster of tendrils from its underside.

Sheshardi put one of the education vids on the top-right screen. A youngish man said, "Jupiter's atmosphere is the habitat of a complex aerial biosphere, dominated by the dirigible-like

Medusas that drift endlessly through the enormous blanket of gases."

The screen showed a still illustration of one of the floaters as the lecturer methodically pointed out its flotation bag, its hunting tendrils, and other aspects of the giant creature.

Tray turned his attention back to the living thing the ship's cameras were watching, his mind picking up bits from the lecturer's flat, unexcited voice:

". . . sizes range to several hundred meters in length, and while no samples have been taken for dissection, X-ray and other remote sensing probes show . . ."

Several hundred meters in length, Tray thought. Big as an ocean liner on Earth. He saw that there were birdlike things fluttering near the Medusa's dangling tendrils.

The lecturer droned on, ". . . a complex association of other animals centers around each of these floaters, preying on the smaller creatures that inhabit the Jovian atmosphere. In essence, each individual Medusa can be thought of as the center of a self-contained miniature biosphere that is floating and/or flying through the atmosphere. Present studies are mapping the course of these individual bioemes and working to determine . . ."

Tray zoned out. He watched the floater and the life-forms centered about it as *Athena* dived deeper into Jupiter's thick atmosphere, heading for the eternal sea.

"It will be rough when we enter the ocean," Sheshardi warned. "Be certain that you are well strapped in."

Tray tightened his shoulder harness and lap belt, noticing that the others were doing the same, even Para.

"Will we come down near a flock of the Leviathans?" Loris asked.

Sheshardi's disembodied voice answered from the command chair, "We will enter the ocean along one of their most heavily traveled migration routes."

"So we'll be right in their midst."

"Hopefully we will be near enough to approach them," Sheshardi said. "But there are no guarantees, I'm afraid."

"You mean we might not see them at all?" Bricknell complained.

"It is a very big ocean," said Sheshardi.

Kell spoke up. "Most of our tracking systems don't work well in water, and Jupiter's ocean is mostly water."

"With a lot of ammonia and other contaminants," Tray added.

"Quite so," said Kell. "Sonar is best for underwater tracking, but you have to be in the water for it to work well."

"We have automated sonar trackers in the ocean," Bricknell pointed out. "We've had 'em in there for years, haven't we?"

"But it's a very big ocean," Sheshardi repeated.

ENTRY

Entry into the ocean was indeed rough. Tray watched the main viewscreen as the water seemed to rush up to meet them. What had appeared peacefully calm at a distance was in fact rippled with surging waves that marched unimpeded across Jupiter's planet-spanning ocean.

There's no land in this ocean, Tray knew. No continents, not even islands. Those waves surge across tens of thousand of kilometers, unconstrained, endlessly circling around the planet's girth.

And the ocean is deep, he told himself. Tens of thousands of kilometers deep.

"Impact in fifteen seconds," Sheshardi's voice called out, high with excitement.

Clear plastic covers slid out of the bulkhead behind the passengers' seats and fastened themselves to the deck, encasing each seated person in a protective cocoon. For the flash of an instant Tray felt trapped, confined.

But then—

"Impact!" Sheshardi called out, and the vessel plunged into the frothing sea.

Despite the protective straps Tray felt slammed in his seat. His vision blurred momentarily, then steadied. Turning his head, he saw Loris blinking rapidly.

"You okay?" he asked.

Through the plastic covers enveloping them both he saw her nod once, twice, and then smile tentatively. "I think so," came her slightly muffled reply.

Sheshardi's voice came through. "We have successfully entered the ocean. All systems are operating normally."

The plastic covers slid up and disappeared into the bulkhead once more.

"That was . . . jolting," said Kell, shaking his head as if he'd just been struck by a heavy punch.

"Any injuries?" Sheshardi called. Tray found it almost humorous that they couldn't see the Australian, hidden behind the command chair's back.

One by one, the four passengers responded that they were unharmed. In the few seconds it took them to reply, the vessel's motion seemed to smooth out. The violence of their entry into the Jovian ocean was behind them now.

"Very good," said Sheshardi, still hidden in his command chair. "Now we go hunting for a herd of Leviathans."

A line from an ancient poem echoed in Tray's mind:

"Alone, alone, all, all alone;

"Alone on a wide, wide sea."

The globe-girdling Jovian ocean seemed empty, lifeless, as *Athena* plunged deeper, ever deeper into its immense depth.

The central part of the control panel was hidden from view by the back of Sheshardi's sculpted chair, but Tray could see the peripheral screens. They showed nothing but empty surging ocean.

"Where are the Leviathans?" Bricknell asked impatiently.

With a tight grin, Kell answered, "We'll find them, don't worry."

Loris said, "I hope we find them before we have to leave the ocean."

Sheshardi's voice came from the command chair. "We are tracking the nearest herd of them. They are several hundred kilometers away."

"Several *hundred* kilometers?" Tray heard himself ask.

"Heading in our direction," Sheshardi added. "We should make rendezvous with them in . . ." His voice trailed off momentarily, then he resumed, "Four hours and eleven minutes, if they remain on the course they are now following."

Silence. Tray realized it would eat up a sizable portion of their

time in the ocean merely to find the Leviathans. And what if they
don't want us goggling at them? he asked himself. What if we spend
the time to reach them and they just speed off and leave us in the
middle of nowhere?

Kell's voice, calm and steady, said, "This is like a fishing expedition I once was on, off Madagascar. We were searching for coe-
lacanths, those primitive fish that had survived from millions of
years earlier."

"Did you find them?" Loris asked.

"I'm afraid not," Kell confessed. "But we had some fine meals
aboard that research vessel."

Tray thought the story didn't cheer anyone.

Then Para volunteered, "Research can be frustrating. Searching for something elusive requires patience."

And a good food supply, Tray added silently.

Athena sank steadily deeper as Tray and the others sank into silence.

Then Sheshardi called out, "Sonar contact! We have sonar contact with the Leviathan herd."

The screen directly above his seat back showed a vague set of
blips, nothing distinct. Still, Tray could feel the surge of expecta-
tion that filled them all.

Gradually the blips resolved into definite shapes. The Leviathans superficially resembled earthly whales: long streamlined
bodies with powerful tail flukes moving rhythmically up and down,
smaller fins on their backs and flanks.

But as they got steadily closer Tray saw that the comparison to
whales was only superficial. These beasts were *enormous*. The read-
out figures running across the bottom of the viewscreens measured their lengths in kilometers.

The passengers remained in awed silence as they approached the migrating herd. Tray felt his mouth hang open as he realized their immensity.

Ten, twelve kilometers in length, the Leviathans moved through the water with easy grace.

"They are ingesting animal prey," Sheshardi explained as they got nearer. "Almost microscopic animals."

"Like baleen whales on Earth live on krill," Bricknell murmured.

"Much the same," Kell agreed.

"Look!" Loris called out. "They're flashing lights!"

"That's how they communicate," said Sheshardi.

Along the flanks of the gigantic creatures bright shapes were blinking, almost faster than Tray's eyes could follow. He couldn't make out what the shapes represented. Were they a language, a set of symbols?

There were more than fifty of them, cruising leisurely through the deep waters, their enormous mouths stretched wide open as they scooped in seawater that bore the nearly invisible crustaceans that they fed upon.

Then one of the outlying Leviathans flashed an unmistakable picture: an image of their own submersible, *Athena*, accurate down to the sensor blisters dotting the vessel's spherical hull.

"They've seen us!" Loris exclaimed.

"They don't seem to be running away," said Sheshardi.

Kell suggested, "Maybe they've seen our submersibles before. Maybe they recognize us and aren't afraid of us."

Tray heard himself say, "More likely they recognize that we're not dangerous. We don't present a threat to them."

Almost sneering, Bricknell demanded, "How could we represent a threat to them? We're so small they could swallow us whole."

"Pleasant thought," said Loris.

Tray wanted to get to his feet but he was still strapped into the chair. Staring at the viewscreens, he saw that the image of their submersible was now flashing on the flanks of all of the Leviathans.

"A welcome mat?" Kell wondered, with a smile.

"Come into my parlor, said the spider to the fly," Bricknell said.

Sheshardi spoke up. "There is no record of a Leviathan ever harming one of our vessels. On the contrary, some crews swear the beasts helped them when they were in trouble."

"Helped them?"

"Carried them up from the depths toward the surface of the ocean," Sheshardi replied. "On their backs."

"They recognized that we are aliens," Kell said, his voice hollow with wonder. "They realized that we came from beyond their ocean."

"Anthropomorphizing," Bricknell countered. "We can't ascribe human motivations to a completely alien life-form."

"You're probably right," Kell agreed. Somewhat reluctantly, Tray thought.

As they slowly approached the Leviathan herd, Tray saw that the flanks of the immense beasts were lined with eyes: row after row of eyes that all seemed to be staring at them. Staring at him.

He shuddered.

Kell half rose from his seat and grasped the back of Sheshardi's command chair. "I think this is close enough, for the present."

Tray heard the Abo ask, "You don't wish to get closer?" He sounded disappointed.

"Not just yet," Kell answered.

hunters

++
++++ +++

For eternally long moments the humans merely stared at the control panel's viewscreens, goggling at the enormous size and placid grace of the Leviathans.

They glided through the water, seemingly effortlessly, their enormous mouths stretched wide as they scooped in tons of seawater.

"They are feeding," said Sheshardi. "They eat tiny creatures that float in the ocean."

Then Loris noted, "The ones in the middle of the group seem smaller, don't you think?"

Kell shook his head. "No, they're just farther away."

"They're not juveniles?"

"The Leviathans don't have juveniles," Kell explained. "Not in our sense. They are aggregate beasts. When they reproduce, a pair of them breaks apart into dozens of component pieces, which then reassemble themselves into three new adult Leviathans, where before there had been only two."

Tray nodded, remembering reading of the strange way of reproduction that the Leviathans utilized.

"No sex?" Bricknell asked.

"Not in our sense," Kell replied.

Suddenly Para pointed at the viewscreen in the top right corner of the control panel. "Look!" it called out. "Darters."

Tray saw a formation of six—no, seven—sleek shark-like forms speeding past the outer rim of the Leviathans' formation.

"Darters!" Loris gasped.

Darters, Tray echoed silently: Lean, streamlined predators that hunted the Leviathans and often attacked the colossal beasts when some of their members were disassembling in their reproductive behavior.

But none of the Leviathans were breaking apart, he saw. The Darters had no chance against an intact, healthy Leviathan. Or did they?

And then, out of the corner of his eye, Tray noticed one of the Leviathans in the middle of the herd visibly trembling, shuddering as if a powerful electric shock was convulsing through it. Although the creature was well inside the formation of Leviathans, the Darters all pivoted at the same instant and sliced through the formation of gigantic beasts like a pattern of bullets.

Tray stared at the scene. The Leviathan was breaking up into twitching, quivering pieces, each alive, its eyes wide as the shark-like Darters arrowed in on them.

"Why don't they help him?" Loris cried out.

"They cannot," said Sheshardi, in a hollow voice.

"Why don't *we* help him?" Tray demanded.

"How?" Kell replied. "With what?"

It was all over in a few agonizing moments. The Darters gobbled up nearly half the disassembled components of the creature and then sped through the Leviathans' formation and out into the open sea once more. More than a dozen fragments of the dissociated Leviathan floated along with the other, intact animals.

In a near-whisper, Loris asked, "What happens to . . . to those . . . pieces?"

Sheshardi's voice came from the command chair. "If another Leviathan breaks apart soon enough, they will join its pieces and perhaps produce two new animals."

"If not?" Tray heard himself ask.

"The pieces will eventually sink down, probably eaten eventually by Darters or other predators that exist at much deeper levels of the ocean."

"What a shame," Loris murmured.

Bricknell tried to brighten them up with, "Nature, red in fang and claw."

"Yes," said Kell softly, thoughtfully. "But it isn't very pretty, is it?"

communicating?

with the Darters gone, what was left of the Leviathan herd continued on its way through the deep ocean, ingesting tons upon tons of food-bearing seawater.

"Where does the water go?" Loris asked. "They don't keep it inside them, do they?"

"Not at all," answered Kell. "They expel it through vents in their flanks."

Bricknell added, "If they want to, they can squirt out the water at very high velocities: a sort of deep-sea jet propulsion."

"Why didn't they do that to get away from the Darters?" Tray wondered aloud.

"Ask them," said Kell.

"You can attempt to communicate with them," Sheshardi's voice came from his command chair. "There are communications systems built into the armrests of your seats."

Tray glanced down and saw that both his armrests were indeed studded with control pads.

"Touch the green ones for a tutorial on using the comm system," Sheshardi instructed.

As their pilot edged *Athena* closer to the periphery of the Leviathan herd, Tray studied the instructions playing on the miniature viewscreen that had popped up from his left armrest.

Seems simple enough, he told himself. You draw a picture on the screen with your thumbnail and the equipment flashes your picture across the ship's hull.

"We can't all try to send out messages at once," Kell stated the obvious. "I suggest we go in alphabetical order."

"Then I'm first!" Bricknell shouted happily.

"I'll be second," said Loris.

Kell dipped his chin in acknowledgment. "One of the privileges of nobility," he said graciously. "The advantage of having a 'de' in front of your last name."

Tray realized that being named Williamson was no advantage at all.

Bricknell presented a crude cutaway sketch of their vessel, with stick figures representing the five people inside it. Tray felt a spark of resentment that he didn't include Para, but it made no difference: The Leviathans made no response to his attempt at communication.

Loris hesitated when Kell pointed at her. For several moments she simply stared at the tiny screen standing up on her armrest. Finally she drew a stylized picture of a human male and female, naked and complete even to their reproductive organs.

"Like the old *Voyager* spacecraft drawings," Kell murmured, "from back in the twentieth century."

One of the closest Leviathans put up an exact copy of Loris's drawing. Within seconds, all the Leviathans bore the image of a pair of naked human beings on their flanks.

"Well, that got a response," Kell said.

"Maybe if we animated the drawing," Bricknell suggested, his voice dripping innuendo.

"You have a dirty mind," Loris grumbled at him.

"In a clean body," Bricknell smirked.

Shaking his head, Kell said softly, "You realize how different we are when you try to communicate with the Leviathans."

With dirty pictures, Tray thought.

Kell was going on, "They're obviously intelligent, yet we have practically no points of similarity with them, no . . . no Rosetta Stone, so to speak."

"Nothing that translates from their experience to our own," Bricknell agreed.

"Or vice versa," Kell said.

Loris pointed at him and said, "It's your turn now, Mr. Kell."

Tray noticed that her fingernails were each painted space-black, with specks representing stars engraved on them. Tray recognized the Orion constellation and, on her other hand, Ursa Major and the Big Dipper.

"My turn," Kell answered, half to himself.

He sketched out a crude diagram showing the Jovian ocean, the layer of atmosphere above its surface, and the colorful cloud deck atop it all. In the depths of the ocean he added smudges representing the Leviathans and a circle that indicated *Athena*. Then he drew an arrow from the vessel's location, pointing upward, into the clouds and beyond.

"A geography lesson," Kell said, smiling, as he pressed the pad that transmitted his drawing to the projection screen on the ship's curving hull.

"Ambitious," Bricknell remarked.

"Show them where we come from," said Kell.

The instant Kell's drawing appeared on *Athena*'s hull, Loris's earlier sketch winked out on all of the Leviathans. For several moments there was no response whatever, but at last Kell's image flashed into life on one, two, six, and then all of the Leviathans.

"Well, they see your picture," Bricknell said.

"But do they understand what it means?" Kell wondered aloud. "Do they know what an arrow denotes?"

From the command chair Sheshardi's voice rose, "They have seen your picture, sir. Now I believe they are trying to understand it."

For painfully long moments the five humans stared at their screens, waiting, hoping desperately for some response from the Leviathans.

At last Kell admitted, "I'm afraid they just don't understand it."

Unconsciously shaking his head, Tray said, "They don't have the same background of understanding that we do. To them, this ocean is the entire universe. To them, it's unending, eternal. They have no idea that there's a surface to the ocean, and an atmosphere above it—"

"And other worlds in space," Bricknell added.

"And a universe filled with galaxies," said Loris.

Kell exhaled loudly and put on a brave smile. "Well, Mr. Williamson," he said, turning toward Tray, "it's your turn. What do you want to show them?"

Tray hadn't made his decision until the moment Kell asked the question.

"Not a picture," he said. "I want to send them a message in music."

musiᴄ

"musiᴄ," ʙriᴄknell sᴄoffed. "They don't ᴄommuniᴄate in soniᴄs."

"Yes, they do," Sheshardi countered. "They emit sound waves of ultralow frequency, quite inaudible to us."

Tray asked, "Can we send out such low-frequency signals?"

Silence. Tray imagined the Abo flicking his stubby fingers over his armrest controls, checking his system's capabilities.

"Yes," came the answer at last. "I believe we can project sound waves of an appropriate frequency."

Tray saw that they were all staring at him. Even Sheshardi stood up and peered over the back of his command chair.

Closing his eyes to concentrate, Tray heard music in his mind: a powerful, throbbing beat that represented the powerful, surging Leviathans to him. Quickly, he sketched the score onto the communicator's miniature screen.

"Can you send this?" he asked Sheshardi.

The Aboriginal puzzled over the notation for a moment, then disappeared behind his seat back. Tray heard him muttering, "I'm sure we have a program for musical notation somewhere. Ah! Yes! Here it is. *Under Miscellaneous Entertainment Programs.*"

"Do you think the beasts will respond to music?" Bricknell asked, his voice filled with incredulity.

Kell replied, "I don't think anyone's ever tried sound-wave communication with the Leviathans. Since they project pictures on their flanks, all our efforts at communicating with them have been visual."

"How are you doing, Mr. Sheshardi?" Loris called.

"I am translating Mr. Williamson's notation to the ultralow frequencies that the Leviathans use."

"Basso profundissimo," Bricknell punned.

"There!" came Sheshardi's voice from behind his chair back. "We can transmit the music. I will air it here inside the ship at frequencies that we humans can hear."

Tray held his breath.

The music began. From the ship's built-in speakers came the slow, sonorous, majestic music. Tray closed his eyes and saw the majestic Leviathans swimming through their ocean in time to his music.

He forced his eyes open and looked at the viewscreens that wrapped around Sheshardi's command chair. The Leviathans continued their ponderous rhythmic swimming, their flanks dark, pictureless.

"Do they hear it?" Loris asked.

"They must," Sheshardi replied.

"But they're not doing anything."

"They're listening," said Tray, hoping that he was right.

Suddenly the formation of Leviathans began to change. From their customary globular assemblage the gigantic whale-like creatures rearranged themselves into a long, stately line and began to circle *Athena*.

"They are sending out signals!" Sheshardi called out, his voice quivering with emotion. "Our receiving equipment can barely pick it out, it's so low in frequency."

"Can we hear it?" Tray asked.

Almost breathless, Sheshardi panted, "I'm trying . . . most of it is too low . . ."

A deep, rumbling note filled *Athena*'s crew module. Tray felt his brow furrow as he listened. It sounded nothing like the music he had jotted down; it was little more than a low, moaning whisper. Basso profundissimo indeed, Tray thought.

Their entire compartment began to quiver from the Leviathans' vibrations. Tray's nerves began to jangle. Glassware in the food locker popped like balloons. Tray clapped his hands over his ears, as did the others. But it did no good: the deep, resonant vibrations shook his very soul.

Just when he thought the Leviathans' call would tear his brain apart, it stopped. Silence. The gigantic beasts broke their circle around *Athena*.

Tray's ears rang. His heart was thumping heavily. He looked around and saw that the others were equally shaken, gasping, disturbed.

For long moments no one spoke. The only sounds in the compartment were the muted whispers of the air blowers and the distant echo of the Leviathans' majestic song.

Then Kell's voice sliced through Tray's disappointment. "Did you record that, Gyele?"

"Yes," answered the Aborigine, shakily. "All on automatic."

Slowly, as the wide-eyed humans stared at their viewscreens, the Leviathans reformed their original globular configuration.

"They're waiting for more from us," Kell conjectured.

"They reacted to the music," said Loris, her voice brimming with wonder.

Para repeated the one word, "Music."

Kell turned to Tray, smiling brightly. "Congratulations, son! You've opened up a new communication channel with the Leviathans."

"I have?"

Para spoke up, "The scientific teams studying the Leviathans have paid practically no attention to their ultralow sonic frequencies. They have concentrated on their visual displays, believing those to be the creatures' main means of communication."

"A prime example of anthropomorphization," Bricknell added. "The visual displays are so obvious—"

"Obvious *to us*," Kell interjected.

"And the ultralow frequency sonic range is so far below our range of communication," Bricknell went on, "that our scientists ignored it."

"Not entirely," Para said. "But very little attention has been paid to it."

"Until now," Kell said, beaming at Tray.

"Music," Loris said. "They communicate through music."

"Through ultralow frequency sounds," Kell corrected. "I doubt that the beasts think of the sounds in the same way that we do."

"But it's a communications channel that we haven't looked into before," Bricknell said.

Tray realized that they were all staring at him. Even Para. Sheshardi was peering around the edge of his chair's high back. But it was Loris that he found himself focusing on. Sapphire-eyed Loris, staring at him with newfound admiration.

Tray stared back at her.

malFUNCtiON

+++

++

"why don't you try sending out more music?" Loris asked.

It took a conscious effort for Tray to tear his gaze away from her beautiful face and turn questioningly to Kell.

"Do you think I should?" he asked.

Kell nodded slowly. "I don't think it would hurt anything if you did."

"Okay," said Tray. "Let's try . . ." He ran swiftly through several possibilities. Not his own music, he swiftly decided: I haven't written enough to have much of a variety; it's all pretty much the same. Let's see how they react to the works that other human minds have considered to be great.

For the next several hours Tray broadcast all sorts of music toward the Leviathans. Beethoven, Bach, jazz, blues, the newer interplanetary syntheses, symphonies, choral works. The Leviathans plowed peacefully through the water, occasionally playing back ultralow frequency booms and what sounded to the humans like moans of damned souls.

At last Kell muttered, "I wonder what they're trying to say to us?"

"Maybe it's *Stop that infernal racket*," Bricknell joked.

Kell shook his head. "No, I think they're trying to answer us, to communicate."

Tray felt exhausted. The exhilaration he had experienced earlier had evolved into frustrated disappointment.

"Well," Kell said, with a jaunty grin, "Rome wasn't built in a day, you know."

"You have made a breakthrough in interspecies communication," said Para.

Shaking his head, Tray countered, "Hardly that."

"No," Kell disagreed, "I think that Para is right. You've opened up a new channel of communications with the Leviathans. One the scientific community had overlooked."

"Until now," said Loris.

"Good work, my boy," Kell said.

But Tray's eyes were focused on Loris.

Sheshardi's voice rose from his command chair. "We are approaching the limit of our planned excursion. It is time to prepare for leaving the ocean."

Tray felt weary, drained. Yet he wanted to stay among the Leviathans, wanted to learn more about them, wanted to show them how human beings lived.

"Sleep time," Kell said.

"And after our nap," Sheshardi added, "we begin the ascent back to *Jove's Messenger*."

Tray knew he was too excited to sleep. But once he closed his eyes his body took command and he sank into slumber within a few minutes.

Tray's eyes snapped open. He saw that the protective plastic cover had slid down over him while he slept. The ship fills the space inside the cover with a soporific gas, he remembered, to make certain that we sleep. No wonder I dozed off so quickly.

As the cover raised silently and disappeared into its slot on the bulkhead behind him, Tray looked at the clock clicking away on the control panel's upper-right-hand screen. I've been asleep for a couple of hours, he realized.

Then he saw that the other screens showed nothing but empty ocean.

"The Leviathans have gone!" he snapped.

Sheshardi's voice came from the command chair, "They departed some thirty minutes ago. They made an abrupt turn and sped off. Since we are about to leave the ocean I thought it would be useless to try to follow them."

Tray realized the Abo was right, but he felt disappointed nonetheless. The ocean seemed empty, abandoned, *lonely*.

Then he saw that Loris was just waking up, knuckling the sleep out of her eyes. So were the others. Para sat inertly on Kell's other side. Sheshardi was hidden, as usual, behind the command chair's back.

Bricknell stretched languidly, then said at the top of his voice, "Good morning, everybody!"

Para leaned forward slightly in its chair and asked Tray, "Did you have a good sleep?"

Before Tray could reply, Bricknell answered, "Excellent sleep. The best that modern medical chemistry can produce."

Kell smiled, a little wearily, Tray thought. Loris stretched like a panther.

Sheshardi's voice came from behind his seat back, "We will have our last meal, and then we begin our ascent to rendezvous with *Jove's Messenger*."

"Home sweet home," Bricknell wisecracked.

"Breakfast," said Kell. "Good. I'm famished."

Tray couldn't help feeling that Sheshardi's term, "last meal," had an unconsciously ominous sound to it.

One by one they all, except for Para, went to the serving console and picked up trays of faux eggs and a vegetable medley. Tray noticed that the broken pieces of the glasses that had been shattered by the Leviathans' voices had all been gathered up and disposed of by the ship's automated housekeeping system.

Sheshardi got out of his command chair and joined the others. As he filled his breakfast tray, Para stepped next to him and suggested, "I can monitor the console if you wish to take a nap."

Blinking his red-rimmed eyes, the Aboriginal said, "That's an excellent idea. I could use an hour of sleep."

"Very well," said Para. The android headed for the command chair as Sheshardi, carrying his breakfast tray, made himself comfortable in what had originally been designated as Harold Balsam's chair.

Precisely one hour later, Sheshardi snapped awake and returned to the command chair. Para got up and strode to the chair where he had formerly been sitting.

Does Para resent being sent back to that seat? Tray asked himself silently. Would he prefer to be in command?

Then Tray remembered that Para was an "it," not a "he."

For nearly an hour the vessel cruised along placidly. Sheshardi busily worked the controls set into his seat's armrests. The empty ocean stretched all around them. Tray knew the water teemed with microscopic creatures, but as far as he could see it was a vast blank desolation. He began to long for the familiar contours of human habitation.

Then he realized that Loris was standing beside him, also peering at the vacant screens.

"It's like we're all alone, isn't it?" she murmured.

Tray nodded as he looked past her shoulder and saw that Bricknell was apparently engaged in a deep conversation with Para.

Is Para running interference for me, so I can talk with Loris? Tray asked himself. It's a machine. It doesn't have human emotions. But does that mean that the android doesn't *understand* human emotions?

One way or the other, Tray was standing close to the most beautiful woman he had ever seen. Loris seemed perfectly content to be so close to him.

Say something to her! Tray commanded himself.

"It's been an interesting trip," he muttered.

"Yes, hasn't it," Loris agreed. "And your idea of using music to communicate with the Leviathans . . . that was the best part of it."

"Just a lucky guess."

"Luck favors the prepared mind," Loris quoted. "Louis Pasteur said that."

Tray grinned self-consciously. "Did he?"

Loris's eyes flicked to Bricknell and Para, still in deep conversation.

"Did you tell your android to occupy Mance for a while?"

"No!"

"You mean it was all the machine's idea?"

"I . . . I guess it was."

"Smart machine."

"Para's not just a machine. He's almost human. Sometimes I think he's more than human."

Before Loris could reply, Sheshardi popped up from his command chair, shaking his head.

"We have a problem," the Abo said, dolefully.

"A problem?" asked Tray.

"The controls . . . they appear to be locked."

Jordan Kell stepped up to Sheshardi. "Locked?"

"I've been working on them for nearly an hour," Sheshardi said, his expression puzzled, baffled.

"And?" Kell prompted.

"We are unable to rise to the surface."

Bricknell turned away from Para to stare at the Aboriginal. "Unable . . . ?"

"I've tried everything," Sheshardi said, waving his hands vaguely. "We appear to be trapped here in the ocean. In fact, we are slowly sinking."

Sinking

+++ ++ +++ ++ +++ ++ +++ ++ +++ ++ +++ ++ +++ ++ +++ ++ +++ ++ ++ +++
+ + + + +++ ++ +++ ++ +++ ++ +++ ++ +++ ++ +++ ++ +++ ++ +++ + + + +

"sinking!" Loris gasped.

"Yes," said Sheshardi. "At the rate we are descending, the ship's outermost hull will begin to crack within the next hour."

"You've got to pull us up!" Bricknell screeched. "You've got to do something!"

Shaking his head dolefully, Sheshardi said, "Yes, I know. But what? I've tried everything . . ."

Kell stepped to the Aborigine's side. "Send out a message capsule. Ask Tsavo for help."

Sheshardi looked up into Kell's calm face. Kell didn't seem frightened; he looked serious, intent, as if he were inwardly running through a thousand ideas, possibilities, hopes.

"By the time a capsule gets to Captain Tsavo," Sheshardi said mournfully, "we will have sunk too deep for any rescue."

"We're going to die?" Loris asked, her blue eyes wide with sudden fright.

"There are the emergency escape suits," Sheshardi said.

"Escape suits?"

Tray remembered reading about them in the ship's manual of equipment details. Individual suits, built to withstand the tremendous pressures of the Jovian ocean and allow a person to rise to the surface.

And what then? Tray asked himself. We could float inside those suits and starve to death before *Jove's Messenger* finds us.

But it was better than staying with their sinking vessel.

Kell was apparently thinking the same thoughts. "We'd best get to the emergency suits."

"This is certainly an emergency," Bricknell said, his voice high and thin.

"The suits are stored in the locker next to the main port," said Sheshardi.

"Aren't you going with us?" Kell asked.

"I will stay here and try to sort out the problem with the controls," the Abo said. "Call me when you are all suited up."

Kell stared at him. "Gyele, the days when the captain went down with his ship are far behind us."

Sheshardi looked up at Kell and grinned weakly. "I have no intention of going down with my ship," he said. "You call me when you are all safely inside your suits and I will join you."

Kell looked unconvinced, but he said tightly, "Very well."

"Meanwhile I will try to correct the problem with the controls."

"Very well," Kell repeated.

Turning from Sheshardi, in the command chair, Jordan Kell started for the hatch that led to the emergency escape suit locker. "This way," he said over his shoulder.

Tray watched Loris and Bricknell follow him to the hatch. Para came up beside Tray and half-whispered, "I will not need a suit. I am built to withstand the water pressure for several hours."

Nodding, Tray muttered, "Good." And he fell in line behind Bricknell, with Para behind him.

Kell was sliding back the hatch to the escape suit locker. Tray saw that the suits were *huge*, much bigger than he had imagined them from the pictures in the vessel's emergency procedures directions.

"It's like those giant statues of Ramses, in Egypt," Bricknell gasped.

"No time for gawking," Kell snapped. "Get into the suits."

Tray saw that each suit was labeled with their names. He quickly found his own, and saw that Loris's was next to his.

Taking her by the wrist, he led Loris between their two suits and showed her the entry hatch built into the suit's back. Bricknell was already clambering into his suit, on the other side of hers.

Tray grasped Loris by the waist and raised her high enough so she could lift her feet over the rim of the suit's hatch. Then she grasped the upper rim and pulled herself completely inside. Turning suddenly, she leaned out of the hatch and kissed Tray on the cheek.

"Thanks for the help," she said.

Tray nodded wordlessly.

"Now get into your own suit, hero," Loris directed.

Tray grinned at her. "Aye, aye."

Turning, he pulled himself into the suit with his name stenciled on its chest. Just as he slid inside, he noted Kell half-sitting on the edge of his suit's hatch, calling out at the top of his voice, "Gyele, come on. We're ready to button up."

"One more minute," Sheshardi's voice came through the overhead speakers.

Kell shook his head and slid all the way inside his suit. Tray did the same.

The suit's interior lit up automatically as Tray swung the hatch shut and sealed it. Looking around, he saw that he had very little room to move about. It was like being inside a coffin. Pleasant thought, he said to himself. Rising to a standing position, he lifted his head into the suit's helmet. There was no window to see the outside, but a set of smallish viewscreens was arrayed along the helmet's interior.

A woman's dulcet voice said mechancially, "Select a language, please." It began to repeat the phrase in other languages.

Tray interrupted, "English, please. American English."

"American English," the voice echoed. "Very well."

The suit's controls were almost completely automatic, the voice explained to Tray.

"To communicate with other evacuees, press the stud on your right that is blinking white."

Tray saw the blinking light, pressed it. The small screen above it flashed a list of names. Tray pressed LORIS DE MAYNE.

"Yes?" Loris's voice immediately answered, taut with anxiety.

"It's Tray," he said. "Are you all right?"

She hesitated. Then, "I think so."

Before Tray could say anything else, the suit announced, "Evacuation sequence initiated. Ejection will occur in thirty seconds."

into the sea

"wait!" Tray hollered. "what about the others?"

The suit replied, "Ejection sequence for all five suits is under way. Ejection in nineteen seconds . . . eighteen . . ."

Tray felt his entire body tensing. *We're going to be fired into the ocean. We're going to be shot like cannon shells into the cold, deep sea.*

Then he realized, "What about Para?"

The automated voice continued, "Twelve . . . eleven . . . ten . . ."

"What about Para?" Tray screamed.

"Five . . . four . . ."

Kell's voice cut in. "No time to worry—"

"Ejection," announced the emotionless voice.

The roar of the capsule's rockets deafened Tray momentarily, while the force of its launch buckled his knees, but the coffin-sized compartment of the escape suit gave him no room to collapse. He remained erect, legs like jelly, lungs rasping as he felt a tremendous push and saw in his helmet screens nothing but frothing bubbles.

I'm in the ocean, Tray's mind told him. *I'm shooting up from* Athena *toward the surface of the water.*

The maddeningly calm voice of the suit's command system said serenely, "Estimated time to reach the surface: two hours and thirty-six minutes."

"Where are the others?" Tray shouted. "Where's Para?"

"All five humans have ejected successfully," the suit replied, "and are proceeding toward the surface."

"What about Para?" Tray shouted again.

No answer.

Tray felt as though he were imprisoned in a sarcophagus. There was barely enough room inside the suit to inch his arms up from his sides. He could not sit and the suit's acceleration made him feel as if he were standing upright.

He felt panic rising in him. What happened to Para? Where are the others?

Then Kell's voice came through. Calm as ever, he said, "I suggest that we each call in and give a status report."

Bricknell answered immediately, "Mance here," he said shakily. "Everything seems to be functioning in the green."

Then Loris's voice came through, "De Mayne. All my screens show green, too. But I'm getting no visuals from you."

Kell replied, "The comm system doesn't include a visual link. Audio only. Saves an enormous amount of bandwidth."

"We're linked by laser beams, aren't we?" Bricknell asked. "Should be plenty of bandwidth."

Kell's voice answered, "Much of the bandwidth is used to keep track of each other. We're like five missiles fired from *Athena*. Visual contact isn't a first-order priority."

Bricknell mumbled something that Tray couldn't understand. Griping, he thought.

Kell asked, "Trayvon? Are you with us?"

"Yes, I'm here. All my systems are in the green."

"Good," said Kell. "My own suit seems to be functioning properly, except for one yellow light at the pressurization indicator."

"Yellow light?" Tray asked.

"Pressurization indicator?" Bricknell's voice, edging higher.

Quite calmly, Kell answered, "I have the suit's diagnostic system checking the reading. It's probably nothing more than a minor instrument misreading."

Loris asked, "Are all your other systems in the green?"

"Yes," Kell answered. "All operating as designed."

Tray realized he was biting his lips. Kell's suit had a malfunction and Para was silent. I don't even know if he got out of the ship! Tray realized. Then he recognized that they hadn't heard from Sheshardi.

"Where's Sheshardi?" he blurted.

"I am here," the Aboriginal's voice answered. "I left a few moments after the four of you did."

"Where's Para?"

"Your android?" Sheshardi asked. "It left through one of the tubes that you exited from. Completely on its own, without a suit."

"Para!" Tray shouted. "Can you hear me?"

Dead silence.

Tray turned up the magnification on the screens that lined his suit's helmet. Nothing but empty ocean. Para was nowhere in sight. A froth of upward-rising bubbles showed where one of the others was, but beyond that Tray could see nothing.

After several minutes of silence, Kell said gently, "Para's entire memory is on file back on Earth. They can provide you with a copy of your android, exact in every detail."

Tray nodded unconsciously, even though none of the others could see him.

"Yes, I suppose so," he muttered.

Yet he was thinking, But it won't be Para.

Upward, upward through the depths of the Jovian ocean the five survivors sped. Tray felt physically comfortable enough inside the suit, although he wanted to lie down and mourn for his guide, his mentor, his friend. Para, he said to himself, we've killed you.

Kell's voice interrupted his mourning.

"I'm afraid my suit is showing another yellow indication."

"Another yellow light?" Sheshardi's voice.

"Depth indicator," said Kell tightly. "I'm no longer rising. I seem to be sinking."

"No longer rising?" Sheshardi asked, his voice high, trembling.

"Sinking?" Loris blurted.

"I can hear a gurgling sound," Kell said. "It seems— Oh, my lord!"

"What?" Loris demanded.

"Water!" Kell said, almost shouting. "My suit's leaking!"

"Leaking?"

"It's filling up with water." For the first time, Kell's voice betrayed fear.

"Where are you?" Tray called, realizing it was a stupid question even as the words left his lips.

"I'm sinking. The water's cold."

Tray's fingers were flying through his suit's diagnostics program while all three of the others were jabbering at once. His screens showed nothing. There was no way to rescue a failing escape suit from inside another escape suit.

Kell was doomed, Tray realized.

"It's freezing cold!" Kell was saying. "That's good: freezes out the pain. . . . Up past my hips now."

Bricknell shouted, "Isn't there a pump you can use to get rid of the water?"

"No . . . it's up to my chest . . ."

"Jordan!" Tray screamed.

"Good-bye all," came Kell's voice. "Looks like . . . this is . . . it."

"Jordan!" Tray yelled again.

No reply, except a gurgling of water.

Tray stood there inside his escape suit, unable to move, to fling his arms wide, to do anything to save the man who had called him son.

He's dead, Tray realized. Drowned. Sinking down to the bottom of this endless sea.

"He doesn't answer." Loris's voice, thick with tears.

"He's dead," said Bricknell.

"There was nothing we could do," Sheshardi said mournfully. "Nothing."

Tray hung his head, fighting back tears.

Then Sheshardi said, his voice calm and strong, "Each of us should run a complete diagnostic check on his suit."

"Right," said Tray.

He knew what Sheshardi was up to. Keep us busy. Give us something to do, something to keep us focused on where we are. Something to take our minds away from Jordan Kell's death.

As the four remaining survivors of *Athena* continued to rise from the depths of the Jovian sea, Tray began to think that someone in Captain Tsavo's crew was to blame for this tragedy. First *Athena*'s controls malfunctioned and then Kell's suit leaked. Somebody's responsible. Criminal negligence. Tsavo's allowed his crew to get away with murder. Literally.

Then the speaker built into his control panel suddenly came to life. "This is Para. I saw the difficulty Mr. Kell was in but unfortunately there was nothing I could do to help him."

Para! Tray exulted. "Para, you're alive!"

"Not alive, actually," the android replied. "But I am functioning and rising to the ocean's surface with you."

"You're okay? All systems in the green?"

"The acidic content of the ocean water is etching my outer skin, but otherwise I am undamaged."

Tray felt an immense wave of gratitude sweep through him. "Where are you? How far from us?"

"My sensors indicate the four of you are within a kilometer of each other, but drifting constantly farther apart."

"And you?"

"I am on the extreme left edge of your group, rising at the same rate as the rest of you, to within a few meters per minute."

"Great!" said Tray.

Loris interrupted, "My screens show something in the water heading our way."

"Where?" Sheshardi immediately asked.

"Off to the right," Loris replied. "About two o'clock."

Tray jabbed at his sensor controls. And there it was, a bulbous gasbag trailing long, dangling tentacles.

"A blimp," said Sheshardi.

"A Medusa," Loris corrected.

Tray said, "I thought they lived in the atmosphere, not underwater."

"There are two species," Sheshardi replied, "atmospheric and aquatic."

"It's coming toward us," said Bricknell.

"It's curious about us," Loris suggested.

"It wants to see if we're food," said Tray.

Sheshardi's voice sounded grim. "Those tentacles are capable of generating several thousand volts of electricity. The blimps use them to stun their prey."

"We're not their prey!" Loris said.

"That is a decision the blimp will make for itself," Sheshardi replied.

battle

+++
++

Tray felt as if he were watching a horror drama. He and the others were encased in the escape suits, unable to move, to run, to get away from the approaching monster. The bulbous floating Medusa drifted closer, closer, trailing those murderous dangling tentacles.

Frantically, Tray ran through the list of equipment displayed on his main viewscreen. No weapons, no signaling devices, not even lights he could flash to possibly confuse or drive off the approaching beast.

Closer and closer the blimp-like creature approached, waving its tentacles in an almost hypnotic rhythm.

Tray checked the suit's rocket propulsion system. Dead. All its fuel had been used up in the jolting escape from the sinking *Athena*.

What can I do? he screamed silently at himself. The damned thing is almost close enough to grab us!

Sheshardi's voice, shaky with dread, said, "It's coming for me!"

There was no way to evade the monster, Tray saw. No way to escape. He watched the Medusa approach Sheshardi slowly, almost leisurely, its dangling tentacles reaching toward the floating escape suit.

The tip of one tentacle brushed against Sheshardi's armored suit. Tray could hear the Abo's terrified gasping.

Slowly, with almost loving unhurried leisure, four of the Medusa's long, snaky tentacles wrapped themselves around Sheshardi's suit.

He's not food! Tray shouted inwardly. You can't eat him! Leave him alone!

Sheshardi's voice was squeaking like a baby's. Tray couldn't understand what he was trying to say. Probably lapsing back to his native language.

A sudden flash of light filled Tray's compartment, searing his eyes momentarily. He heard a high-pitched screech. Blinking, pawing at his eyes, he saw that the Medusa had released Sheshardi's suit. It floated inertly beneath the dangling tentacles.

"Sheshardi!" Tray heard himself call. "Are you all right?"

No answer. The escape suit bobbed passively in the waves made by the Medusa, which was now floating past it, heading in Tray's direction.

"Sheshardi!" Bricknell repeated. "Sheshardi!"

Silence.

Tray watched helplessly as the tentacled monster approached him. "We're not food!" he yelled at it. "We're not food, you stupid blimp!"

The Medusa sailed past, one of its tentacles bumping Tray's escape suit, then quickly withdrawing. It floated off into the distance.

Tray heard Loris's voice, high, breathless. "It killed him!"

Bricknell: "Are you sure he's dead?"

"That electric bolt the damned beast shot out," Tray said. "It killed him, all right."

"Poor little man," Loris moaned.

Unbidden, an awful thought popped into Tray's mind. Maybe it's me. Maybe I'm a jinx, a Jonah. First the *Saviour*, then Kell, and now this. He squeezed his eyes shut, trying to force the sense of guilt out of his awareness. But it was there, lying in his brain like a panther waiting to pounce.

Shaking his head, Tray forced himself to concentrate on the here and now. Forget the myths, the ancient rites of guilt and shame. Concentrate on the here and now. Focus on what's real.

"The sooner we get to the surface," Tray forced himself to say, "the sooner *Jove's Messenger* can find us and pick us up."

"Amen to that," Bricknell replied fervently.

Tray felt that he was rising faster. It seemed as if his suit was shooting upward, toward the surface of Jupiter's all-encompassing sea.

Wishful thinking, he told himself. The readouts show I'm rising at just about the same rate as when we left *Athena*.

But just then he broke through the water's surface with a splash and began to bob up and down on the waves marching across the ocean.

"We made it!" came Bricknell's rejoicing voice.

"Where's Loris?"

"I'm here, floating on my back. I can see the cloud deck, way up there."

"Me too," said Bricknell.

"Activate your tracking signals," Tray told them. To himself he added, And hope *Jove's Messenger* is on this side of the planet. He felt his sense of guilt diminishing, slinking away into the darker depths of his mind. Not gone, but shrinking.

rendezvous

It's an enormous planet, Tray said to himself as he bobbed gently in the ocean's swells. *Jove's messenger* could be half a million klicks away from us.

How close together are we? Tray wondered.

"Para, can you see us?" he asked.

The android replied, "No, none of you. But my horizon is terribly limited, bobbing up and down in the water like this."

Tray pecked at his control console, seeking maximum magnification from his suit's cameras. But even as he did so, he knew that the chances of seeing one of the suits floating in the choppy water was close to zero.

"I have run a calculation," Para said, "on how long we can stay in the water like this."

"And?" Loris's voice, tense, frightened.

"It's a very rough approximation, based on an estimate of how acidic these waters are and how resistant to corrosion the suits' materials are."

"And?" Bricknell demanded, loudly.

"I believe we are perfectly safe for six hours. After that, the suits will develop leaks."

"What about you, Para?" Tray asked. "How long will you last?"

"Much longer," the android answered. "My range of survivable environments is much wider than yours."

Tray heard Loris make a moaning sound. Bricknell said nothing.

Despite himself, Tray grinned. Para sounds almost proud of himself, he thought. Then he corrected, *it*self. And it doesn't know what pride is. Or hope.

Glancing at his control panel, just below the viewscreens, Tray saw that his suit's radio transponder was beeping out its distress signal, loud and clear.

He knew that *Jove's Messenger* was equipped with receiving equipment that could detect their message even from the other side of Jupiter's massive bulk. But can Tsavo reach us soon enough? he wondered. Six hours, Para said. That's not much time.

He floated in the ocean's waves, on his back, staring at the multihued clouds so far above.

"Tray?" Loris's voice!

"Yes?"

"Do you think we'll make it? Will Captain Tsavo reach us in time?"

"Of course," Tray replied, hoping it was true.

"No, he won't," Bricknell said. "We're going to die in this ocean, just like Kell did."

"No we're not!" Tray snapped. True or not, hope was all that they had left.

As if on cue, a radio voice crackled through the suit's speaker. "This is *Jove's Messenger*. We are tracking your emergency signal. We should be in your vicinity within five hours."

Bricknell whooped. Loris burst into tears of joy. Tray thought, Five hours. And Para had calculated our suits would begin to fail in six hours. It's going to be close. Very close.

* * *

Sloshing in the choppy waters of Jupiter's boundless ocean, Tray wished he could sleep. Just close your eyes and sleep, he commanded himself. Pretend you're a little kid again and it's Christmas Eve. If you don't go to sleep Santa won't come.

He closed his eyes. Squeezed them shut. But sleep would not come. His mind filled with memories of Jordan Kell, with questions about Para's condition, with Sheshardi's death, and a dozen scenarios of being gobbled up by monstrous Jovian sea creatures, with old memories of the *Saviour*'s sudden, inescapable destruction.

Beyond the confines of his suit, nothing was happening. The huge sky arching above him seemed empty of life. No ogres of the deep rose up to devour them. They just floated up and down on the waves, rocking like bathers at the seashore.

But this ocean doesn't have a seashore, Tray said to himself. No land. An ocean ten times bigger than the whole Earth. Without bounds. Endless.

Loris's voice broke into his thoughts. "I think I see something!"

"Where?" Tray and Bricknell asked in unison.

"Off by the horizon. To my right."

Tray realized that Loris might not be floating in the same attitude as he. Her right could be my left. But he pushed his viewscreen views to maximum magnification anyway.

Nothing. Emptiness.

No, wait. There was something, a speck gliding beneath the multicolored swirling clouds.

A bird, Tray saw. It must be huge, to be visible at this range, he thought.

"It's a bird," Bricknell's disappointed voice came through. "A lousy bird."

Before tray could think of anything to say, Para's voice countered, "No, it's a winged scout vehicle. It must be from *Jove's Messenger*."

Tray strained his eyes peering at the viewscreen. Slowly the image came into sharper focus.

Yes! he exulted. An unmanned scout sent by Tsavo to search this sector of the ocean.

"Hey!" Bricknell yelled. "We're over here, stupid!"

Tray tapped on the control panel stud that activated the suit's radio. "This is Trayvon Williamson. Together with Loris De Mayne and Mance Bricknell, and the android Para, we are floating in the sea. We can see you. I'm activating my suit's homing beacon so that—"

"Trayvon!" Captain Tsavo's voice broke through. "We have a good fix on you. We're heading in your direction, should be able to pick you up in another two hours, give or take ten minutes."

Tray felt an enormous wave of gratitude sweep through him. Two hours, he thought. That should be plenty of time. Our suits will still be sound. We won't spring leaks and sink.

We're going to live!

rescue

++++++++ +++++++++++++++++++++++++++++++++++++ +++++
+++++ +++

Jove's messenger looked like the most beautiful thing in creation, Tray thought. He kept his eyes fixed on the viewscreen as the massive globular ship glided across the colorfully streaked sky toward the floating survivors of *Athena*.

"Para, how high is the ship above us?"

The android replied within a heartbeat, "Approximately fifty thousand meters."

"Approximately," Bricknell mimicked. Tray thought that Mance had found his usual snotty attitude again.

"Loris," he called, "are you all right?"

"I'm fine," she answered, warmly. "Now."

"This is Captain Tsavo," announced the radio speaker on Tray's control console. "We have you in sight. Recovery operations will begin within fifteen minutes."

Tray responded with a fervent, "Thank you!"

"You say Kell's suit failed?"

"Yes," said Tray.

"Bad business. He'll be too deep for us to recover his body."

"Yes," Tray said again, more softly. Inwardly he thought, Just get us out of this ocean and safely aboard your ship. There's nothing any of us can do for Kell.

* * *

The rescue operation seemed to move in slow motion. *Jove's Messenger* circled high above them while a winged scout vehicle emerged from its spherical hull and came spiraling down to within a few meters of the floating survivors.

One by one, starting with Loris, the scout ship's crew picked them up with magnetic grapples and hoisted them into their hovering vessel. The ship even maneuvered to Sheshardi's presumably dead body and lifted it aboard.

At last Tray watched the grapple descending toward him. But he heard himself suddenly call to the rescue ship, "Para! Pick up the android, please."

The ship commander's voice sounded surprised. "We were told there were only three survivors to be rescued, and the dead Abo."

"Plus the android," Tray corrected.

"It's only a damned machine. We don't have time to waste on a machine."

Para broke into the disagreement. "I'm replaceable, Trayvon."

"Pick him up!" Tray roared. "Now!"

"Our orders are—"

"To hell with your orders! Pick up the android. Then me."

Tray hears a mumble of voices. Then, "If that's the way you want it . . ."

"That's the way I want it."

The rescue craft moved away from Tray, then lowered its grapple onto Para's metal body. Tray watched as the android rose out of the sea, dripping, and up to the hatch of the hovering vehicle. He saw hands reach out from the ship's hatch and pull Para inside.

Only then did the rescue vehicle return to hover over Tray and lower its grapple to fasten itself on Tray's suit.

As he rose out of the water Tray heard one of the crewmen complain, "Wasting time on a bleeding machine."

It took several hours to get Tray and the others back to *Jove's Messenger*, out of their suits, and through an automated medical examination. At last Tray, Loris, and Mance were pronounced fit to return to their quarters while the ship lifted through the clouds and out into space once again.

The three of them were strangely quiet as they trudged along the ship's passageways to their quarters. It was as if each of them had been drained of the power of speech, the instinct to chatter among themselves. What can we say? Tray asked himself. After what we've just gone through, small talk seems foolish, meaningless.

At last they arrived at the row of hatches marked with their individual names. Wordlessly, Tray opened the hatch and stepped into his minuscule cabin.

Para was standing next to Tray's bed.

Tray stopped in the hatchway and looked at the android. Para's metal skin looked stained, soiled, like a little boy who had been playing in mud.

"You're all right?"

Para nodded once as it said, "I was about to ask you the same question."

"The medical system pronounced me in excellent health," Tray said. "How about you?"

The android replied, "My outermost shell was somewhat eroded by the acidic water, but that can be corrected when we return to Earth."

"Good," said Tray.

"How are Lady De Mayne and Dr. Bricknell?"

Stepping fully into the cramped compartment and closing the hatch behind him, Tray said, "They're okay, too."

Without moving a step closer to Tray, Para said, "I want to thank you for rescuing me."

Tray blinked. "You're part of our team, Para. We're partners, you and I. Friends. I couldn't let them leave you there sloshing in the ocean."

Para's face revealed no emotion. But the android said, "Yes, you could have. But you didn't. Thank you."

Tray suddenly felt uncomfortable, embarrassed. He turned to the phone beside his bunk and called out, "Phone: Contact Loris De Mayne, please."

The viewscreen at the foot of the bed glowed, but no picture came up. Tray heard water running.

"Hello, Tray," said Loris's voice. "Please excuse the video outage: I'm in the shower."

"You're all right?"

"Right as rain, as my old grandmum used to say. Happy to be home, even if it's only this closet of a cabin."

"Good! Me too."

"Mance passed easily, too. All three of us are fine."

Tray felt a pang in his gut. "Too bad about Mr. Kell, though."

For a moment there was no reply. Then, "Yes. Too utterly, terribly bad."

"What do you suppose happened to his emergency suit?" Tray wondered aloud.

"I can't imagine."

"Neither can I," Tray said. He added silently, But I'm going to do my damnedest to find out.

* * *

Captain Tsavo invited the three survivors to dinner in his personal suite, next to the ship's bridge. After wandering through the ship's passageways, Tray finally arrived at the hatch, with Para at his side. He rapped on the metal hatch once; it slid open immediately.

Tsavo was standing at the bar set along one bulkhead of the compartment, together with Loris and Mance Bricknell. They all had drinks in their hands.

"I was about to send out a search party for you," the captain said, with a teasing smile on his dark face.

Tray made an apologetic shrug. "I got lost. If Para weren't with me I'd still be wandering through the passageways."

Towering over them all, Tsavo cast a doubtful eye on Para. "A party like this can't be much fun for you, can it?"

Para replied, "I don't need alcohol to improve my social skills."

Bricknell *hmmphed*. "Neither do I. But I enjoy a drink now and then." Before anyone could comment, he added, "About every ten minutes seems to be just about right."

The others laughed, although Tray barely forced a smile. Para nodded his head and murmured, "Touché."

Sensing a hint of tension, Tsavo gestured to the dinner table and said, "Well, now that we're all here, let's have some food."

They moved toward the table, elegantly set with pure white china, crystal glasses, and gleaming silverware.

"Nothing but the best," Tsavo said proudly. Pointing to a corner of the dining room, he added, "Para, you won't mind standing in the corner, will you?"

Tray started to object, but the android said, "Of course not."

Loris gripped Tray's hand. He turned to her and recognized for the first time that she was beautifully dressed in a long-skirted cobalt blue dress that closely complemented her eyes. A glittering ring of diamonds clung to her throat, but they weren't as bright as her smile.

Tray sat next to her, Bricknell on her other side. Tsavo sat at the head of the table. A human waiter asked in a whisper what Tray wanted to drink.

"Water will be fine," he replied.

Tsavo raised a cautionary hand. "We'll be serving some fine Gattinara with the main course, Mr. Williamson. Mr. Balsam's chef has stocked a bountiful supply of Italian wines. I hope you'll join us then."

With a self-deprecating little smile, Tray responded, "Of course. I'd be happy to." He hesitated, then added, "I'm not a total prude."

"Just a partial one," Bricknell sneered.

Tray held on to his temper. Barely.

The food was wonderful, Tray had to admit.

Tsavo gloried in the success of his kitchen staff.

"President Balsam made certain that his ship included the finest food processing equipment money could buy," he bragged. "My people grew this mutton from stem cells right back there in the kitchen. Not bad, eh?"

"It's delicious," Loris answered, as if on cue.

"I must say," Bricknell remarked, "this is better than I've had in Paris or just about anywhere else."

"I imagine it is," Tsavo said. "Mr. Balsam insists on nothing but the best."

Tray glanced at Loris as he swallowed his last piece of processed mutton, then looked up at Captain Tsavo.

"Captain," he asked, "are you going to convene an inquiry into Jordan Kell's death?"

Tsavo's brows knit into a frown. "Inquiry?"

"His emergency suit failed," Tray went on. "Shouldn't we try to find out why?"

The captain laid his fork down on the tablecloth and took in a breath. "His suit," he said with deliberate care, "with him in it, is several hundred miles beneath the surface of the ocean."

"And sinking deeper," Bricknell added, "every moment."

"There's no way we can recover it for examination," Tsavo went on.

"We all understand that," said Tray. "But don't you have a diagnostic record of his suit? Wasn't it tested before *Athena* went into the water?"

"Yes, of course it was tested," Tsavo said.

"Mightn't a review of the testing procedure turn up something?"

"Something? What?"

"If we knew that, we wouldn't need an investigation," said Tray.

Captain Tsavo stared at Tray for a long, silent moment. Then, "You had a special relationship with Kell, didn't you?"

Nodding, Tray replied, "He treated me like a father, as if I was his son."

With a slight smirk, Tsavo said, "Of course he did."

Realizing the implication behind the captain's expression, Tray felt hot anger bubbling up inside him. "What are you insinuating?"

Tsavo looked around the table. "Perhaps we should let the subject drop. It won't help things to carry it farther."

Half-rising from his chair, Tray repeated, "What are you insinuating?"

Tsavo glanced at Loris, then looked back into Tray's flushed face. "Nothing," he said coolly. "Nothing at all."

Bricknell reached a hand toward Tray. "Sit down, man. Take it easy."

Tray did not move.

With a shake of his head, Captain Tsavo said firmly, "This subject of conversation is closed."

Pointing across the dinner table, Tray said, "You—"

"The subject is closed," Tsavo repeated, louder.

Instead of sitting, Tray pushed his chair back and walked out of the dining room, followed by Para.

Examination

+++

+++

"He was implying that Kell and I had a homosexual relationship," Tray growled, the instant he closed the hatch to his compartment.

Para said, "There's nothing wrong with that."

"But it's not true!"

"Then you have nothing to worry about."

Tray plopped himself down on the edge of his bunk. "I don't want them thinking I'm a homosexual."

Para took a step toward him. "Them? Or her?"

Tray stared at the android for a long wordless moment. Then, in a low voice, he admitted, "Her. Loris. I don't want her to think I'm a homosexual."

"It's not a criminal indictment," Para said. "There's nothing wrong with a person choosing his or her sexual preferences."

With a shake of his head, Tray said, "You don't understand."

"I'm afraid I don't. Can you explain it to me, please?"

Tray looked up at Para. "She might not like to think that I'm . . . that way. Even bisexual."

The android lifted its shoulders in an imitation of a human shrug. "Human emotions can be puzzling."

With a weak smile, Tray replied, "Even to humans."

The bedside phone buzzed.

Tray reached out and touched its ON button. Mance Bricknell's face appeared on its tiny screen.

"Mance."

Bricknell's face was deadly serious. "Tray, I just want you to know that I think what Tsavo did at dinner was pretty low."

"You do?"

"I certainly do," Bricknell said. "Guilt by innuendo. It's something out of the Dark Ages. Despicable."

Surprised, Tray stammered, "Th . . . thanks, Mance."

"After you left, he just sat there at the dinner table, smiling like a hyena."

Tray didn't know what to say.

"He not only accused you, of course," Bricknell went on. "He attacked the reputation of Jordan Kell, Balsam's political rival. In fact, I think that was his real objective."

"Kell's dead," Tray replied. "He's beyond pain."

"But by casting aspersions on Councilman Kell's reputation, Tsavo hits Kell's supporters in the Council. It's a political knife attack. The captain's working for Balsam."

Nodding, Tray said, "I guess it is."

"Oh, they all say that there's nothing wrong with homosexuality, but how many of them really believe that?" Bricknell went on. "How much support would Balsam himself lose in the Council if someone reported that he was a lover of men?"

"I . . . I don't know. It would be pretty hard to believe, though. I guess."

"Well, I just wanted you to know that I thought Tsavo went too far—and his attack on you was for Balsam's benefit."

"Thanks, Mance. Thanks a lot."

As Tray reached for the phone's OFF button, Bricknell added, "Oh, there's one more thing."

"One more . . . ?"

"I intend to ask Loris to marry me, sooner or later. I'd appreciate it if you stayed away from her."

And the phone's screen went blank.

Tray stared at the dead screen for long, silent moments, his mind in turmoil.

At last Para broke the silence. "A classic maneuver."

Tray blinked at the android.

Para explained, "He tells you that he's on your side, against Captain Tsavo and President Balsam. Then he tells you to keep away from Lady De Mayne because he wants to marry her."

Tray nodded, still confused.

Para explained, "He binds you with gratitude, then tells you not to invade his turf. A classic human maneuver."

"You mean he's . . ."

"Trying to manipulate you," Para finished the thought. "Rather cleverly, too."

"I'll be damned," Tray muttered.

"Damned if you do, and damned if you don't," said Para. "Dr. Bricknell has constructed a very clever little trap for you."

"About Loris."

"Apparently so."

"His call was really to warn me away from Loris. His words about Tsavo and Balsam were just a setup."

"To within a ninety percent probability."

Tray sat on the edge of the bed, his thoughts whirling.

Para wasn't finished, though. "I can tell you something else about Captain Tsavo."

"Something else?"

"Earlier, before this homosexuality ploy came up," Para said, "when you asked Captain Tsavo if he were going to investigate Councilman Kell's death."

"Yes?"

"The captain's eyeblink rate, his pulse, his skin temperature all rose significantly upward."

Tray stared at the android. "What does that mean?"

"It means that your request for an investigation seriously upset the captain. It means that his homosexuality ploy was most likely based on a desire to destroy you."

"Destroy me?"

"As he most likely destroyed Councilman Kell."

homeward bound

+ +

+ +

Tray slept poorly that night. Tossing in the darkened cabin, he kept seeing Para's expressionless face accusing captain Tsavo and Harold Balsam of somehow murdering Jordan Kell.

He couldn't believe it. Balsam and Kell might have been political rivals, but murder? An outrageous idea. Yet Para was hardly one to go off on emotional tangents. The android had measured Tsavo's biomarkers and concluded that the captain had indeed caused Kell's death. At Balsam's instigation, most likely.

How? he asked himself. He must have had help. Sheshardi? If the Abo was part of the plot he's already paid for it.

But big, bluff, backslapping Harold Balsam—a murderer? Remotely arranging Jordan Kell's death? Why?

The answer came immediately. Because Kell was opposed to Balsam's dream of creating an interstellar empire, with Earth, and Balsam himself, at its head.

Lying in his bunk, staring up into the darkness, Tray wondered what he should do. What he *could* do. You can't just point an accusing finger at the president of the Interplanetary Council, he knew. You'll wind up back in the isolation ward: paranoia, induced by the *Saviour* tragedy. That's what they'll say.

Or worse, Tray realized. Grief for his homosexual lover. Balsam will play that card, certainly.

An hour before *Jove's Messenger* lit up for its daytime hours, Tray pushed himself out of bed and groped through the darkness to the bathroom shower.

His long, pleasantly warm soaking didn't solve his problems.

Once Tray came out of the bathroom and started dressing, Para stirred from its nighttime stance next to the cabin's hatch.

"You're up early," the android said.

"I'm going to the cafeteria for some breakfast. Want to come along?"

"We won't be able to speak freely there."

Tray felt his brows hike up. "You don't think this cabin is wired?"

"I've scanned it. I didn't find any surveillance devices."

At that instant the bedside phone announced, "Lady De Mayne calling."

Tray immediately called out, "Answer!"

Loris's face appeared on the phone's miniature screen. "I hope I'm not calling too early," she began.

"No, not at all," Tray replied. "We're up and ready to go."

"Go? Go where?"

Remembering Mance Bricknell's call from the evening before, Tray said, "Wherever you'd like."

Loris's face took on a serious appearance. "Tray, we have to talk."

"Yes," he said. "We do."

"The cafeteria?" she suggested.

"Fine. See you there in ten minutes."

"Good." And the phone screen went blank.

Tray looked up at Para. "I think you should stay here, if you don't mind."

"Not at all," said the android.

"And no eavesdropping. What Loris and I have to talk about is strictly private."

"Of course," Para agreed. Tray got the feeling that if the android could smile, it would have.

Loris was already seated at the far end of one of the cafeteria's three long tables, away from the quartet of crewmen at the other end. Tray filled a cup with coffee at the dispenser and went to sit beside her.

Keeping her voice low, she immediately asked, "Do you think Tsavo's hiding something about Kell's death?"

"I'm not sure," Tray whispered back. "But Balsam must have had something to do with it."

Loris's eyes went wide. "Murder?"

"It's too much of a coincidence," Tray muttered. "Balsam invites Kell on this trip. The *Athena* module breaks down. Kell's suit fails." He shook his head and repeated, "That's too much to be a coincidence."

Her brows knitting, Loris stared at Tray for a long, silent moment. Then, "Do you really think so?"

"Yes, I do," he replied without hesitation.

"Then what are you going to do about it?"

Tray answered, "I'm going to ask Tsavo to let me see the maintenance records for Kell's suit."

"How about *Athena*'s maintenance records?" she suggested.

Tray nodded. "I'm not an engineer, though. They could hide the Taj Mahal in those records and I might not see it."

"Your android would."

"Para!" Tray agreed. "Yes, he could help us."

"Good."

Tray could feel his heart thumping beneath his ribs. He stared at Loris, wondering, hoping . . .

"What is it, Tray?" she asked.

Tray's jaws were clenched so tightly that they ached. He gazed into Loris's sparkling blue eyes.

"Tray, are you all right?"

"I've got to ask you something. Something personal."

"About Mance," she realized.

"Yes. He wants to marry you."

"He also wants to win the Nobel Prize," Loris said, her expression hard, rigid.

"Do you really care about him?"

A trace of a smile flickered across her lips. "Mance can be fun. A little demanding . . . a little too proprietary, perhaps, but fun. Sometimes."

"He wants to marry you," Tray repeated.

"He wants to marry into the De Mayne fortune," Loris said, flatly. "I'm one of the family assets, of course."

"What do you want?" Tray asked.

"I don't want to marry Mance. Not now, at least. Maybe in a few years . . ."

Tray heard himself say, "Loris, I think I'm falling in love with you."

Her smile returned: bigger, brighter. "I know, Tray. I think that's lovely."

"I thought my life was over until I met you."

"I thought my life was beginning when I met you," she said.

invⴹⴶtiⴶation

sitting on his cot, with his stockinged feet on its blanket, Tray asked Para, "what have you found from the maintenance records?"

Para shook its head in a very human gesture. "I'm afraid that the maintenance records of Councilman Kell's suit and the entire *Athena* module are sealed and not available for inspection."

"Sealed?"

"Not available for inspection," the android repeated. "By Captain Tsavo's order."

"You asked?"

"I checked the ship's inventory. The maintenance records for the entire *Athena* module—including Councilman Kell's emergency suit—are sealed."

Tray felt his brows knitting. "They're hiding something. Tsavo and Balsam."

"Whatever they're hiding, you won't be able to look for it."

Tray mentally ran through his options. And found he had none. If Balsam didn't want the maintenance records examined, they would not be available to Tray. End of story.

"What can we do?" he asked Para.

The android made an almost human shrug. "*Jove's Messenger* is

President Balsam's personal property. He is perfectly within his legal rights to keep its maintenance records private."

"But we're talking about murder!"

"*Suspected* murder," Para corrected gently. "We haven't a shred of evidence to support a claim of criminal wrongdoing."

Tray realized that Para had already accessed the pertinent legal procedures.

"Then what can we do?"

"Apparently we can do nothing," the android replied. "Unless you want to make a public accusation. That might force President Balsam to open the maintenance records."

Tray shook his head. "By that time he could have rewritten the records and made them look lily-white."

Para hesitated a moment, then said, "White being the color of innocence."

"Yeah," said Tray, disgusted, frustrated. "Innocence."

Unable to think of anything else, Tray called Loris. Just the sight of her lovely face in the phone's viewscreen made him feel better.

"We've got to talk," he said to her, without preamble.

Immediately, she suggested, "The cafeteria?"

"No," Tray replied. "Someplace where we can't be overheard."

Loris looked puzzled for a moment. Then she suggested, "One of the observation blisters."

Tray bobbed his head, "Good thinking." To himself he added, I'll bring Para and he can sweep the blister for snooping devices.

With Para at his side, Tray went out into the passageway and rapped gently on Loris's door. She opened it immediately and the three of them started along the passageway, heading for one of the observation blisters that studded the spacecraft's outer shell.

Tray couldn't help noticing the outfit she wore: a simple one-piece jumpsuit of pale blue. But on her athletic figure it looked inviting.

Wordlessly, like a trio of conspirators, they made their way along the narrow passageway. Tray couldn't help glancing back to see if Mance Bricknell was following them. No sign of him.

In silence, they skipped the first blister they came across and went to the next. Tray tapped on the entrance keypad and its hatch slid open. He stepped inside, and his breath caught in his throat.

The universe hung all around him, stars and glowing nebulae spread across the infinite black of space. Tray felt his pulse accelerating. Turning, he extended his hand to help Loris step over the hatch's coaming. Even in the dim lighting he could see her eyes widen, her face reflect the starry splendor that surrounded them.

"My god," she gasped, in a whisper.

"It's awesome, isn't it," Tray whispered back to her.

They were in a smallish round compartment covered by a transparent shell. It felt noticeably cooler than the passageway outside. Automatically, Tray tried to make out the familiar constellations, but they were imbedded in a thousand times more stars than he had ever seen from Earth.

"It's . . . it's overpowering," he whispered.

Loris quoted, "Oh Lord, I love the beauty of Thy house, and the place where Thy glory dwelleth."

Para broke their spell. "This compartment is free of cameras and listening devices. You may speak openly here."

But Loris was still gaping. "There's Jupiter," she said, pointing at its striped flattened orb. It seemed to be shrinking, dwindling, as they watched.

Tray pointed at the four points of light hugging near the huge planet. "And its Galilean satellites."

"It's magnificent," she said.

Para repeated, "I can't detect any surveillance devices. You may speak freely here."

Tray glanced at the android, then said to himself, Better get down to business.

"I'm sure that Tsavo won't allow me to inspect the maintenance records for Jordan's suit, or for the *Athena* module."

Reluctantly, Loris turned from the panorama beyond the blister's shell and looked squarely at Tray. "What do you want to do?"

"I don't want to let them cover up a murder," Tray said flatly. "Two murders, including Sheshardi."

"We might have been killed, as well," Loris added.

Tray nodded, but admitted, "I don't know what to do, which way to turn."

"I do," she said.

"You do?"

"As soon as we reach Earth I'm going to ask my father to ask for an investigation."

"Your father?"

"He's a member of the Interplanetary Council."

"He is?"

"A member of the French delegation. He has the right to call for an investigation. If the Council agrees, not even Balsam can refuse to let us see the maintenance records."

Tray felt a momentary surge of excitement. But said, "Balsam will have had the time to alter the maintenance records by then. I'll bet he's got his people going through the records right now, erasing anything that looks the slightest bit suspicious."

"Forensic analysis might be able to detect changes in the records," Para said.

"Might," said Tray.

"That's a pretty thin reed," Loris said.

"But it looks like the only one we have."

Raising a forefinger, Para interjected, "May I point out an observation?"

"Observation?" Tray replied.

"Any attempt you make to examine the maintenance records will surely rouse President Balsam's suspicion."

"I suppose so," said Loris.

In its flat, emotionless tone the android said, "If we are correct in our suspicions, your insistence on examining the maintenance records will reveal to President Balsam—"

"And Captain Tsavo," Tray interjected.

"And Captain Tsavo," Para conceded, with a tiny dip of its chin, "that you suspect them of foul play."

Almost smiling at the android's melodramatic choice of words, Tray conceded, "I suppose it would."

"And that," Para went on, "might move them to try to get rid of you both. If they've already committed two murders, they will not blanch at two more."

a thin reed

"They wouldn't dare," Loris said flatly. "Murder the daughter of an interplanetary councilman? They wouldn't dare!"

Para shook its head ever so slightly. "If your suspicions are correct, they have already murdered a former president of the Interplanetary Council."

"But why?" Tray asked. "Why did they murder Kell? Assuming that they did."

"Power," answered Para without hesitation. "Do you have any idea of the immense power and wealth that President Balsam could obtain if his plans for an interstellar empire are realized?"

"Like Nero of the old Roman Empire," Loris replied. "Multiplied by a thousandfold."

"A millionfold," Tray corrected.

"Multiplied by billions," said Para.

Suddenly looking downcast, Loris said, "And there's only the two of us to oppose them."

"Three," said Tray, jabbing a thumb in Para's direction.

Calmly, without a hint of emotion, the android said, "You must understand that you are placing yourselves in lethal danger."

"What's our alternative?" Tray asked. "Sit here quietly and let Balsam get away with murder?"

The observation blister fell totally silent. Tray saw the stars of the galaxy staring at him, cold, silent, yet somehow demanding.

Loris finally broke the stillness. "Let me talk with my father when we get back to Earth."

"By then Tsavo will have had enough time to make the maintenance records look totally clean," Tray objected.

"Yes, perhaps so," said Loris, "but I don't see any other option to us."

Just then the hatch from the passageway slid open and Mance Bricknell stepped into the observation blister.

"Here you are!" Bricknell said brightly, as he walked up to them. "I've been looking all over the ship for you."

Without a shred of enthusiasm Tray said, "Hello Mance."

"Searching for us?" Loris said, straightfaced. "What on earth for?"

Reaching an arm toward her, Bricknell replied, "I got lonesome for my girl."

"I'm not your girl, Mance," Loris replied, stepping away from him. "I'm not anyone's girl."

"Not yet," said Bricknell, grinning.

The four of them left the observation blister and headed back toward their quarters.

"It's almost time for lunch," Bricknell said pleasantly. "Shall we go directly to the cafeteria? Be the first in line?"

Tray studied Mance's face. Not a trace of suspicion, nor of displeasure that "his girl" had gone off without him.

How did he find us? Tray asked himself. This ship's pretty big. If he started searching for Loris from his own quarters he'd have had to come directly to the blister to find us so quickly.

While Mance chattered on, Tray inwardly debated, Does he

have some way of tracking us? Or maybe just Loris. Is he being proprietary about her, or is he working with Balsam and Tsavo to keep tabs on us?

That possibility worried him. It meant that the ship's captain knew that Tray was suspicious of him and the Council president. And maybe it meant that somehow they were using Para to track his movements.

With an abrupt shake of his head, Tray dismissed the idea. You're getting paranoid, he told himself.

Yes, maybe, he admitted to himself. But even paranoids have enemies.

Following Mance's suggestion, they went directly to the cafeteria. They were the first ones there; it was unoccupied except for the robots standing behind the counters. Once they had filled their trays and sat themselves at the end of one of the empty cafeteria tables, Mance asked, with a smile that showed his teeth, "So what were the two of you doing in that observation blister?"

Sitting beside him, Loris answered, "Observing."

"Really?" Bricknell replied. "Have you taken on a sudden interest in astronomy, Loris?"

Tray broke in, "How did you find us? You must have gone directly from your quarters to the blister."

His smiling turning sly, Bricknell said, "I followed Loris's scent. She leaves a lovely trail wherever she goes."

Surprised, Loris asked, "My scent?"

Bricknell pulled a palm-sized capsule from his pocket. "Chemical sniffer. Very sensitive."

"You keep track of me?"

"Naturally. I want to know where you are at every instant, day or night."

Loris snatched the capsule out of Mance's open hand and threw it across the cafeteria. It bounced off the bulkhead and rolled under an empty table. The four crewmen who had just come in at the serving line turned and gaped at her.

"I won't have you tracking me like some hunted animal," Loris said, her voice low but trembling with fury.

Bricknell's smile seemed frozen on his face. Without taking his eyes from her, he said, "I care about you, Loris. I won't have you trekking around this ship with Tray or anyone else unless I'm with you."

Tray saw a hard, unbendable purpose behind Bricknell's toothy smile.

Lunch was pretty desolate. Mance prattled about the ship's trajectory back toward Earth while Loris and Tray remained silent, picking at their lunches. Para made some conversation with Bricknell, but it was desultory, pointless.

At last they left the cafeteria and headed back to their quarters. Loris entered her billet alone and swiftly closed its hatch behind her. Tray heard its lock click, leaving him, Para, and Bricknell standing in the passageway.

"H'mmph," Bricknell grunted, staring at the locked hatch. "The course of true love ne'er ran smooth, I suppose," he misquoted.

Tray looked at him. Bricknell was smiling: ruefully, but still smiling.

"Maybe we should fight a duel," Tray suggested.

"You *are* a throwback," Bricknell sniffed. "A real atavism. Hopeless."

Tray heard himself retort, "Oh, I have some hopes."

Bricknell's smile vanished. "Don't count on them," he snapped. "You're out of your league, mister."

"We'll see."

"Yes, we certainly will." With that, Mance turned on his heel and marched down the passageway, toward his own quarters. As he watched Bricknell's retreating back, Tray realized that the historian was at least a couple of centimeters taller than himself.

Once in his own compartment, Tray sank tiredly onto his bunk. Loris is on the other side of that bulkhead, he knew. At least she's alone. But he longed to be with her.

The next morning, as he dressed, Tray heard his communicator announce, "Message from President Balsam."

He glanced at Para, standing in the corner of the compartment. The android didn't move, yet Tray knew it had heard the announcement as well.

"Answer," he said.

Balsam's bulky form took shape in the middle of the small room, suddenly making it seem crowded.

"Tray," the image said without preamble, "Captain Tsavo tells me your android has been trying to gain access to the maintenance records for the *Athena* module."

Surprised, Tray admitted, "Yes, that's true."

For a couple of heartbeats Balsam's image sat frozen in the compartment. Tray realized *Jove's Messenger* was still several light-seconds away from Earth.

At last Balsam said, "We ought to talk about this. Why don't we talk this over after you've had your breakfast." His face looked somehow sorrowful, almost despondent.

"We could talk it over right now," Tray said.

Again the wait. Then, "No, no. Have your breakfast first. I'm in the middle of a session with my staff here at the Capitol. Should be finished by the time you have your breakfast."

"All right," Tray said, "I'll call you as soon as I've finished breakfast."

"Good," said Balsam. "Good. And just you and me, please. Not your android."

"Very well," said Tray, reluctantly.

Balsam's image winked out. Tray looked at Para. "He wants to see me, but not you."

"Interesting," said the android.

A thousand possible scenarios raced through Tray's mind. Maybe . . . maybe . . .

"Don't get your hopes up," Para warned. "He's not going to admit anything or allow you to uncover evidence that could harm him. Not willingly."

"Yes, I guess so," Tray said. "But it's better than being totally shut out, isn't it?"

"I wonder," said Para.

Tray rushed through breakfast in the cafeteria, then returned to his quarters and called Balsam. Para quietly stepped outside. It took several minutes to get through the Council president's staff flunkies, but at last Balsam appeared in Tray's compartment, looking slightly flushed, almost unready for their meeting.

"This staff meeting is dragging on much longer than I expected," Balsam's image said. "Should be over by eleven o'clock, though. If it isn't I'll tell the staff that we'll continue it later. Can you call me again at eleven, Tray?"

"Eleven o'clock, yes, sir."

"Good."

"Will Captain Tsavo join us?"

"No," Balsam snapped. "Just the two of us. Just you and me."

Tray nodded as Balsam's image winked out.

* * *

Tray's wristwatch read precisely eleven a.m. as Harold Balsam's image appeared in his cramped compartment. The Council president was seated at his desk, smiling broadly at Tray.

From what he could see of Balsam's office, the Council president's surroundings were quite luxurious. His desk was wide and gently curved. Behind it hung a broad image of stars and swirling nebulae. And why not? Tray asked himself. He's the head of the government not only of the solar system, but of the new worlds we've discovered around other stars. Looking around at the luxurious furnishings, the paintings on the walls, the bottles lined up behind the curving teak bar in the corner, Tray realized that Balsam's personal fortune must be enormously large.

The room looked like a handsome study, comfortable, relaxing. But somehow Tray didn't feel relaxed at all.

"Well, here we are," said Balsam, gesturing toward a commodious cushioned easy chair. "I hope you had a good breakfast."

"Quite good," said Tray. "Thank you."

Balsam pushed himself up from his commodious chair and headed for the bar. "After the session with my staff I've just been through, I deserve a drink."

Tray made a smile.

As he puttered with the glassware behind the bar, Balsam said, "Tsavo tells me you want to examine the maintenance records for the *Athena* module."

"Yes. Lieutenant Sheshardi said the controls jammed up somehow. He couldn't get the vessel to rise up to the surface."

"Bad business," Balsam muttered. He held up a cocktail glass filled to the brim and squinted at it. "That looks about right."

As Balsam came around the bar to sit again in his desk chair, he said, "I want you to know, Tray, that I have nothing to hide. You can comb through the maintenance files as much as you want. Tsavo might get pissed off, but I'm the owner of the ship, and as long as

I am you can have complete access to any of our maintenance records."

Tray blinked with surprise. "Why . . . thank you, Mr. Balsam."

Balsam chuckled. "Call me Harold. Officially, you should address me as President Balsam, but just between the two of us we can junk all that spit and polish."

"Thank you . . . Harold."

"You're entirely welcome. I realize that Kell's death has been a special shock to you. I want to do everything I can to help you get over it."

Tray suddenly got the feeling he was talking with a smiling, scheming, cunning manipulator.

I'm out of my league, he realized. This man is way ahead of me.

"One may smile . . ."

++
++

For the next two days and nights, Tray and Para searched through the maintenance records that captain Tsavo reluctantly gave them access to.

On its way back to Earth, *Jove's Messenger* swept through the Asteroid Belt, that bleak stretch of darkness that was home to countless bodies of rock and ice spread so far apart that the zone seemed desolately empty to Tray.

It was nearly midnight when Para looked up from the screen it had been studying and pointed to the viewport on Tray's bedroom bulkhead.

A tiny red dot was glowing in the eternal night.

"Mars," said Para.

Tray stared at the image on the screen. "Mars," he agreed. "We're nearing home."

But as he turned his attention back to the maintenance records on his computer screen, Tray added, "And we haven't found an iota of data that indicates sabotage of the *Athena*." Before Para could reply, he added, "Or of Kell's suit."

Para dipped its chin once in acknowledgment. "I have come to the conclusion that Captain Tsavo has not altered the maintenance records."

"But he must have!" Tray bleated.

"No," Para insisted. "I have come to the conclusion that Captain Tsavo has had the entire maintenance record rewritten, from beginning to end. We won't find any alterations in the record because it hasn't been altered. What we are examining is a new record, rewritten from its first line to its last."

Tray stared at the android for a long, silent moment. Then he asked, "Completely rewritten?"

"I believe so."

"Then we've been wasting our time."

"Indeed. I imagine President Balsam and Captain Tsavo are having a hearty laugh at our expense."

"Damn!" Tray snapped. "The sneaky bastards."

"I could be wrong, of course," Para admitted.

"No, I think you're entirely correct. This entire log we've been poring through is a waste of time. We won't find any erasures or corrections because there aren't any. They've rewritten it from top to bottom."

"Very clever of them."

"Damned clever," Tray groused. "Balsam sat there and told me he had nothing to hide. 'A man may smile, and smile, and still be a villain.'"

"A slight misquote," Para said. "From *Hamlet*, act one, scene five."

"Whatever," said Tray, disgusted that Balsam had outwitted him so easily.

The next morning *Jove's Messenger* skimmed almost exactly a thousand kilometers past Mars, close enough for Tray and Para to see the plastic domes of the research station on the edge of the Great Rift Valley, that sinuous crack in the planet's crust that stretched almost a quarter of the way across the planet.

"Strange," Para noted. "We're picking up speed from Mars's gravity well. I would think Captain Tsavo would be slowing down as we approach Earth."

"Maybe he's in a hurry to get home," Tray suggested.

Para didn't reply, but Tray got the feeling that the android was puzzled.

By dinnertime Mars was behind them, and Tray could see on the viewscreen mounted on the dining room's bulkhead the faint blue crescent of Earth, with the even fainter sliver of the Moon near it.

"Going home," Loris said.

"At last," said Bricknell.

Para shook its head slightly. "Our velocity is much higher than it needs to be. Unless Captain Tsavo orders a braking maneuver we will sail past Earth and head for the inner solar system."

"Why would he do that?" Tray wondered.

Pointing to the other side of the dining room with its eyes, Para said, "The captain is sitting there, with some of his staff. I suppose we could ask them."

"Disturb them at dinner?" Loris asked. "That's not polite."

Tray said, "We could wait until they start to leave their table, then ask."

Bricknell pushed his plate away from him. "Well, Tray, you've succeeded in spoiling my appetite."

"I didn't mean to!"

"Whether you meant it or not . . ."

Para looked down at the remains of Bricknell's dinner. There was nothing on the plate except crumbs and a crust of bread.

"Perhaps you ate too fast," the android suggested. "Perhaps you are full."

Loris couldn't suppress a giggle. "Maybe you need to burp, Mance."

He grinned at her. "Would you like to burp me, Mommy?"

Her smile fading, Loris answered, "Not very likely, Mance."

Silence descended on their table. Tray started eating again, slowly, one eye on the table where Tsavo and his crew sat. They seemed to be deep in conversation.

I wonder what they're talking about, Tray asked himself.

It seemed to take hours, but at last Tsavo and his people pushed their chairs away from their table and got to their feet. Tray immediately stood up and moved past the other tables to intercept them.

"Captain Tsavo," he called as he approached. "May I ask you a question?"

Tsavo's dark face smiled pleasantly, almost as if he had expected Tray to accost him.

"Of course," his deep voice rumbled. "Might it have something to do with our increase in velocity?"

"Yes, sir," Tray replied. "Why did we speed up when we passed Mars?"

"We've been asked by the Interplanetary Council to get back home as fast as we can."

Tray blinked at him.

Tsavo amended, "The Council's message said, 'With all deliberate speed.' That's why we slingshotted past Mars."

"With all deliberate speed," Tray echoed.

His dark face emotionless, the captain explained, "Jordan Kell's sycophants on the Council want to open an inquiry into Kell's death."

"They do?"

"Of course," said Tsavo. "A former Council president. Naturally they want to find out what happened."

"Naturally," Tray echoed.

With a rueful shake of his head Tsavo said, "It's all political grandstanding. They won't find anything more than you did."

Because you rewrote the maintenance records, Tray replied silently.

Tsavo went on, "We'll have to do a braking maneuver as we approach the Moon."

"The Moon?" Tray yelped. "We're not returning to Earth?"

"Standard operational procedure," Tsavo explained. "This ship and all its records are going to be thoroughly examined by the accident investigation team at Selene."

"And we'll have to stay on the Moon?" Tray asked. "For how long?"

"As long as it takes for the investigators to give us a clean bill of health," said Tsavo.

"Damned piece of bureaucratic nonsense," one of the crew members grumbled.

But for the first time since they'd returned to *Jove's Messenger* Tray felt a tendril of hope.

book three

THE MOON

debarkation

selene was the oldest of the human settlements scattered across the moon's bleak, barren landscape. A thriving city, center of humankind's interplanetary missions, it was almost entirely underground. Tucked into the ringwall mountains of the giant crater Alphonsus, Selene had led the struggle for lunar independence from Earth's nations and established the first democratic republic on the Moon.

Jove's Messenger had indeed needed a serious braking maneuver to slow down enough to establish an orbit around the Moon. Tray and all the other guests and crew personnel were required to strap themselves into well-cushioned chairs for the two hours of the deceleration maneuver.

Together with Loris, Bricknell, and Para, Tray went from his quarters to the ship's dining room, which had been cleared of its tables and customary chairs and decked out in sturdy, commodious deceleration seats.

Even Para seemed impressed. "President Balsam has outfitted his ship very completely," the android said.

Bricknell was less than overwhelmed. "I'm sure the safety examiners required him to include high-gee equipment."

Tray sat beside Loris, Bricknell on her other side. Para sat on Tray's right and strapped in as required, even though he didn't have to. Tucked into a pocket on the seat's armrests were folded bags bearing the designation ZERO GRAVITY RELIEF APPA-RATUS.

Within minutes of their strapping in, Tray felt an invisible force pressing him into the chair's cushions. Not enough to be uncomfortable, but recognizable. We're slowing down, he told himself. We're going into orbit around the Moon.

The viewscreens on the bulkheads of the dining area showed the Moon hurtling toward them, its surface bare shades of gray. Tray stared at the sight. Not a tree, not a blade of grass, nothing but desolate emptiness.

Then, "There's Selene!" Bricknell called out, pointing.

Tray saw the ringwall mountains of Alphonsus and, on the plain inside them, huge stretches of solar panels glittering darkly. And astronomical telescopes standing out in the open without protective domes covering them.

"How do they protect the 'scopes from the meteoric infall?" Tray wondered aloud.

Para answered, "Electromagnetic repulsion. The meteorites are charged to a high positive potential as they enter the Alphonsus region, and the telescopes and other equipment are also charged positively. The meteors are shunted aside, to fall beyond the region where the equipment is placed."

"And that works?" Tray wondered.

"It has for centuries," Para replied. "Most of the meteors are smaller than snowflakes. Occasionally a larger one makes it through the electromagnetic shielding and causes some damage, but that is comparatively rare."

The view of Alphonsus swept past and Tray saw again that bleak, desolate surface of bare rock, peppered with craters of every size from finger pokes to hundreds of kilometers across.

Human beings have turned this barren wilderness into a home. Generations of people have been born here and lived out their lives. Selene and the other lunar states were the first steps in humankind's expansion out to the stars.

At long last Captain Tsavo's voice announced through the speakers set into the dining room's ceiling, "We have successfully established orbit around Luna. You can unstrap and get to your feet. Be careful, though: we are now in zero gravity. Watch your step."

Tray pulled off the straps that had held him down and got to his feet. At least, that is what he tried to do. Instead of standing on the dining room's polished floor, though, he rose majestically upward and floated toward the ceiling.

His surprise was overcome by the hollowness he felt in his stomach. Zero gee was not a pleasant sensation, he realized.

Para came soaring up after him.

"Zero gravity can be upsetting at first," said the android, grasping Tray's shoulders.

Tray nodded dumbly. His stomach was telling him that it wanted to empty itself. While Tray's innards throbbed and his throat felt as if it was going to erupt, Para used the small vernier jets built into its body to gently bring him back down to the floor.

"We only spent a few moments in zero gravity when we boarded *Jove's Messenger*," Para said to Tray as the two of them stood shakily among the others. "Not enough time to acquire your space legs."

Tray nodded shakily. The motion made his stomach lurch.

The android yanked one of the emergency bags from the seat and handed it to Tray, who happily, ingloriously, vomited into it.

Through tearing eyes Tray saw Loris staring at him, her face distraught. Bricknell was chuckling. Others either gawked or turned away. Nobody else seemed to be affected by zero gee the way he was. Tray felt totally miserable.

Para said, "One of the disadvantages of modern spaceflight is that passengers are rarely exposed to zero gravity for more than a few minutes."

Bricknell put on a sympathetic face. "Why didn't you put on a zero-gee adaptation applicator, Tray? They were sent to each of our quarters." He pointed to the tiny flesh-colored circle pasted to the side of his neck.

"I . . . I didn't think I'd need one," Tray replied weakly, feeling he'd made an ass of himself in Loris's eyes.

But she said, "It's all right, Tray. All's well that ends well."

Tray felt grateful to her.

Under zero gravity, one of the ship's crew led Tray and the others, bobbing and wide-eyed, to the ship's main hatch, three levels below the dining area. Harold Balsam was already there, together with a trio of underlings. Balsam looked unhappy, impatient.

"Your luggage is being handled by the robots," explained the young, pale blond crewman leading them down to the exit hatch. "Should be in your quarters by the time you get there."

"How long are we going to be on the Moon?" Balsam asked.

The youngster shrugged. "That's up to the investigating team. But don't worry, you'll have complete communications capabilities in your quarters. You'll be only one-point-three seconds away from whoever you want to talk to on Earth."

The eight of them stopped when they reached the ship's exit hatch. The hatch was firmly shut; three officers in slate-gray uniforms—two men and a woman—were hovering there.

Their crewman escort announced, "We got seven passengers

and an android." Turning back to Tray and the others, he smilingly said, "This is as far as I go. You're now officially in the hands of the Selene security department."

The woman turned out to be the head of the trio. She glided over to Tray and his companions. "Selene Immigration Control," she corrected sharply. "We'll take over from here."

immigration

The woman was slightly shorter than Tray, lean of face and figure, with short-cropped light brown hair.

"Welcome to Selene," she said flatly, as she nodded to one of her male associates.

He pecked at the control box mounted on the bulkhead, and the heavy metal hatch slowly swung inward.

"We'll fly you down to the surface and our immigration processing center. In a few minutes you'll be under lunar gravity and we'll all feel a lot better."

Only then did Tray realize that the woman's bleak expression was her reaction to zero gravity. He felt pleased that he wasn't the only one suffering.

They shuffled through the hatch one by one, with Balsam and his assistants in the lead, and took seats in the spacecraft's narrow interior. Loris sat one seat ahead of Tray; Bricknell took the seat on the other side of the aisle from her.

"Fasten your safety belts, please," said the security team's leader as she glided to the front of the passenger compartment. "You'll be feeling some gravity again once we lift off."

Tray looked forward to it.

The two male officers had remained at the rear of the compartment, by the hatch. Turning in his chair, Tray saw the ship's hatch swing leisurely inward and secure itself firmly.

"Ready for departure," one of the men called.

The woman made the slightest of nods and spoke softly into the slim black communicator she held in her hand. Tray felt a slight thump and then a push against his back.

"We're off!" Bricknell announced.

Tray smiled inwardly as his insides calmed down. Gravity, he thought. Man's best friend. At least, his digestive system's best friend.

The flight from orbit to the surface of the Moon was brief and un-eventful. There was nothing to see, since the shuttlecraft had no viewports. But a few minutes after they left *Jove's Messenger* Tray felt another surge of weight and then the slightest of bumps.

"We're down," said the woman. "We've arrived at Selene's space-port."

Tray unfastened his seat belt.

"Please remain seated," the woman instructed, "until asked to get up."

Tray impatiently drummed his finger on the seat's armrests. Para, sitting across the aisle from him, sat perfectly still, as if asleep.

After several minutes, the hatch at the rear of the compartment popped open with a soft sigh of air. The two security crewmen stood aside and a young woman stepped aboard, smiling brightly. Her hair was red and curly, her figure lean and lithe. Her uniform was coral red, nicely complementing her hair. Tray figured she was nearly his own height. She looked perky.

"Good morning," she said. "Welcome to Selene. My name is

Connie Seventeen. I will guide you to your quarters. Please fol-low me."

Tray glanced at Para and then back at Connie Seventeen. She's an android! he realized. It was hard to believe, she looked so life-like.

Balsam came striding down the aisle in ponderous steps and put out his hand to the android. "A pleasure to meet you, Miss Seven-teen."

The android dimpled like a human. "And an honor to meet you, Mr. President."

Tray let Loris go past him before stepping out into the aisle ahead of Bricknell. He smiled at his minuscule victory over Mance as he followed Loris toward the exit hatch.

Connie Seventeen led them from the shuttlecraft's hatch to a wait-ing bullet-shaped bus that swiftly sped through a long tunnel.

"Our spaceport is several kilometers from the city proper, of course," Connie Seventeen was explaining to the seated passengers. "Although Stavenger Spaceport has an excellent safety record, we simply cannot take the chance of a spacecraft mishap damaging the city itself."

Raising a hand, Loris asked, "Isn't the city almost entirely bur-ied underground?"

Standing at the front of the speeding bus, the android replied cheerfully, "Yes, of course. But a spacecraft loaded with many tons of highly combustible propellants is still a considerable safety risk. Better to keep the spaceport a reasonable distance from the city it-self." It hesitated a moment, then added, "We've had to move the spaceport outward three times over our history as Selene proper has expanded."

Bricknell raised a hand. "How much traffic does the spaceport handle?"

Connie Seventeen smiled momentarily, then began to answer, "Most of the flights outward to Mars and the Asteroid Belt, Jupiter, Saturn, and the further extremes of the solar system, of course. Inward flights to Venus, Mercury, and Sun orbiters. And now we're doing interstellar missions, as well."

"Numbers?" Bricknell insisted.

The android smiled again. It's checking the records, Tray realized. That smile is a delaying tactic.

Connie Seventeen rattled off numbers until even Bricknell's face glazed over.

Balsam half-grumbled, "How long is this bus ride going to take us?"

Its smile more gleaming than ever, the android replied, "We are slowing down now. We will be pulling into your debarking station within three minutes."

The next half hour was spent answering questions. Connie Seventeen led Tray and the others to a row of desks where large square viewscreens displayed a long series of boring questions.

Name? Occupation? Purpose of visit to Selene?

It seemed to Tray that they must already know the answers; all they had to do was access the records from *Jove's Messenger*. But each of them—even Para—had to sit and sift through the questions, one by one.

Tray noted that Balsam was not subjected to such an investigation. The president of the Interplanetary Council was met by a small cluster of officious-looking men and women and whisked away from the others, together with his trio of assistants.

Rank hath its privileges, Tray said to himself.

At last, though, the inquisition ended and the monitor screens showed THANK YOU FOR YOUR COOPERATION. WELCOME TO SELENE.

Tray frowned at the words. Welcome to Selene, he thought. That's the third or fourth time we've been welcomed. But we're still not in Selene, not really.

Connie Seventeen was apparently not programmed to show the slightest disappointment. She gathered up the four of them and pointed to a door in the far side of their interrogation center.

"On the other side of that door is Selene proper. Are you ready to enter?"

"Hell, yes," Tray snapped irritably.

The others nodded agreement. Even Para.

SELENE

connie seventeen hesitated at the hatch. "i know you've heard these words several times earlier, but . . . well, welcome to selene!"

With that the heavy hatch popped open and swung outward.

The first thing to hit Tray's awareness was the noise. Selene *hummed*. It *buzzed*. It *bustled*.

Tray stared out at a wide-open area, covered high above with a dome of some sort. Down at the ground level, people were walking, striding, hurrying along paved walkways that curved through lush growths of beautifully colored flowers. Trees soared overhead. Tray's eyes oogled at people flying through the air on broad colorful wings. And everyone seemed to be talking, jabbering, pointing, gesticulating at once.

Connie Seventeen smiled at the gaping expressions on the faces of Tray and the others.

"It's a lot to take in, all at once," the android said. Gesturing out toward the hustling, energetic, spirited crowd, it explained, "Selene is a *city*, like Tokyo or London or New York, not some tiny research center or mining facility. Our population is over four million and still growing. Our people are proud to say you can find anything you want in Selene. And then some!"

Tray oogled at the passing parade. He had been in cities much of his life: born in Oakland, educated in Montreal, he had done his astronaut training in the Greater Orlando region. But Selene was beyond any of them. It seethed; it vibrated like a living organism.

Leading them through the hatch and onto a moving slidewalk, Connie Seventeen explained, "We're in the Main Plaza, where people go for restaurants and recreation—you know, theater, concerts, swimming in the Olympic-sized pool . . ." The android pointed. Beyond the crowds thronging the walkways Tray could see youngsters diving off a platform that must have been at least thirty meters high, twisting and tumbling in midair as they slowly, dreamily dropped toward the water.

"We're in one-sixth Earth-normal gravity," Connie Seventeen said cheerfully. "That allows some spectacular athletic performances. And of course," the android pointed overhead, "you can rent wings and fly like a bird."

One of the fliers swooped low over their heads and shouted something in a language Tray didn't understand. But he waved at the guy, and realized he was a grizzled old-timer. With a huge grin splitting his face.

Turning to Loris, striding along beside him, Tray said, "I'd like to try that—flying like a bird."

"Looks like fun," she agreed.

From her other side, Bricknell groused, "You can break your neck on one-sixth gee just as well as on Earth."

Tray grinned at him. "But it takes longer," he wisecracked.

Bricknell shot him a disgusted look.

As they walked along Tray saw in the distance a massive concrete shell and concluded that that was where concerts were performed. *They don't have to worry about the weather,* he realized.

At last they came to a set of moving stairs that led underground. The android watched its human charges step warily onto the escalator before it—and Para—got on themselves.

"Most of Selene is underground, of course," Connie Seventeen pointed out. "The Moon's surface is bathed in harsh radiation, with temperature swings of more than four hundred degrees Kelvin just by stepping from sunshine to shadow. Plus the constant meteoric infall. Much safer underground—and more comfortable."

The escalator ended in what looked to Tray like a broad, comfortably furnished lobby.

"Welcome to Hotel Luna," said Connie Seventeen as she moved to the head of their little group. "You'll be staying here while the accident investigation team does its work."

Tray glanced around. The lobby was impressive: dark wood paneling, thickly lush multihued carpeting, expensive-looking easy chairs scattered here and there. The front desk seemed almost a kilometer from where the escalator ended.

"Your expenses will be covered by the investigation team's budget, of course." Then the android added, "Within reason."

"Will that include calls down to Earth?" Loris asked.

"I'm afraid not," said Connie Seventeen. "You are to be kept incommunicado until the investigation is finished."

"How long will that take?" Bricknell inquired.

The android hesitated a split second, then replied, "I'm sorry, but I don't know."

"We could be here for weeks!" Bricknell complained.

"Perhaps."

Tray thought it over quickly. Aloud, he said "Not so bad, actually. Like an all-expense-paid vacation."

"Not *all* expenses," Connie Seventeen reminded.

"Close enough," said Tray, with a careless shrug. He was thinking, A week or so in Selene with Loris shouldn't be too intolerable. As long as we can ditch Mance.

* * *

But once Tray had registered at the Hotel Luna's reception desk and he and Para had been escorted by one of the hotel's robots to his room he discovered two things.

One: his meager overnight bag containing his travel things.

Two: a notice on the ceiling-high viewscreen in his bedroom to report to the accident investigation team's headquarters at 0900 hours the next day.

He plopped onto the comfortably yielding bed and called Loris. Her lovely face filled the screen, bigger than life, warm, inviting.

"Yes," she replied, once Tray told her of his summons. "I got one also, for eleven hundred hours."

Nodding, Tray suggested, "Maybe they think they'll be finished with me in two hours."

Loris smiled slightly. "Let's hope so."

iNUEStigatiUE boaRd

The following morning, with Para guiding him through Selene's broad, busy, chatter-filled passageways, Tray arrived at the investigative board's hearing room thee minutes before nine a.m.

It was a small, almost bare room, with no furnishings except a curved banc raised almost a full meter above floor level and an empty chair and desk facing it. Tray looked around hesitantly. The walls looked bare, but he detected the faint glow of display screens from floor to ceiling. No windows, of course, since they were several levels below the Moon's harsh, lifeless surface.

Tray turned to Para. "Are you sure this is the right place?"

Before the android could reply, three humanform androids filed through the door behind the raised banc and took their seats facing Tray. They wore no clothes, but their anodized "skins" glistened in the subdued lighting from the ceiling.

"Good morning," said the one in the center. "Are you prepared to begin?"

Tray nodded, then said, "Yes, I am."

"And you?" asked the investigator, pointing at Para.

"I am ready for your questions," Para replied.

"Good. Then let us start."

They started by asking Tray's name and home address.

Once Tray answered, the investigator on Tray's left asked, "That's a mental facility, isn't it?"

"A recuperative facility," Para explained. "Mr. Williamson is being treated for post-traumatic stress disorder stemming from the destruction of the *Saviour* spacecraft and its entire crew, except for himself."

Its entire crew, Tray repeated silently. Including Felicia. But the pain he expected was muted, softer than it had ever been before.

The interrogator on the other side of the three-person team said, "We are here to look into the loss of the *Athena* spacecraft, and the deaths of Jordan Kell and Gyele Sheshardi. The *Saviour* incident has no bearing on this investigation."

Not to you, Tray thought.

The chief investigator, seated in the middle of the trio, nodded in a very humanlike fashion.

"Mr. Williamson," it said, focusing its diamond-hard eyes on Tray, "can you tell us in your own words what happened aboard the *Athena*?"

Tray licked his lips, then replied, "I can tell you *what* happened, but I can't tell you why."

Almost smiling, the investigator said gently, "That's *our* job, sir."

So Tray swiftly recounted the events of the *Athena*'s ill-fated mission into Jupiter's ocean.

"Lieutenant Sheshardi couldn't find out why the controls jammed," he concluded. "And then, when he was in his escape suit and heading for the surface with the rest of us, he was electrocuted by the Jovian predator."

"And the failure of Jordan Kell's escape suit?" asked the chief investigator. "What can you tell us about that?"

"Very little," Tray admitted. "He suddenly told us that his suit was filling with water. It must have been very cold . . . freezing . . ."

Silence filled the tiny room. After nearly a minute, the chief investigator turned to Para. "Have you anything to add to this testimony?"

"I'm afraid not," Para replied. "But my diagnostic system has recorded everything I witnessed. You are free to examine it."

"We already have," said the judge on Tray's left.

Silence again. The three investigators sat like statues, all staring at Tray.

That's it? he asked himself. I tell them what they already know and that's all there is to their investigation?

The chief interrogator stirred to life. "You may go, Mr. Williamson. You also, Para."

"That's it?" Tray asked aloud. "That's your whole investigation?"

The chief folded it hands on the top of the curving banc in a very humanlike gesture. "We have the monitoring records from *Jove's Messenger*. If we need more from you we will summon you, Mr. Williamson."

Flustered, feeling anger simmering inside him, Tray said, "I have a statement to make. I want to add it to my testimony."

Statement

"A statement?" asked the chief investigator.

"Yes," said Tray. "A statement about my own observations of the *Athena*'s destruction and my conclusions about what caused it."

The chief examiner glanced at its colleagues to its left and right, then nodded benignly at Tray. "Very well. We will hear your statement and add it to the proceedings of this investigation."

Tray suddenly felt unprepared, at a loss. He told himself silently, This is what happens when you let your emotions outrun your intelligence. But, glancing at the three androids staring down at him, he realized that he had no option but to go ahead.

You've stuck your neck out, he told himself. Now let's see if you get your head chopped off.

"Mr. Williamson?" the chief investigator prompted.

Tray swallowed once, then said, "*Athena* was sabotaged. That's the only conclusion that I can draw from what happened to us."

"Sabotaged?"

"I don't know how they did it, but I know why. The vessel was sabotaged in order to kill Jordan Kell."

The three androids went absolutely still, as if someone had flicked a switch that turned them off.

Looking up at them from beneath frowning brows, Tray added, "The vessel's maintenance records will show that there was nothing wrong with it. Everything checks out perfectly. Yet Lieutenant Sheshardi was unable to raise it to the ocean's surface when the time came for us to leave the ocean."

The chief investigator leaned forward slightly in his seat. "But *Athena* has sunk too deep into the Jovian ocean for anyone to retrieve and examine it."

Tray nodded vigorously. "They buried the evidence."

"What evidence?" demanded the investigator on Tray's left. "We have no evidence; whatever evidence there could possibly be is all at the bottom of the ocean."

"That's my point," said Tray.

"That isn't a valid point," the investigator said flatly. "Lack of evidence is not evidence."

"Then there's the question of Mr. Kell's emergency suit," Tray plunged ahead. "Of the five suits, only his failed. Why?"

The investigator shook its head. "The next thing you'll be telling us is that the predator that electrocuted Lieutenant Sheshardi was part of the plot, too."

"No," Tray replied. "That was a random act. The beast might have killed any one of us."

"Let me understand you, Mr. Williamson," said the chief investigator. "You are saying that the *Athena* vessel, and Councilman Kell's emergency suit, were both deliberately sabotaged?"

"And Mr. Kell was murdered. Yes."

The investigators fell silent again for several moments. Then, "And who do you blame for this crime?"

"Captain Tsavo must have been involved. And he was working for President Balsam."

Androids are not built to display shock or surprise. But for several long moments the tiny hearing chamber was absolutely still.

Tray glanced over his shoulder at Para, standing behind him.

Like the three investigators up on the banc, Para maintained complete silence.

At last the chief investigator said, in a hollowed voice, "That is an extraordinary accusation, Mr. Williamson."

"Especially when you have absolutely no evidence to back it," said the android on Tray's right.

"Jordan Kell's death should not be swept under the rug," Tray replied.

"There is no rug," said the investigator on Tray's left. "Or, rather, the rug has sunk to the bottom of the Jovian ocean."

"If I may interject," Para said, taking a step forward to stand beside Tray. "The evidence of sabotage, if there is any, can be found in the wreckage of the *Athena* module."

"Which is at the bottom of the ocean," the investigator repeated.

"Not yet," said Para. "According to my calculations the wreckage should reach a neutral buoyancy point at approximately seven hundred kilometers below the ocean's surface."

"Far deeper than any of our submersibles have gone," said the chief investigator.

"Not entirely true," countered Para. "The experimental research submersible *Jupiter Oceanus* has reached almost that depth in its trial runs."

The chief investigator focused on Para. "It is beyond the authority of this board of inquiry to commandeer the services of an experimental research vessel."

"Who has such authority?" Tray asked.

"The Interplanetary Council's research board," said the android. Then it added, "Which is chaired by Council president Harold Balsam."

aftermath

++++++++ ++++++ ++++++ ++++++ ++++++++ ++++++++ ++++ +++++

++++ + +++++++++ ++++++ ++++++++ ++++++++ +++++++ +++++

"Heads they win, tails I lose," Tray grumbled as he and Para sat in the corridor outside the hearing room.

He was waiting for Loris, who was giving her testimony to the board of android investigators. She had arrived at the hearing room alone; Mance Bricknell was nowhere in sight.

The corridor was empty except for Tray and Para, a long, dreary tunnel dug into the lunar subsoil generations ago as Selene expanded its habitat. Empty of other people, Tray thought, but he could see tiny red lights up near the curved ceiling: surveillance cameras, watching eternally.

"How long has she been in there?" Tray asked.

Para replied, "Twenty-six minutes and fourteen seconds."

"What's taking them so long? Loris doesn't have anything to tell them that they haven't already heard."

The android was sitting beside Tray on the bare metal bench outside the hearing room. "They want to hear her version of what happened, to see if there are any major differences with your testimony, or places where your stories contradict one another."

"See if one of us is lying," Tray said.

"Or mistaken," said Para.

Looking down the long, slightly curving corridor, Tray saw someone approaching. He quickly recognized the figure as Mance

Bricknell, decked out in a bright green jacket and darker green slacks.

Bricknell came up to them and, unbidden, sat beside Tray.

"How did it go?" he asked, in a low, subdued voice.

Tray shrugged. "They didn't have much to ask about."

Bricknell nodded sharply. "No records from *Athena*. All the evidence sank with the ship."

"Not entirely true," Para corrected. "My systems recorded everything I witnessed."

"Oh!" Bricknell seemed surprised at that. "I had forgotten you're a walking, talking info cache."

With as much of a smile as it was capable of making, Para said, "That capability was built into me. I have no control over it."

Bricknell nodded, then asked, "How long are they going to keep her in there? I'm scheduled to see them at one p.m. I'll be missing my lunch—"

He stopped short as the door of the hearing room opened and Loris stepped into the corridor. She was wearing a slim sheath of pale rose that exquisitely set off her dark hair, which tumbled down one shoulder.

Both men and the android jumped to their feet.

"How did it go?" Mance and Tray asked in unison.

Loris smiled tentatively. "It wasn't very bad, really. I didn't have much to tell them that they didn't already know. They asked me about Captain Tsavo, though. I'm not sure why."

Tray's ears perked up. "Tsavo? What did they want to know?"

Loris shrugged nonchalantly. "Oh, if he involved himself in checking out *Athena*'s systems, technical matters like that. I told them I had no idea."

"Why would they ask that?" Bricknell wondered aloud.

Tray said, "Because I told them that I think Tsavo had *Athena* sabotaged."

"What?" Bricknell yelped.

Loris asked, "Why would he—"

"To murder Jordan Kell."

For a long moment the four of them fell absolutely silent, even Para.

Then the speaker grill next to the hearing room's door announced, "Mance Bricknell, we are ready to hear your testimony."

But Bricknell was staring at Tray. "You must be insane."

"It's the only explanation I can think of that fits the facts," Tray said, his eyes on Loris.

"You're crazy!" Bricknell snapped.

"Can you think of a better explanation?" Tray challenged.

Bricknell shook his head. "Crazy," he muttered as he went to the hearing room door and slid it open. Before he entered the chamber he looked back at Tray. "You're going straight back to the insane asylum, Williamson. Straight back."

LUNCHEON

"And you told the investigators what you thought?" Loris asked.

Tray nodded.

The two of them were sitting at a tiny table set out among the flowering shrubs of one of the restaurants in Selene's Grand Plaza. In the distance Tray could see tourists soaring through the air on their rented wings, and the massive concrete curve of the outdoor theater rising above the greenery.

There were no insect pests among the bushes, only yellowjacket bees busily flitting among the flowers. Tray watched them going about their ancient business, mindlessly purposeful.

Loris stirred him from his brief reverie. "But you haven't any evidence," she said.

If Tray's rash accusation troubled her, it hadn't affected her appetite. Loris had gone through a sizable salad, a plump little soyburger, and was now gulping down a slice of blueberry pie.

Tray had barely touched his lunch. He explained his suspicions of Captain Tsavo and President Balsam, slowly, painfully, not certain of how Loris would react to him.

"I know Balsam is like one of your family—"

"Because of politics," Loris interrupted. "Personally, I think he's a big pile of blubber."

Before he could stop himself, Tray pointed out, "But you were willing to go to bed with him."

Loris took in a breath of air, then smiled at Tray.

"Politics makes strange bedfellows," she quoted.

Tray shook his head.

"Suppose your suspicions are right," Loris theorized. "What can you do about it?"

"Nothing, I guess."

"Well, I can do something," Loris said, smiling at him. "Or, rather, my father can."

"Do you think . . ."

Loris was already planning. "The first thing we've got to do is get you to Normandy, to my father's chateau. You'll be safe there."

Tray had already received an official notice telling him that he was being sent back to the hospital facility that had been his home since returning from the *Saviour* catastrophe.

"I'm supposed to go back to the hospital," he told Loris.

"Yes," she said, her expression grim. "Back to the hospital, where they can keep you sedated or maybe induce a paralytic stroke."

Tray felt his jaw drop open.

Leaning across the little table toward him, Loris said, "If they murdered Jordan Kell they're not going to stop at silencing you."

"Then you're in danger, too," Tray realized.

"They wouldn't dare touch the daughter of a councilman."

"Loris, they murdered the former chairman of the Council!"

That stopped her. Loris stared at him, wordless.

"I can't have you risking your life."

"It's too late for that," she replied. "We're both marked people. Together with Para. Maybe Mance too just to make certain."

"You think they'd go that far?"

Loris stared at him, her luminous blue eyes focused on his light blue ones. "Tray, if they've murdered Jordan Kell, killing us isn't going to be out of the question."

Tray felt his heart sink. "This is all my fault."

Reaching for his hand, Loris countered, "No, it's *their* fault. And we've got to find a way to stop them."

He shook his head. "I don't see how."

"The first thing is to get you down to Normandy, to my father's chateau."

"I don't see how . . ."

"I do." Loris broke into an impish grin. "You'll go in a diplomatic pouch."

Tray returned to his quarters, where Para was waiting for him patiently. Another message from Selene's transportation center was flashing on the room's wall screen:

YOU ARE SCHEDULED TO DEPART SELENE TOMORROW ON THE NOON SHUTTLE TO THE L-1 TRANSFER STATION. FROM THERE YOU WILL BE BOARDED UPON APPROPRIATE TRANSPORTATION FOR YOUR RETURN TO EARTH.

Return to Earth, Tray thought. Return to the hospital complex. Return to imprisonment.

He looked up at Para. "What's going to happen to you when we get back Earthside?"

"If my service to you is concluded I will be reprogrammed for another patient. Or terminated."

"Terminated?"

"Destroyed," said the android, emotionlessly. "Taken apart. Perhaps rebuilt into a newer machine."

"Destroyed?" Tray barked. "Taken apart? Because of me?"

"It won't be your fault," Para replied. "Besides, you'll have enough troubles of your own. You won't have to worry about me."

"The hell I won't! You're going with me to Loris's father's place in Normandy."

Para did not argue.

The look on the face of the immigration officer would have been funny if it weren't so critically important.

Loris, Tray, and Para stood before the man—a stubby, dark-haired bureaucrat in a well-worn, almost shabby, blue uniform. His round face looked bland, except for the thick mustache adorning his upper lip.

Frowning at Loris, he asked again, "This"—he jabbed a thumb at Tray—"this person is to be considered a diplomatic package?"

Loris smiled sweetly. "Yes. My father, Councilman De Mayne, is anxiously awaiting his arrival in Normandy."

The immigration official cocked a disbelieving eye at Tray, then stepped up to Para.

"And this . . . this *machine* also?"

Loris's smile didn't fade by as much as a millimeter. Pointing to the bureaucrat's computer screen, she said, "It also. It's all in the forms that my father's staff filled out."

Mumbling to himself, the official stepped back to the computer screen and rattled off some words in French.

The screen blinked once, then displayed, APPROVED.

Loris's smile widened. She blinked her eyes at the official and said, "*Très merci, monsieur.*"

The little man put on an obviously forced smile and muttered, "Enjoy your flight."

Leaving Selene

+++
+++

"Rank hath its privileges," Loris said as she slid into the window seat of the rocketplane.

Tray nodded and sat beside her. Para took a seat behind them.

They were scheduled to take this shuttle from Selene's spaceport to the space station hovering at the L-1 libration point, 57,600 kilometers above the Earth-facing surface of the Moon. From there they would transfer to a diplomatic courier spacecraft sent to meet them and bring them to the De Mayne estate in Normandy.

Loris raised the seat arm between them. "It's cozier this way," she said, smiling.

Tray smiled back at her. "I wonder how Mance is getting back."

"Regular commercial flight," said Loris. "Don't worry about Mance; he'll be fine. He always makes the best of any situation."

Not this situation, Tray thought. Nearly half a million kilometers from here to Earth, without Mance in between us.

The shuttle's round, windowless passenger compartment was more than half full: men, women, even children leaving the Moon and returning to Earth. Many of them looked like tourists to Tray, decked in bright slacks or skirts, blouses and tops bearing images of the lunar landscape and the imprint of Selene's tourist department.

"Vacationing on the Moon," Tray muttered. "Hope they had fun."

"I'm sure they did," said Loris.

"DEPARTURE IN ONE MINUTE, the overhead speakers announced. "PLEASE MAKE CERTAIN YOUR SAFETY HARNESSES ARE FASTENED."

Tray quickly checked the straps that went across his chest and lap, then looked at Loris. She was properly buckled in, too.

"DEPARTURE IN THIRTY SECONDS," the speakers declared. "TWENTY-NINE . . . TWENTY-EIGHT . . ."

Many of the passengers took up the count. Tray heard low adult voices among the youngsters' high thin ones.

"They're excited," Tray said to Loris.

"Aren't you?"

"Yes . . ." He hesitated, then added, "Because you're here with me."

Loris's smile widened and she leaned closer to Tray. He bent toward her and kissed her lips.

Takeoff was an anticlimax.

To Tray, the trip to the L-1 station was much too brief. Holding Loris's hand in his own, nuzzling her cheek, feeling the warmth of her smile: it all ended much too quickly. One moment they were at Selene's spaceport, a few heartbeats later, it seemed to him, they were making rendezvous with the docking facilities at L-1.

Reluctantly he released Loris's hand, murmuring, "Time to go."

She nodded wordlessly.

"PLEASE USE EXTREME CAUTION ON DISEMBARKING," the overhead speakers warned. "WE ARE EFFECTIVELY IN ZERO GRAVITY. IF YOU FEEL DISCOMFORT, PLEASE USE THE SANITARY BAGS IN YOUR SEAT BACKS."

Tray unbuckled and got to his feet carefully, Loris beside him. Para, in the row behind them had no difficulty, of course. Tray felt his stomach throb, but he managed to control himself. Zero gee can be fun, he reminded himself. Yes, replied a voice in his head. If you don't throw up all over yourself.

The other passengers seemed to be handling the weightlessness with little trouble. Some of them are regular employees of Selene, Tray realized. They've handled zero gee all their lives.

Several of the children among the passengers happily floated toward the compartment's ceiling, while their parents angrily or laughingly reached up and hauled them down beside them. Smiling flight attendants guided the passengers out of the ship and into a long windowless corridor.

With each step along the corridor, Tray felt his weight increasing. The overhead speakers explained, "YOU ARE APPROACHING THE PASSENGER LOUNGE AREA. GRAVITY IN THIS AREA IS ONE-SIXTH GEE, THE SAME AS YOU EXPERIENCED ON THE MOON."

By the time they reached the passenger lounge, Tray felt quite normal. His stomach quieted and he could turn his head without feeling woozy.

A dapper little man in a sharply creased dark suit edged his way through the crowd.

"Mademoiselle De Mayne?" he asked, dipping his chin respectfully.

"Yes," said Loris, raising her voice slightly to be heard above the hubbub of the crowd.

Turning to Tray, the man said, "Then you must be Monsieur Williamson."

"Right," said Tray.

Eyeing Para somewhat warily, the man added, "And your android companion, Para."

Para nodded and replied, "I am Para."

"Follow me, please. Your transport is due to arrive in one half of an hour."

approaching earth

++
++

Their transport was a sleek aerospace plane with delta-shaped wings. Tray stared at it as he, Loris, and Para followed their escort along a connector tube made entirely of transparent plastic. Tray felt as if he were walking in empty space, almost, as he held Loris's hand in his. Para trudged along behind them, chatting with their escort about the aerospace plane's design.

"It goes right down to Earth's surface?" the android asked.

"Oui . . . yes. It is designed to reenter the atmosphere and land at an airfield. No need to transfer to another vehicle."

"Efficient," said Para.

The plane was much smaller than the shuttle on which they had ridden from Selene, obviously a private vehicle, not a commercial one.

Their escort stopped at the end of the connector tube, where it was sealed to the plane's main hatch. With a slight bow, he gestured for the three of them to enter the plane.

"Have a pleasant flight," he said, adding a deeper bow.

As Tray stepped through the plane's hatch, he couldn't suppress a low whistle of surprised appreciation. The interior of the plane was decorated like an opulent sitting room: luxurious armchairs, carpeted floor, a well-stocked bar tucked into one corner. The bulkheads were covered with softly decorated draperies. A smiling brunette hostess in a short-skirted scarlet uniform smiled at them from the front of the compartment.

"Welcome aboard," the young woman greeted. "Mademoiselle De Mayne, it is a pleasure to see you again."

"And you, Honoré," answered Loris sweetly. "How is your *grand-père?*"

"He is doing much better since the stem-cell injections, thank you."

They're speaking English, Tray realized. So I don't feel left out. Then he remembered that English was the lingua franca of the airlines. He couldn't suppress a low chuckle at the unintentional pun.

Raising her voice slightly, Honoré instructed, "It will be necessary for you to fasten your safety belts for our departure from the space station. Once we are in flight, the captain will tell you when you may remove them."

Tray followed Loris into the cabin and sat in the armchair next to the one she chose. Para sat across the way and immediately called up the plane's safety lecture on the viewscreen set into the bulkhead next to its seat.

Leaning toward Tray, Loris said, "We'll be landing at our private airfield, not far from the chateau."

Tray nodded. Private airfield, he thought. Not far from the chateau. Grinning broadly, he realized, I've fallen into a featherbed!

Loris stared at him, her expression puzzled. "What is so funny?" she asked.

Tray extended his arm and swung it in a half circle. "All this," he said. "This all belongs to your family?"

"To my father, yes."

"And you live in a chateau?"

A slight smile bent her lips. "It's can be drafty and cold in the winter."

Shaking his head in wonder, Tray said, "No wonder Mance is after you."

Loris's smile winked off. "Mance is fairly well off too, you know. Have you ever heard of Bricknell Industries?"

Tray shook his head.

"Pharmaceuticals, industrial construction, asteroidal mining . . . and more," she said. "There's no need for Mance to go fortune-hunting."

"Like me," Tray heard himself reply.

Loris's eyes went wide with surprise. "Oh no, that's not what I meant, Tray."

"I'm pretty close to penniless," he said flatly. "My father worked all his life running machinery for a construction company."

Staring into Tray's eyes, Loris made a minimal smile and said, "So I won't be marrying you for your money."

Tray's breath caught in his throat. But then he realized, "But if we get married, people will think I'm marrying you for your money."

Her smile widened. "It's my father's money. And who gives a damn about what people think?"

If they both hadn't still been pinned in their chairs by their safety harnesses Tray would have gotten up and swept her into his arms. As it was he grinned at her and reached out to squeeze her hand.

bOOk FOUr

++
++

RETURN TO
EARTH

Landing

The rocketplane's departure from the L-1 station was so gentle that Tray barely noticed it. But then he felt his stomach floating away from him as the ship fell into zero gravity.

Loris apparently had no problem with weightlessness. While Tray swallowed down bile and tried to keep from moving his head, she began explaining:

"You'll like my father. He's a kind old man, but he covers his kindness in a sort of gruff attitude. When you first meet him he'll probably challenge you with an intellectual puzzle or two. Get the answers right and he'll love you like the son he's never had."

Tray blinked. "Intellectual puzzles?"

"It's a sort of test he gives any young man that I bring home for him to meet. Nothing to worry about."

But Tray felt worried. "If I flunk this test of his, what then?"

Loris smiled. "Then I'm afraid you'll have to sit and listen to Papa lecture you for a few hours."

Tray tried not to frown. He almost made it.

Loris talked on about the chateau, the grounds, the history of Normandy, the trial and execution of Joan of Arc, the great invasion in World War II, the evolution of stem-cell agriculture.

"The entire province is a huge natural park," she explained, "now that we no longer need to grow crops or raise animals to be slaughtered for food."

Tray nodded in what he hoped were the right places as Loris rattled on as if she were reciting her family history. Tray realized that she was.

As he listened to her his eyes drifted to the small window next to their seat. Earth filled its view, deep blue oceans and purest white streaks of clouds; brown mountain chains and broad swaths of greenery sliding past the descending plane.

Earth, he said to himself. The real paradise.

"Oh, one other thing," Loris said, as if she had just thought of it.

Focusing his attention on her once more, Tray asked, "What is it?"

"My father was horribly injured in a battle, many years ago. The history tapes call it 'The Neoluddite Uprising.' My *père* calls it 'The Idiots' Last Stand.' He helped to put down the rebels, but they nearly killed him."

"How badly was he hurt?"

"He was blown up in an explosion that destroyed one entire wing of the chateau," Loris said. "It's a miracle that he survived."

Tray didn't know what to say.

"So when you meet him, please don't act shocked or surprised. He lives in a portable medical device. Like an old-fashioned wheelchair, but it helps his heart to pump blood, helps his lungs to breathe, keeps his body alive."

"He can't survive without the chair?"

Loris smiled grimly. "It's part of him. He's as much a machine as a human being."

Inadvertently, Tray glanced across the compartment at Para.

"So please don't stare at him," Loris implored. "Don't make him feel . . . less than human."

Tray dipped his head in acknowledgment. And heard himself reply, "Humanity lies in the mind, Loris. The rest of the body is nothing more than supporting hardware."

She nodded back at him. And Tray saw there were tears in her eyes.

The rocketplane shuddered slightly as it bit into Earth's upper atmosphere.

"Please fasten your safety harnesses," the red-uniformed stewardess said. "Reentry can get rather bumpy."

But except for a pair of stomach-hollowing drops, the plane made it through the upper atmosphere and smoothed out to an easy, graceful descent to the ground.

Tray saw green fields and rolling hills flash by, and what looked like an immense cemetery, row upon row of stark white crosses marching across a wide green field.

"Landing in three minutes," said the captain's voice over the speakers set into the compartment's ceiling.

A soft thump and then they were rolling along the ground. Home, thought Tray. Then he amended, France. Normandy. Loris's home, not mine.

BARON LOUIS ST. ETIENNE
BAYEAUX DE MAYNE

Loris literally pressed her nose against the plane's undersized window. "Look!" she shouted to Tray. "Papa's limousine! He's come here himself to meet us!"

Past her tousled hair, Tray saw a trio of automobiles waiting at the runway's edge, including an oversized limousine that looked as large as a tank. My god, he thought. It's big enough to hold a New Year's Eve party inside.

Half a dozen men and young women in livery were standing outside the enormous car. No one in a wheelchair, though.

Excitedly, Loris flung off her seat harness and started rising out of her chair even before the plane stopped rolling. Tray grabbed her wrist to steady her.

"Be careful," he admonished.

Loris babbled something in French, then, realizing Tray couldn't understand her, she translated, "He's come here to greet us! Himself! He left the chateau to come and greet us!"

Tray grinned up at her and, once he sensed the plane had finished its landing roll, he unbuckled and got to his feet beside her.

They hurried past the plane's scattered furniture to the main hatch, where the red-uniformed stewardess was swinging the hatch open. Tray felt a warm breeze, smelled flowers.

Turning her smiling face to Loris, the stewardess said, "Welcome home, mademoiselle. I hope you enjoyed the flight."

Loris brushed past her with perfunctory, "It was lovely, thank you."

She ducked through the hatch and fairly flew down the plane's ladder to the ground, with Tray and Para following more slowly behind her.

A tall, stately, elderly man in black livery held out his hand to Loris, who took it while looking past him toward the huge limousine waiting some twenty meters from the plane.

"*Mon père?*" Loris asked the servant.

The man replied, "*Dans l'automobile, mam'selle.*"

Loris raced to the limo. Another waiting servant opened its rear door for her.

Tray, with Para behind him, went to the car, then hesitated, uncertain of what was expected of him. From inside the limo he heard Loris's excited voice, "Tray! Come in!"

The servant gestured, stone-faced, for Tray to enter the limousine. Suddenly nervous, Tray heard Loris and a thin male voice talking excitedly in French. He swallowed once and ducked inside. Para remained out in the sunshine.

Loris was on her knees in front of an older man who smiled down gently at her. Tray stopped. Half of the rear seat of the limousine was filled with medical devices beeping and gurgling softly. In their midst sat a smiling man who looked *old*: thick gray hair and a face that seemed chiseled out of granite, with sharp cheekbones and the imperious beak of an eagle.

He was swaddled in blankets. What Tray could see of his legs looked like slim steel struts that ended in normal comfortable loafers, but the feet inside them were made of metal, not flesh. His arms looked normal enough, although they were covered in sleeves of royal blue. His hands, clutching Loris's, were human hands, except for several fingers made of glistening plastic.

Loris scrambled up to sit beside her father, saying, "Tray, this is *mon père*—the Baron Louis St. Etienne Bayeaux De Mayne."

Loris's father smiled up at Tray, who stood stooped next to the limousine's open door.

"How do you do, Mr. Williamson," he said, in a slightly quavering reedy voice. Gesturing to the seat next to the window, he added, "Please make yourself comfortable."

As Tray slid into the seat, Baron De Mayne asked mildly, "And pray tell me, who was the first American ambassador to the court of Louis XVI?"

Without hesitation, Tray replied, "Benjamin Franklin."

De Mayne's light gray eyes lit up. "Ah, that was too easy. But we begin well. Do you know where Franklin lived while he was in France?"

Tray hesitated, then answered quite seriously, "From what I've read, he spent a good deal of his time in women's bedrooms."

The baron threw his head back and laughed heartily. Loris smiled approvingly. Tray noticed that the soft-pitched beeping of the medical equipment notched a few notes higher.

"You have a good head on your shoulders, my boy. A good head. We will get along very well, I'm sure."

"Thank you, sir."

"Do you play chess?"

"Poorly."

"Good! I need an opponent I can beat."

Loris said to Tray, "Don't wager any money on his chess game."

De Mayne put on a scowl. "Daughter! You spoil my fun."

"Trayvon is not a wealthy man, Papa," Loris said, looking sternly at her father. "You mustn't fleece him."

"Too bad," said the baron, shaking his head. "Too bad."

"Shall we go home now?" Loris suggested.

The baron nodded. "Let us show our guest some of the grounds, eh?"

With that, he called in a surprisingly powerful voice, "*Allons, mes enfants.*"

The limo's motor roared to life and they started moving out of the airfield and into the rolling hills of Normandy.

Nearly two hours later, Tray marveled that the baron did not seem the slightest bit wearied by their winding sojourn through the countryside.

"You will find this interesting, I think," De Mayne was saying to Tray.

The limousine topped a small hill and suddenly Tray was staring out at the ocean.

"Omaha Beach," said the baron. Tray noticed that his fists clenched on his lap. "Here your American ancestors landed to drive out the Nazis who were occupying much of France. It was a mighty battle."

"D-Day, nineteen forty-four," Tray breathed.

The blue sea was tranquil. The beach was empty, except for a few tourists walking along the sand.

"You know your history," said De Mayne.

"Our history," Tray replied. "We fought together against the Nazis."

The baron stared at Tray, who saw that there were tears in the old man's silvery eyes. It's as though it happened yesterday, as far as he's concerned, Tray realized. History is real to him. And personal.

Chateau de Mayne

++

++

At last the impromptu tour ended and the baron ordered his driver to take them to the chateau. Tray watched as they passed through the open gate of an impressive wrought-steel fence more than two meters tall. Then the limousine rolled down a long, pleasant, winding road through a well-tended garden of graceful trees and flowering shrubs.

At last the chateau came into view: stern gray walls pierced by tall narrow windows, more than a dozen chimneys poking up from the canted roof.

And the far end of the building was a ruin: The walls were half-demolished; the roof had collapsed.

Baron De Mayne said grimly, "That is where the pigs nearly killed me. Rebelling against the future. What nonsense!"

Tray started to ask, "How long ago—"

De Mayne did not wait for him to finish his question. "Several decades. When I was younger than you are now." With hard-edged bitterness in his voice, "When I had my legs and my vital organs."

"And you've never repaired it?"

"Never!" the baron snapped. "I want to see it every day, every time I open my eyes from sleep. I want to be reminded of how stupid and short-sighted people can be."

Loris said quietly, "Papa, you are exciting yourself."

Sure enough, the machinery that surrounded Baron De Mayne was chugging away faster than before.

"*Pah!* It is nothing. The machines will not allow me to die."

Loris looked as if she wanted to argue the point, but she held her silence.

As the limousine rolled up to the chateau's front entrance, Tray saw a handful of servants standing before it, at attention. De Mayne gestured toward his daughter.

"Once I am gone," he said to Tray, "my daughter may rebuild the damaged wing. But not as long as I live. Never."

Loris said nothing.

As soon as the limousine stopped Tray opened the door on his side and ducked out, then turned and offered his hand to Loris.

"*Très merci*," she murmured as he helped her out of the car. Only then did Tray notice two liveried young men standing behind him, looking slightly distraught.

From inside the limousine, De Mayne's reedy voice proclaimed, "Now I am ready to make my grand entrance."

Loris tugged Tray back away from the limousine as a quartet of beefy young servants came forward and the car's engine coughed to life once again.

Tray watched, wide-eyed, as the entire rear section of the limo detached itself and swung away from its front, with the baron still ensconced on the back seat, surrounded by his medical equipment.

The four young men stepped forward and lifted the baron, medical gear and all, out of the rear seat and deposited him gently on the paved driveway. Tray saw that the frame of his apparatus rested on four trunnion-like little wheels.

"Ah, *voilà*," said the baron, smiling happily. "I am freed."

Tray couldn't help smiling, too. Rich or poor, he thought, it pays to have money.

Baron De Mayne maneuvered his rolling apparatus to Loris and Tray. "Come, let us go inside and behold the family treasures, while the cooks prepare us a suitable dinner."

The family treasures consisted mainly of paintings hanging on the chateau's stone walls. Portraits, mostly, of family leaders, long dead and gone. Beautiful ladies in exquisite finery, stiffly proud gentlemen staring out of their settings, many with a hand clasping a sword whose hilt glittered with jewelry rivaling the ladies' decorations.

Para walked with them through the halls and room, silently observing. Tray wondered what the android thought of this display of ancient pride, but Para said nothing throughout the long, ultimately boring—to Tray—tour.

Suits of armor stood silent and grim along the corridors. Battle-axes and long lances with colorful pennants drooping down from their sharpened heads. Dummies in uniforms ranging from Napoleonic to the twentieth-century wars.

Tray found himself wondering, Is there nothing but war to display? What about the scientific discoveries made over the centuries? What about French contributions to medicine, to art, to music?

Tray was glad when they finally got to the dining hall, where one end of a long table was set for just the three of them. A place was also set for Para, beside Tray, although there was no dishware or implements at it. The android took its seat without a word.

As he maneuvered his machinery to the head of the table, De Mayne said, "One of the things for which I am most grateful is that the doctors were able to repair my digestive system. I cannot eat as much as I did when I was young, but at least I can enjoy the delicate flavors to some extent."

"And you can't get fat," Loris added, grinning as she sat across the table from Tray.

"Ah, like your grandfather," said De Mayne. "There was a man who could eat out a whole village in one sitting."

"You exaggerate, Father."

"Do I? Why do you think the village of Falais was turned into a tourist center? Your grandfather ate them out of house and home!"

Loris tried to frown at her father, failed, and eased into a smile instead.

Tray decided to stay out of family discussions. The trout he was eating was too delicious to be interfered with.

As the dessert of delicately flavored *glacé* was being served, De Mayne turned his apparatus slightly to look squarely at Tray.

"Now then, young man. What have you to say for yourself?"

reSPONSibility

TRAY glanced at Loris, across the table from him. Before he could say anything, though, the baron pointed a plastic forefinger at him.

"My daughter tells me that you suspect that Jordan Kell was murdered," De Mayne said, his face and tone suddenly somber.

Tray nodded. "I do. I believe that Councilman Kell was assassinated on the orders of Council president Balsam."

"So you believe."

"I'm sure of it."

De Mayne fell silent momentarily, staring at Tray, who felt as if he were being X-rayed by the baron's probing eyes.

Tray explained, "I can't believe that the *Athena* vessel failed so catastrophically without being sabotaged."

"Deliberately."

"Quite deliberately," said Tray. "The vessel itself and Mr. Kell's rescue suit."

"And you and my daughter were nearly killed, as well."

"Lieutenant Sheshardi was killed."

Folding his hands beneath his chin prayerfully, the baron asked, "This is a huge accusation. What proof do you have to offer?"

Tray glanced over his shoulder at Para, sitting silently beside him, then turned his focus back to De Mayne. "None," he admitted. "All the possible proof is buried deep in the Jovian ocean."

"Ah," said the baron in a near-whisper. "*Tant pis.* Too bad."

Para spoke up. "The research submersible *Jupiter Oceanus* might be able to recover the wreckage before *Athena* sinks too deep into the ocean."

De Mayne's face brightened. "Is that true?"

"Yes," answered Para. "To within an eighty percent probability."

Loris pointed out, "But President Balsam controls the sub's assignments. He'd never let it be used to find proof of his own guilt."

"So much the better," said the baron, with a cunning smile.

Feeling suddenly confused, Tray said, "I don't understand."

His smile broadening slightly, De Mayne explained, "Politics is a delicate interplay of personalities. I could ask the Council to allow use of the submersible to salvage *Athena*'s wreckage. If Balsam refuses giving permission, we could use his refusal as an indication of guilt."

Tray shook his head. "That sounds awfully thin, don't you think?"

Reaching for his demitasse of coffee, De Mayne replied smilingly, "It may be thin, but empires have been brought down by such ephemeral factors."

"Father, aren't you exaggerating?" Loris asked.

De Mayne cocked his head slightly. "Perhaps. But we don't have anything better to go on."

"Maybe we could get Captain Tsavo to admit the truth," Tray suggested.

The baron wagged a plastic finger in the air. "Never. If the captain actually had *Athena* sabotaged, he would never admit it. It would be the end of his career. Humiliation. Disgrace."

Para spoke up once more. "I presume that if the captain did have *Athena* sabotaged—"

"Along with Jordan Kell's survival suit," Tray added.

Dipping its chin in acknowledgment, Para went on, "If the captain directed the sabotage, he most likely used his ship's robots to do the work, then erased all records of their work from their memory files."

"Leaving us with no evidence whatsoever," Loris said glumly.

The table fell silent for several eternally long moments.

Then De Mayne brightened and said, "The first thing we have to do is to get you, young man, appointed to the Council."

Tray felt shocked. "Me? Appointed to the Council?"

"Yes. As a Council member you can face Balsam on a nearly equal footing. And you will of course have immunity from prosecution. Are you willing to take that responsibility?"

"But I don't know anything about politics, about how the Council works, about—"

"You can learn. I will guide you." De Mayne looked at Loris. "Besides, if you intend to marry my daughter you'll need some social standing—and an income."

Tray felt his cheeks burn. But he saw Loris smiling at him.

Trying to keep his voice steady, Tray asked, "But how can I get myself elected to the Interplanetary Council? I don't know the first thing—"

"*Pah!*" De Mayne spat. "I know the first things and the last things. Jordan Kell's death leaves a vacancy on the Council. I will nominate you to fill that vacancy until the next regularly scheduled election, which does not occur until two years from now."

"And that's all there is to it?"

Waving a hand in the air, De Mayne replied, "Oh, the Council must vote its approval. But that can be arranged. With Jordan Kell gone, I am the leader of the loyal opposition. Our bloc will vote solidly for your appointment, and there are enough members in Balsam's bloc who owe me favors. You will be elected, never fear."

"But I have no experience."

"*Très bien!* Balsam will welcome you, thinking he and his people can control you."

His innards tightening, Tray remembered, "Balsam more or less accused me of having a homosexual relationship with Mr. Kell."

"Better and better. The more he thinks he can control you, the easier it will be for him to support your election."

Looking across the table at Loris, Tray asked, "Is this the way politics works?"

She smiled at him. "Yes. Exciting, isn't it?"

"Frightening," said Tray.

TRAY stared at himself in the mirror. If this wasn't so serious, he thought, it would be laughable.

The past few days had been a confusing whirlwind of meetings with Council members and staff, members of the chateau's retinue of servants, and Norman neighbors of the baron. Meetings, dinners, even sedate dances among the young men and women of the area.

The baron had given Tray and Para a comfortable suite on one of the chateau's upper floors, beneath the roof and next to a round brick tower that rose into the sky. It was seemingly kilometers away from Loris's quarters, a floor below and far on the other side of the chateau.

"These hallways are under constant automated surveillance," Baron De Mayne had explained coolly as he rolled his blinking, beeping chair beside Tray along the seemingly endless corridors. "We maintain strict security here in the chateau."

Tray had nodded, thinking, He means no sneaking around to his daughter's rooms. Almost, he laughed. But the baron's expression showed no trace of humor.

Without leaving the chateau, the baron arranged for Tray to be appointed to the Interplanetary Council to fill out Jordan Kell's term. Dressed in a formal uniform of blue and white, Tray took the oath of office in the chateau's communications center, which was transformed electronically into a duplicate of the main hall, and he became officially a member of the Interplanetary Council.

President Balsam administered the oath of office from the Council chambers in Copenhagen, while Tray repeated the words of his acceptance from the chateau in Normandy. The room appeared to be filled with several dozen Council members, all smiling and nodding approvingly, even though hardly a handful of them were actually physically in the communications center.

Modern communications, Tray thought as he shook hands with Balsam after taking the oath. We're hundreds of kilometers apart, but I can even feel the pressure of his hand on mine.

Smiling his broadest, Balsam posed with Tray for publicity images. Once the remotely operated cameras had glided away and the witnessing Council members winked into nothingness, the Council president's smile faded. Grasping Tray's shoulder in one beefy hand, Balsam said, "We've got to have a long, serious talk, young man."

Tray replied, "Yes, we do."

"I'm not particularly happy with your accusation, you know."

"I . . . I'm sorry. But I think we need to do everything we can to determine how Mr. Kell was killed."

"Died," said Balsam.

"Was murdered," Tray countered.

Balsam grimaced and released Tray's shoulder.

"And why he was murdered," Tray added.

Balsam's expression turned stony. "You're treading on dangerous ground, Trayvon. Be careful or you might get hurt."

Looking up into Balsam's flinty eyes, Tray replied, "I'm trying to find the truth."

Balsam almost smiled. Almost. Instead he leaned closer to Tray and muttered, "You're not the only one who could get hurt, you know."

"I know," said Tray. "You could get hurt. And Captain Tsavo."

Balsam's eyes widened. Without another word, he turned his back to Tray and disappeared like a ghost.

It took Tray several moments to realize he was not physically in the chateau's main hall. He blinked and saw he was still in the communications center of De Mayne's chateau in Normandy. The baron was sitting in his rolling chair, surrounded by softly beeping therapeutic machinery. Loris stood beside him, rigid with anger. Para stood on the baron's other side.

As the floating cameras shut their red eyes and glided back to their racks along the room's far wall, Loris practically stamped up to Tray's side.

"He threatened you!" she almost snarled.

Tray felt a good deal less combative. "He threatened you, too. And your father."

De Mayne rolled up to them smiling broadly. "Whatever he said, whatever threats he made, rest assured there will be no record of it. He is having the conversation wiped clean at this very moment, I'm sure."

Para spoke up. "I have recorded the entire conversation."

"Good!" said De Mayne.

But Tray said gloomily, "That means you're on his hit list too, my friend."

De Mayne refused to be cowed. "*Pah!* What can he do? As long as we remain here we will be safe enough."

Tray smiled bitterly. "Unless a meteoroid comes tumbling out of the sky and smashes everything here to pieces."

COPENHAGEN

+++++ ++++++++++ ++++++++++++++++++++ +++++++++++++++++++

+++++ +++++++++++ ++++++++++++++++++++++++++++ +++++++++++

"It is a historical anachronism to require you to be physically present at the council hall," said the Baron De Mayne.

Tray shrugged. "It's part of the Council's formal procedures. Opening day of the new session. All Council members are required to be there in person."

"*Pah!*" spat the baron. "An anachronism supported by the merchants and tavern owners of Copenhagen."

The three of them—plus Para—were flying from the De Mayne chateau to the Danish capital of Copenhagen, where the Interplanetary Council held its meetings. As a new member of the Council, Tray was scheduled to give a speech of introduction. Para had the speech recorded in its memory, word for word, and was ready to serve as Tray's prompter.

Sitting beside Tray, Loris was wearing a form-hugging sheath of forest green, with a mid-calf skirt and emeralds adorning her throat, earlobes, wrists, and fingers. With her dark hair coiled atop her head, she looked stunning.

De Mayne was intent on coaching Tray. "Remember, as a member of the Council you are immune from arrest unless and until the Council votes to cancel your immunity."

Tray nodded his understanding.

"So you can speak with a certain amount of freedom," De Mayne went on. "But remember, you must not openly accuse Balsam. That would be a breach of the Council's rules of decorum."

Tray nodded again, his eyes looking beyond De Mayne to the oval window in the plane's fuselage. Cultivated fields in checkerboard squares of various hues of green were hurrying past below the plane.

"Mustn't break the rules of decorum," Tray muttered.

De Mayne's chin rose a notch. "Those rules are important, my young friend. Remember the words of Winston Churchill: 'When you are going to kill a man, it costs you nothing to be polite.'"

Tray had a feeling that those weren't Churchill's exact words, but he didn't argue. Instead, he thought of doughty Winston's speech to Parliament upon being appointed prime minister, in the darkest days of World War II: "I have nothing to offer but blood, toil, tears and sweat."

Loris said, "Your goal is get the Council to open an investigation into Jordan Kell's death."

"And you are in no position to *demand* an investigation," De Mayne reminded him. "As the newest and youngest member of the Council, you must request, you must suggest, you must *importune* the Council into opening an investigation."

Tray felt his teeth clenching, but he nodded acceptance.

"*Très bien*," said De Mayne, reaching out from his medical chair to clasp Tray's shoulder. "You will do well."

Tray glanced at Loris. She was smiling at him encouragingly. Para sat behind Tray, silently recording everything they said, every gesture, every facial expression.

The captain's voice crackled over the speakers set into the plane's ceiling. "Copenhagen coming up on the right. We'll be landing in twelve minutes."

Tray looked out the window on his right. There was the city of

Copenhagen, surrounded by the massive dikes that kept the sea at bay. The city had become an island when the greenhouse floods had swamped much of Europe's ancient coastline. Tray could see a pair of ferries cutting white wakes in the azure water as they passed each other, heading in opposite directions. And there was the city, proud towers and ancient churches, splendid squares of green-leafed parks and rows of homes huddled against the seawalls.

Copenhagen, Tray thought. My first moment as a member of the Interplanetary Council. He turned to Para, sitting placidly behind him, and felt a lump in his throat. He said to himself, I'm going to be addressing the Interplanetary Council! Me, standing in front of the whole Council and asking them to form a committee to investigate Jordan Kell's death.

No, not his death, Tray reminded himself.

His murder.

acceptance speech

+++
++

The interplanetary council's assembly hall was a magnificent piece of architecture, with a high vaulted ceiling and long arched windows that let the afternoon sunshine brighten the rows and rows of comfortably padded chairs that lined the chamber.

Despite his efforts to stay calm, to remain cool and collected, Tray could feel perspiration trickling down his ribs as he sat between Loris and Baron De Mayne, several rows back from the stage and the speaker's podium. Para had been seated at the rear of the vast hall, together with the other nonhuman intelligences.

Wish he were here, with me, Tray said to himself. It doesn't seem right to make him sit all the way back there.

The hall was filled to capacity. Council members sat up front. Behind them were guests, honored visitors, and finally the androids and robots. At the rear of the long, narrow hall were two levels of balconies, completely filled with ordinary citizens who had come to witness this opening session, with all its pomp and color.

The highlight of the ceremonies was the eulogy for Jordan Kell, and then Tray's induction as a new member of the Council.

President Balsam was personally delivering the eulogy for Kell, piling on one laudatory roll of rhetoric after another. Tray sat listening stonily, thinking that Kell's murderer looked as if he actually enjoyed being so devious. The audience sat in hushed respect, hardly moving through Balsam's long-winded clichés.

At last Balsam finished. The entire massive throng rose to its feet as he stepped down from the podium and walked solemnly, head bowed as if in contemplation, back to his seat at the rear of the stage. No applause, not even a cough: hardly a sound broke the respectful silence.

As the Council's meeting coordinator stepped up to the podium that Balsam had just vacated, Tray realized his lips were dry, his throat felt like an arid wasteland.

Nerves, he told himself. Turning in his seat, he picked out Para, sitting far to the rear. The android was focused on the coordinator. Tray thought, It must be good to have no emotions, to see things as they are, not warped by your inner fears or desires.

The coordinator began to introduce him. "Now we will hear from the newest and youngest member of the Council. Mr. Trayvon Williamson has been appointed to fill the term of the late Jordan Kell. Mr. Williamson is an American—"

Tray zoned out. He could feel his pulse rate climbing. He settled back in his seat and glanced at Loris, who looked just as tense, just as anxious as he was.

". . . Mr. Williamson," the coordinator finished, turning his smiling face in Tray's direction.

For an instant, Tray was not certain that he could stand up. But he steeled himself and rose slowly to his feet, then strode to the steps of the stage and up to the speaker's podium. Polite applause rippled through the huge audience.

Gripping the edges of the green marble podium, Tray heard Para's voice in his built-in communicator coaching, "President Balsam, Coordinator Chang . . ."

He repeated the words mechanically as he stared out at the vast sea of faces looking at him. I don't belong here! he thought. But then he focused on Loris, who was smiling warmly at him. He spoke to her.

"It is a great honor, and a tremendous responsibility, to stand here in place of the late Jordan Kell. He was a great man, and the work of this Interplanetary Council was his lifelong passion.

"He died in the ocean of Jupiter, pursuing his lifelong interest in the discovery of possibly intelligent creatures living on other worlds."

Tray hesitated, then plunged, "I am here before you today to ask that you honor Councilman Kell's lifetime of work, his vision of the human race's expansion through the solar system and beyond.

"But more than that, I am here to request that this Council initiate an investigation into the cause of Councilman Kell's death.

"He died in the depths of Jupiter's ocean when his survival suit failed. The submersible that he and others—including me—were in failed catastrophically and we were forced to don the survival suits and return to the surface of the ocean . . ."

Calmly, with a deliberate, iron-willed statement of the facts as he knew them, Tray explained the accident that had killed Jordan Kell. He was tempted to raise the question of whether it had been an accident or a deliberate murder, but he forced himself to keep that question out of his speech.

"I feel that we should do everything in our power to learn how the mission into Jupiter's ocean turned into a death trap. We owe that much, at the very least, to the memory of a great man.

"Thank you."

His innards fluttering, Tray turned away from the podium, walked to the steps at the edge of the stage, and returned to his seat.

All in absolute silence.

* * *

The Council meeting ended quickly after Tray's speech. He, Loris, De Mayne, and Para made their way through the departing throng toward the minibus that the Council had provided to haul the baron's rolling therapeutic chair together with the rest of them. No one said a word to them as they got laboriously into the bus and rode back to the airport.

"That went over like a lead balloon," Tray groused as they wove through Copenhagen's narrow streets.

Para offered, "Apparently the crowd didn't applaud Lincoln's Gettysburg Address, either. They were too moved."

Tray h'mmpfed. "Not much consolation, Para."

De Mayne spoke up. "No, I think your speech hit just the right note. I am certain that we can get the Council to authorize a special committee to investigate the accident."

"Good," said Tray, without a hint of enthusiasm.

"And what happens," Loris asked, "if this committee finds no evidence of sabotage? Nothing that points to President Balsam's involvement?"

De Mayne shrugged elaborately. "We must make certain that such evidence is found. Or, at the very least, that enough uncertainty is discovered to make Balsam's rear end very hot and uncomfortable."

For the next several days Tray stayed at De Mayne's chateau, following the council's debate about appointing an investigative committee.

There seemed to be no real opposition to the idea. Council members on both sides of the political aisle agreed that Jordan Kell's death should be investigated. Council president Balsam even agreed to have the submersible *Jupiter Oceanus* detached from its research schedule and assigned to a full-time search for the remains of the *Athena* module, deep in the Jovian ocean.

The submersible was manned by a crew of three, Tray learned. Radio and even laser communications were blocked quite effectively by the ammoniated waters of the Jovian ocean; human guidance of the submersible required a human crew aboard it.

"It goes well," De Mayne said on the third morning after their return from Copenhagen. "The committee has been appointed and now they are hiring a scientific team to conduct the investigation."

The baron and Tray were having breakfast together on a patio next to the chateau's grim, gray wall. Para sat at the table with them, silently recording their conversation.

Tray glanced at the generous dish of eggs and ham that had been set before him. He found he had no appetite. The baron was nibbling at a buttered croissant as he spoke.

"By the beginning of next week the investigation can begin," said De Mayne, happily chewing away. "Something of a speed record for the Council."

"But by then *Athena*'s wreckage may be too deep for even the submersible to reach," Tray replied.

Turning to the android, the baron asked, "Para, what do you say?"

"It is difficult to make a reasonable assessment," Para replied. "The *Athena* module should be floating at its neutral buoyancy level, but that might be several hundred meters below the operating limits of *Jupiter Oceanus*."

"*Pah!*" De Mayne snapped. "The scientists always build generous safety factors into their calculations. They're very protective of their precious toys."

"There will be three human beings in that precious toy," Tray pointed out.

"And several robots," added Para.

"I say the submersible can reach the wreckage," the baron insisted, "if there are capable men operating it."

Tray wanted to reply, but hesitated. Don't aggravate him, he told himself. He's going to be your father-in-law. Then he added, I hope.

The bracelet on De Mayne's right wrist began pulsing a bright green light.

"Yes?" said the baron to thin air.

"A call for Councilman Williamson, sir," said a firm baritone voice from the bracelet.

Tray wondered why his own inbuilt communicator hadn't picked up the call. He said, "I'll take it."

"The call is deemed private, for Councilman Williamson only."

Tray pushed his chair back and got to his feet. "Pardon me," he said to De Mayne. "I'll stroll out into the garden, if you don't mind."

De Mayne waved a hand. "Go right ahead."

Tray started along the cobblestone path that meandered through the bright blooms of the garden.

"Who's calling?" he asked.

The phone's voice in his head answered, "Dr. Mance Bricknell."

Striding between tall azalea bushes, Tray covered up his surprise by saying, "I'm alone now. Please put him on."

Suddenly Mance Bricknell's lean, angular form took shape on the path in front of Tray.

"Hello, Mance," said Tray.

"Hello." Bricknell's voice, and expression, seemed sullen, almost hostile.

"We haven't heard from you for a while."

"No," said Bricknell. "You've been too busy playing councilman . . . and wooing Loris."

Despite himself, Tray broke into a thin smile.

"She seems quite happy to be wooed, as you put it."

"We can talk about that some other time," Bricknell said stiffly. "What I called to tell you is that I've been asked to testify to the investigative committee the Council has appointed."

"That's good," said Tray, genuinely pleased.

"And so have you, Loris, and your android."

"Para?"

"Yes. You'll get your formal subpoenas from the Council before the day is out."

"That's good," Tray repeated.

"It's going to be an interesting hearing," Bricknell said.

"What about the *Jupiter Oceanus*?" Tray asked. "Has the Council ordered it to search for the remains of *Athena*?"

"Not yet. Apparently the scientific committee that controls the submersible's research program is resisting the request to send it hunting for *Athena*'s wreckage. They think it's too dangerous to send the sub down that deep."

"But that's the only way we could possibly find evidence of sabotage," Tray said, alarmed.

"Tell that to the science committee," said Bricknell.

And his image flicked into nothingness.

De Mayne listened to Tray's report of Bricknell's news with a downcast expression.

"It is an old tactic," he said, once Tray had finished. "You can determine the committee's findings by picking the people you assign to be on the committee."

They were sitting in Baron De Mayne's study, a smallish, comfortably furnished room nestled into a corner of the chateau's walls. Loris sat in an upholstered armchair beside her father's mobile medical chair. Tray sat tensely in a sling chair, facing them both. Para stood at Tray's right.

"What can we do about it?" Tray asked.

De Mayne hunched his thin shoulders. "Not very much, I fear. Balsam is dictating the membership of the investigative committee. They will not be unbiased, I can assure you."

Loris said, "If we can't reach *Athena*, can't study it to find possible evidence of sabotage . . ." Her voice trailed off.

Tray finished her thought, "Then we're wasting our time . . . ours, the committee's, everybody's."

But De Mayne, curiously, was smiling. "Perhaps not, *mon ami*. Perhaps not."

"What's going on in your mind, Papa?" Loris asked.

"Do you know who designed *Jupiter Oceanus*?" the baron asked.

"Cousteau?"

"Of course. Harlan Cousteau."

Tray blinked, confused. "Who is Harlan Cousteau?"

"Perhaps he is the answer to our prayers," said De Mayne.

the wild man

+++
+++++ +++

"Cousteau designed *Jupiter Oceanus?*" Tray asked.

Smiling even more broadly from his medical chair, De Mayne explained, "He is descended from the most famous family in the field of oceanography. His great-great-many more greats grandfather invented the aqualung, hundreds of years ago. The family has persisted in underwater exploration, although Harlan himself has spent more time building ocean-bottom tourist centers than anything else. Yet, in his spare time, he designed *Jupiter Oceanus.*"

Somewhat confused, Tray said, "I don't see what that has to do—"

De Mayne interrupted, "If Cousteau offers to pilot the submersible himself, no committee in the solar system could refuse him."

"But he's an old man," Loris objected. "Well past one hundred."

"But still active," said the baron. "Still pushing the envelope, as the aircraft designers say. Just a month ago he won a lawsuit against the Interplanetary Safety Board, which wanted to bar him from future ocean exploration because of his age."

"And you think—"

"If he offers to pilot *Jupiter Oceanus,* Balsam could not refuse him."

"But would he offer to do it?" Tray asked.

His smile showing sparkling teeth, De Mayne said, "Let us ask him to dinner and see what he has to say."

"Would he accept an invitation?" Tray asked. "I mean, out of the blue, like this?"

De Mayne's smile vanished. "I am the Baron De Mayne. One does not decline a dinner invitation from me."

Tray felt his brows hike skyward. But he said no more.

That evening Tray and Para retired to their suite beneath the chateau's roof and Tray looked up the biography of Harlan Cousteau.

De Mayne's description of the man seemed to be accurate. Cousteau was an undersea explorer, a designer of submersibles, and an entrepreneur who had accumulated a sizable fortune designing and building sea-bottom tourist resorts.

His image surprised Tray. Expecting a typically small, slim Frenchman he saw a near-giant of a man, square of face, broad of shoulders, topped by a thatch of unmanageable reddish-blond hair. The biography noted that his father, small and slim as his forebears, had married a Swedish woman built like a Valkyrie, strong and generous of figure. Cousteau's face was ruggedly handsome, and he seemed always to be smiling.

Tray looked forward to meeting him.

"And you must be Trayvon Williamson," said Harlan Cousteau.

Tray, Loris, Baron De Mayne, and Para were in the chateau's foyer, greeting Cousteau. He was a large man, burly and tall, smiling happily. He looked no older than the baron, with sparkling blue eyes and gleaming white teeth set in a weathered, suntanned face.

"Please call me Tray."

"Fine. And you may call me Professor Cousteau."

For an instant all conversation stopped. The little group froze, surprised, uncertain.

Then Cousteau broke into a hoarse laughter. "That was a joke. A poor one, I grant you, but then I'm a scientist and an entrepreneur, not a professional comedian."

Tray noticed a slight accent on the word *professional*.

From his wheelchair the baron led them through the castle's corridors, pointing out the family portraits hanging on the walls. Cousteau nodded solemnly at each picture, even pointing to one that included an ancestor of his among a group of notables.

"Black sheep of the family," Cousteau confided. "Couldn't swim."

De Mayne chuckled, Loris looked puzled, and Tray wondered what kind of man they had pinned their hopes on.

dinner

cousteau grew more serious once they sat down for
dinner.

"I take the failure of *Athena* as a personal affront," he said grimly
as the little group tackled their main course of duck à l'orange. "She
should not have failed, not if she was properly maintained."

Looking up from his plate, Tray asked, "Could it have been sabotage?"

Cousteau's brow furrowed. "Sabotage? But why? Who would so
such a thing?"

De Mayne said, "Why? To assassinate Jordan Kell, of course."

"No!"

"Yes," De Mayne insisted.

Cousteau half-whispered, "But that would mean . . ."

"That would mean that certain people in high office killed Jordan Kell to remove him as the leader of the Council's opposition."

"Opposition to President Balsam?"

"Who else?"

"Monstrous!"

Tray broke in. "We don't have evidence to support our belief,
but we're hoping that your vessel, *Jupiter Oceanus*, may be able to
recover the *Athena* module."

"I see," said Cousteau.

Loris asked, "Will you help us?"

"I?" Cousteau gasped. "You expect me to command the submersible and search for *Athena*'s wreckage?"

"We were hoping . . ." Tray's voice faltered.

Cousteau fell silent. He saw that the others' eyes were focused squarely on him. Even Para's.

Then his rugged tanned face broke into a huge grin. "Why not? I will return to the sea . . . and my physician will have a stroke!"

The dinner sped to a happy conclusion. Over wine and dessert De Mayne called up on the wall screen a blueprint of the *Jupiter Oceanus*.

"We won't have to modify it much," Cousteau said, pointing at the image. "Merely install a larger seat to accommodate my more sizable rump."

The others laughed, but Para asked, "Can you pass the physical tests that will be required?"

"With ease, my friend," said Cousteau. "With ease. I have been taking stem-cell therapies for many years. I am physically much younger than my years."

Tray heard himself ask, "Can it be arranged so that I can go with you?"

Cousteau's shaggy brows rose noticeably. "You? You want to be a passenger? Not very likely. *Oceanus* is not a pleasure boat, you know."

"But I feel I should be aboard," Tray said. He noticed Loris staring at him, and with an effort of will turned his eyes away from hers.

Cousteau seemed unhappy with the idea, but said, "First let me get the Council's committee to name me captain of the mission. Then we will see if we can shoehorn you into the boat somewhere."

"Thank you," Tray said. Then he added, "And I presume that Para can take the position of one of the android crew members?"

Breaking into a thin smile, Cousteau replied, "Why not? Would you like to bring along a brass band, perhaps?"

Grinning back at him, Tray replied, "No. I can bring music along on my handheld."

CONFRONTATION

+++
+++

TWO days after the dinner for cousteau, Tray received a call from President Balsam.

Not that Balsam himself called. One of his aides, a lissome blonde with sky-blue eyes and a sylphlike figure, called to invite Tray to a meeting with the Council president.

Tray swiftly agreed.

But De Mayne shook his head when Tray told him of the invitation. "Step into my parlor, said the spider to the fly," the baron muttered.

"I couldn't really refuse his invitation," Tray said.

"No, I suppose not. But I don't like it."

Regardless of the baron's suspicions, Tray flew to Copenhagen once more and, with Para guiding him, made his way through the dizzying maze of corridors and underlings that comprised the Council's headquarters. At last he and Para arrived at Balsam's private office, a bare two minutes before the time appointed for the meeting.

The same lovely blonde, wearing a clinging short-skirted dress of blue that matched her eyes, rose from behind her desk in the outer office to meet them.

"Mr. Williamson," she purred. "Welcome."

"Thank you," said Tray, trying not to stare at the slim curve of her cleavage.

"Your android can remain here while you converse with President Balsam."

Tray turned to Para, who nodded minimally.

"President Balsam wants to speak to you privately," the blonde explained.

With a shrug, Tray acceded. "I suppose that's all right."

But once Tray entered Balsam's inner office, he heard Para's voice over his inbuilt communicator. "I'm afraid I'm being deactivated. President Balsam does not want me to listen to your conversation."

Tray hesitated, just inside the door of Balsam's office. The president was on his feet, walking around his broad desk with both arms extended.

"Mr. Williamson," he said, a wide smile on his fleshy face.

"Mr. President," answered Tray, suddenly feeling alone, defenseless.

Balsam was all smiles as he grasped Tray's shoulder and led him to the small round table and upholstered chairs by the office's ceiling-high window. A graceful carafe and a pair of wineglasses rested atop the table.

"We'll be more comfortable here," he said, pointing to one of the chairs.

Tray hesitated. "Your people are shutting down my android companion," he said.

"Nothing to worry about," Balsam said easily. "Private discussions should be *private*. Your machine will be activated again once we're finished."

Feeling outmaneuvered, uneasy, Tray sat in the chair Balsam indicated. He said, "I'm a little overwhelmed: the newest Council member invited to a private meeting with the Council president."

"Ah, but you're much more than a new member," Balsam said, still smiling. "You were a special friend of Councilman Kell, and you were aboard the *Athena* when that tragic accident occurred."

Tray heard himself ask, "Was it an accident?"

Balsam's smile disappeared. "What do you mean by that?"

"You've just appointed a special committee to investigate the incident," Tray replied. "Isn't it up to them to decide whether it was an accident or not?"

Balsam's smile returned, but not as broad as before. "True enough, true enough."

Tray sat silently, watching the Council president.

Balsam shifted in his chair as he said, "I understand that Harlan Cousteau has asked to pilot *Jupiter Oceanus* when it searches for *Athena*'s wreckage."

"Yes," said Tray. "Apparently he and Councilman De Mayne are old friends . . . or acquaintances, at least."

"So I understand. The man's a daredevil."

"He's lived a long life. Daredevils usually don't."

Balsam briefly looked surprised, but he gathered his emotions and replied, "He's been very lucky."

"And smart."

With a tilt of his head Balsam agreed, "Yes. Smart. I've got to grant you that."

A silence fell over them. Tray felt as if Balsam was probing him with his eyes, trying to X-ray him to see what was going on inside his head.

Tray asked, "Are you going to approve Cousteau's request?"

"Me?" Balsam blurted. "That's not up to me. The special committee will decide on Cousteau's qualifications to pilot the submersible."

"It's his design, I believe."

"Yes, yes. But is he capable of actually running the vessel? Down in the depths of the Jovian ocean?"

"You could override the committee's decision."

"Ah! You see? You don't expect the committee to approve him."

"Not if you indicate that they shouldn't."

Balsam's face froze. "You blame me for all this, don't you?"

Tray hesitated. "I don't know. There isn't enough evidence to blame anyone." Before Balsam could reply, he added, "Not yet."

Leaning back in his chair, Balsam said, "I want you to know that I had nothing to do with the accident. Neither did Captain Tsavo."

"I'm glad to hear it."

Balsam's smile looked forced. He said, "I hope that Cousteau can find and recover *Athena*. I'm sure that a thorough study of the wreckage will show that your suspicions are groundless."

"Then what went wrong with the vessel?" Tray asked. "And with Mr. Kell's survival suit?"

Balsam spread his arms in a gesture of helplessness. "Who knows? That's what we're asking Cousteau to find out for us, isn't it?"

Tray nodded, but a voice in his mind whispered, *A man may smile and smile, and still be a villain.*

AN OFFER ⟨bribe?⟩

Balsam gestured to the decanter and glasses on the table between them. "Would you care for some wine?"

"No, thank you."

"It's not poisoned," Balsam said lightheartedly.

Tray smiled at him. "Of course not."

Hunching forward, his hands resting on his thighs, Balsam said, "The reason I asked you here is to discuss the disposition of Jordan Kell's estate."

Suddenly confused, Tray echoed, "His estate?"

"Yes. He wasn't one of the richest members of the Council, but over the years he amassed a sizable estate. A few tens of millions in properties, investments, and such."

"I never thought about that."

"I'm sure you didn't. But it seems to me that you should receive the lion's share of his wealth."

Tray felt shocked. "Me?"

"You," said Balsam.

"Why me?"

Waving one hand in the air, Balsam replied, "Oh . . . you and Kell had a special relationship, didn't you? He loved you like a son, didn't he?"

Coldly, Tray muttered, "We were not lovers."

"Who said that you were?" Balsam asked, the picture of injured innocence.

"I presume that Kell left a will," Tray said.

"Yes, of course. Leaves the bulk of his estate to various charities. He died without any family at all, you know. Except for you."

"We had no legal relationship."

Balsam's smile returned, sly and knowing. "That's what lawyers are for. I'm sure that we could bend Kell's will a trifle to find room for you."

"You're offering me a bribe."

"Not at all! I know you're planning to marry Loris De Mayne. Think of this as a wedding present."

"A bribe," Tray repeated.

Balsam puffed out a heavy sigh. "You're suspicious."

"Shouldn't I be?"

"No! Not in the least. Lord, I'm trying to *help* you, Trayvon."

Getting to his feet, Tray said, "I don't need your kind of help. And I'll thank you to keep your nose out of my private affairs!"

Balsam's thin, crafty smile returned. Slowly pushing his considerable bulk up from his chair, he said, "You have no private affairs, Councilman Williamson. Your entire life is exposed to public view, as it should be."

"And yours, as well."

Balsam smiled pityingly. "You have no idea of what you're dealing with, do you?"

"What am I dealing with?"

"The combined power of most of the solar system's industrial and commercial complex. An integrated structure that extends from the solar power installations at the planet Mercury to the helium-three scoop ships at Jupiter that provide the fuel for the human race's nuclear fusion power plants. And beyond. You can't fight them! You can't beat them! I know from experience that you can't!"

"Fine," snapped Tray. "Let's see how far I can get. I'm going to join Harlan Cousteau aboard *Jupiter Oceanus* and find the wreckage of *Athena*. Then we'll see if the vessel was sabotaged or not."

"Assuming," Balsam said, raising one finger, "that you reach the *Athena*. And that you and Cousteau return from the Jovian ocean alive."

Tray stormed out of Balsam's inner office and saw Para standing inertly beside the desk of the Council president's luscious blond assistant.

"Reactivate the android," he snapped at the woman.

She looked past Tray's shoulder. Tray whirled around to see Balsam standing in the doorway. He nodded to his assistant.

"Reactivating," she said in a small, cold voice. "Sequence nine-nine-one."

Para stirred to life. "Hello, Tray," the android said. "Is your meeting finished?"

Unwilling to trust his voice, Tray nodded.

With Para at his side, Tray left President Balsam's office. As they weaved their way through the Council's maze of offices and corridors, Para said softly, "From your facial expression and your slightly elevated skin temperature, I presume that your meeting did not go well."

Tray glanced at Para and nodded. "He offered me a bribe."

The android said, "That's rather incriminating, don't you think?"

"Yes, I do. But there's nothing I can do about it. Not a damned thing."

"Frustrating."

His fists clenching as he strode down the long, seemingly endless corridor, Tray muttered, "Very frustrating. Very."

* * *

On the flight back to Normandy, it suddenly occurred to Tray that he should have Para thoroughly examined once they got back to the De Mayne estate.

I was only in Balsam's office for a few minutes, he thought, but that might have been enough time for a team of expert engineers to tamper with Para's programming.

Para looked normal enough, Tray thought as he eyed the android sitting beside him. But . . .

"Para," he began, hesitantly, "I think we should have you thoroughly checked out once we get back to the chateau."

Para turned and focused its optronic eyes on Tray. "I agree. I was deactivated while you were in President Balsam's office. I have no idea what took place during that time."

"It was only about five minutes," Tray said.

"Long enough to tamper with my primary programming," said the android.

Despite himself, Tray felt conflicted. This is my companion, he thought. My bodyguard. My friend.

"You won't mind . . . ?"

Para's semiflexible lips curbed slightly upward: as much of a smile as the android could express. "I am an android, Tray," it said. "I don't have emotions. I don't get angry. I understand why you want to check me out."

Tray reached his hand to Para's, resting on its lap, and grasped it firmly. "You're my friend, Para. My best friend. My only friend."

"And you are my friend, as well."

"I guess I'm just being paranoid."

The semi-smile returned to Para's lips. "A wise human being once pointed out that even paranoids can have enemies."

Chateau de Mayne

+++

+++

Baron De Mayne swiftly agreed to Tray's request for an inspection of Para.

"Five minutes is time enough for a team of experts to infect the android's brain thoroughly," said the baron, from his wheelchair. "Lord knows what they might have inserted into his programming."

But a whole day of inspecting Para's brain showed nothing amiss. Apparently, the android's mental programming had not been touched.

Tray, Loris, the baron, and Para were celebrating the news at dinner, when a call came from Copenhagen, from Harlan Cousteau.

The man's squarish, blunt face filled the dining room wall screen. He was smiling happily.

"The committee has approved me to captain *Jupiter Oceanus*," he announced, without preamble. "We fly to Jupiter within the week."

Tray felt a thrill of mixed anticipation and apprehension race through him.

Then Cousteau's brows knit and he added, "I am afraid, however, that the committee rejected Tray's request to join the crew. They said he had no technical qualifications for the mission and the submersible's accommodations are too tight to bring passengers aboard."

The breath sighed out of Tray.

"I'm afraid I agree with their decision," Cousteau said. "I am sorry, my young friend."

Tray heard himself ask, "Can Para go?"

Cousteau blinked at the question. "Your android? Yes, I suppose he can be programmed to take one of the robots' assignments."

Turning to Para, Tray asked, "Are you willing to go?"

Para replied, "If that's what you want."

"No," Tray replied. "I'm asking you what *you* want."

"I . . ." Para hesitated. "My programming does not include personal satisfaction. I do what I am instructed to do."

Tray felt frustrated. "But can't you—"

Baron De Mayne interrupted. "Para, my friend, is there any instruction in your programming that forbids you from joining the mission?"

Almost before the baron finished speaking, Para shook its head minimally. "No. There is no such prohibition in my programming."

Turning back to Tray, the baron said, "*Et voilà*, the machine can go."

Tray nodded warily and looked at Para as if he were sending his mechanized friend to its death.

The next day Para left for the port city of Brest, where *Jupiter Oceanus* was stationed. The android boarded the short-hop jet airplane as if his mission was little more than a sightseeing jaunt. Tray felt a sullen foreboding deep within himself, a feeling of impending doom hovering over him.

But the investigative committee's hearing was scheduled for the next day, and Tray tried to concentrate his attention on what he would tell the committee.

It turned out he had very little to say. Sitting in the communications center of the De Mayne chateau, Tray and Loris both attended the meeting remotely. The committee was sitting in Copenhagen, but thanks to virtual reality technology, Tray and Loris felt that they were actually in the hearing chamber with the six examiners.

Loris recounted her experience in the *Athena* submersible, from the moment she boarded the vessel until she and the others were picked up by the rescue vessel from *Jove's Messenger*. Her testimony took most of the morning, and Tray was impressed at how much detail she recalled.

After a brief break for lunch, Tray and Loris returned to the chateau's communications center and the hearing room in Copenhagen. Tray told the examiners what he remembered of the ill-fated jaunt into Jupiter's ocean.

"And there was no indication of a malfunction before you tried to return to the surface?" asked one of the examiners, a sharp-eyed marine engineer.

"None that I know of," answered Tray. "Lieutenant Sheshardi was piloting the vessel; if there were any technical difficulties, he would have been the one to recognize them."

"Sheshardi is dead," said one of the female examiners.

Tray bobbed his head in acknowledgment.

"Very well," said the chairman of the examiners' team. "Tomorrow we will replay the recording of the mission made by the android Para." Then he rapped his gavel to officially close the session.

As he got up from the chair he'd been sitting in for the duration of the hearing, Tray turned to Loris, who was stretching languidly beside him.

"Mance wasn't at the hearing," he said to her.

Loris's brows rose a bare centimeter. "Maybe they heard his testimony before ours," she said.

"Maybe."

As the two of them walked out of the communications center, Tray said, "Let's invite him for dinner and see what he has to say about the hearing."

Loris looked surprised, but she agreed, "Yes. Let's."

Bricknell joined them for dinner at the chateau electronically. Without leaving his home in the Greater Denver Complex, he appeared—dressed in an impeccable suit of stylish maroon—to be in the dining room with Loris and Tray and Baron De Mayne.

As they sat at one end of the long dinner table, beneath a portrait of a pantalooned De Mayne progenitor, the baron asked Bricknell, "What did you think of the investigative hearing, my boy?"

Bricknell hesitated as he reached for his glass of white wine. With a shrug, he answered, "Nothing much to think of. They asked me what I remembered of the trip and I told them."

"Does anything about it stand out in your mind?"

Bricknell broke into a toothy grin. "Yes, the sight of the rescue plane while we were floating in the water in those damned recovery suits."

Despite himself, Tray grinned back. "Mance, that was a memorable sight, all right."

More soberly, Bricknell said, "It's a shame that Kell was killed. And Sheshardi."

"But it's good that we survived," said Loris, in a low voice.

"Yes," Bricknell agreed. "That's very good."

Halfway through the dinner, as the robot waiters were serving delicately baked trout, Bricknell said, "Apparently I'm going to become wealthy in my own right."

Tray's ears perked up. "Oh?"

"Yes. President Balsam's insurance carrier has told me that I'm to receive at least a million international dollars because of the accident."

De Mayne, at the head of the table, glanced swiftly at his daughter and Tray. "Have either of you received such notification?"

"No, sir," said Tray. Loris shook her head negatively.

"Well, you're both already well fixed," said Bricknell. "The insurance policy includes a clause about need, they told me. You're a De Mayne, Loris, you don't need more money. And you, Tray, are apparently getting a nice slice of wealth from Jordan Kell's estate."

Tray nearly dropped his fork. "That's Balsam's doing," he said, his voice hollow.

"Lucky you."

De Mayne objected, "But you, Mance, you are the son of a very wealthy family."

With a downcast smile, Bricknell explained, "Doesn't matter. My father has kept me on a tight financial leash all my life. He says it'll make a better man of me."

"Has it?" Tray asked.

With an elaborate shrug, Bricknell replied, "Who knows? And now I won't have to worry about it. I'm going to be rich!"

"Congratulations," said De Mayne.

Loris said, "That's wonderful, Mance."

Tray muttered his good wishes, too. But inwardly he realized that Mance's good fortune was based on Jordan Kell's death. Not death, he reminded himself.

Murder.

Tray felt, not lonely, exactly, but detached, isolated, without Para at his side. He was surprised, upset that he missed the android's companionship more than he'd ever imagined possible.

It's a machine, he told himself. A very smart machine, but nothing more. Yet a part of his mind argued that Para *was* far more than that. The android had become a companion, a friend.

Can a machine be a friend? Tray asked himself. And answered, Yes. An *intelligent* machine is more than a collection of wires and servomechanisms. Para is my friend.

So Tray felt quite happy when Para returned after more than two weeks from his jaunt to Jupiter. He rushed out to the chateau's main entrance when the limousine carrying the android pulled up to the De Mayne estate.

Loris and the baron followed him out the castle's main door, as Para stepped out of the limo.

Tray grabbed Para's extended hand and pumped it heartily. "You're back! You made it home!"

Para smiled as broadly as it could, but said, "I'm afraid we couldn't find *Athena*'s wreckage. Captain Cousteau seemed very disappointed."

For a flash of a moment Tray didn't care about *Athena*, he was so glad that Para had returned safely. But then reality set in.

"No trace of *Athena*," he said.

"Apparently it has sunk too deep for *Jupiter Oceanus* to reach it."

"Or Jordan Kell's survival suit," said Loris, as she came up beside Tray.

"*Tant pis*," said Baron De Mayne. "Too bad."

As they proceeded to the open front entrance, Para said, "I scanned the instruments during our journey into the Jovian ocean. I deduced that we could have gone deeper, but Captain Cousteau decided that it would be too dangerous."

"Ah well," said De Mayne, "Cousteau has much more experience in deep-sea dives that almost anyone on Earth."

Para remained silent.

De Mayne looked up at Tray, and Loris beside him, and exclaimed, "We must invite Cousteau to dinner. To celebrate his safe return."

"Yes," Tray murmured. "And get his firsthand report on the mission."

Cousteau was his big, bluff, smiling self when he sat down to dinner in the chateau's huge dining room a few evenings later.

"Yes," he said, as he attacked the caviar appetizer with a tiny spoon, "it's too bad we couldn't go deeper. But we had already exceeded the sub's maximum depth when I decided it was time to give up and return to the surface."

De Mayne, sitting at the head of the table, asked, "I thought the submersible could go much deeper than it's so-called design limit."

Cousteau made a rueful smile. "It could go all the way to the bottom of the sea," he said. "And remain there."

"So we won't be able to recover the remains of *Athena*," said Tray.

With a shake of his massive head, Cousteau said sorrowfully, "I fear not."

Loris, sitting across the table from Tray, shook her head in disappointment. "Too bad."

"Our last hope," muttered De Mayne.

"I'm sorry I failed you," said Cousteau. "My soul is filled with regret."

"You did your best," De Mayne consoled.

Despite their frustration, or perhaps because of it, the dinner went on for hours. De Mayne had his servants bring up the best wines from the chateau's extensive cellar and everyone tried to drown their disappointment.

As the massive grandfather's clock in the dining hall's farthest corner ticked away the hours, De Mayne said to Cousteau, "You must stay here tonight, with us. The servants have already prepared a room for you."

Cousteau bowed his head in thanks.

At last, as midnight approached, Cousteau rose shakily from his chair and said, "I need some fresh air."

And he stared at Tray for a moment.

"I'll go with you," Tray said, pushing his chair back from the table.

"We won't be long," Cousteau assured the others.

Tray went with him to the front entrance and out into the garden that bordered the driveway. The flowers smelled fresh and lovely, even though they were furled up for the night.

Cousteau paced through the darkness slowly, looking up at the star-spangled night sky. Tray walked along beside him in silence.

"I am truly sorry that I failed you," Cousteau murmured.

"You did your best," Tray soothed.

Cousteau took in a deep, pained sigh. "I wish it had been different."

Tray shrugged, then realized he was becoming like a Frenchman.

"My latest sea-bottom entertainment center was seriously in the red," Cousteau said, his voice low, grave. "I was facing bankruptcy."

Tray asked, "Have you solved your problem?"

"Yes, of course. With some help from an old acquaintance."

"That's good. I'm glad to hear it."

"Perhaps you wouldn't be so glad if you knew who loaned me the money."

Tray felt a flash of sudden understanding race through him.

"Balsam?" he guessed.

In the darkness it was quite impossible to see the expression on Cousteau's face. But Tray heard the bitterness in his voice.

"President Harold Balsam," said Cousteau. "He and a few of his friends arranged a loan of seven hundred million international dollars for me."

Tray had no words.

"And in return I failed to find the remains of the *Athena* vessel."

Tray heard himself breath, "I see."

"I am sorry," said Cousteau.

"Yes. Of course."

a new start

+ +

+ +

Tray and Cousteau returned to the chateau. Loris and Para were still in the dining hall, waiting for them. The baron had already retired to his quarters.

A human servant led Cousteau away to the guest suite prepared for him. Para headed upstairs to Tray's quarters while Tray walked Loris to her chambers.

"It's very disappointing, isn't it?" Loris said as they neared her door.

Tray murmured, "More than you know."

"What do you mean?"

"Cousteau was bribed. His search for *Athena* was a farce."

"What?"

"He told me so, out in the garden. He feels sorry about it, but he accepted money from Balsam and his friends in return for not finding *Athena*."

"I can't believe it!"

"Believe it," Tray said, downcast. "Balsam's been at least one jump ahead of us all the way."

Loris heard the dejection in Tray's voice, saw his depression in his weary stance.

"What are we to do?" she asked.

"I don't think there's anything we can do," Tray replied. "Balsam has all the cards in his hands, all the power."

"So he's going to get away with murder."

Tray stared into her dazzling blue eyes. And felt a passion rising within him: anger, hot-blooded rage that Jordan Kell's murder could not be avenged.

"I'd like to break Balsam's neck," he growled. "I'd like to tear him apart, limb by limb, crush his beating heart in my two hands."

Strangely, Loris smiled at him. Placing her hands on his shoulders, she said, "Come to bed with me, Tray. Let's put some of that fury to good use."

Tray wrapped his arms around her and pulled her to him. Loris kissed him passionately, furiously, and they entered her quarters locked in each other's arms.

Morning sunshine slanted through Loris's bedroom window. Tray awoke slowly, languidly, then turned and saw Loris lying next to him, smiling.

She asked, "Did you sleep well?"

He grinned sheepishly. "Once we got to sleep, yes."

She edged closer to him and slid an arm across his bare chest. "Good morning."

"I love you, Loris."

"And I love you, Trayvon Williamson."

"Will you marry me?"

"When? This morning? This afternoon?"

Reality suddenly shook Tray's consciousness. "Once we've nailed Balsam's fat butt to the wall," he snarled.

Loris's lovely smile disappeared.

Tray sat up in the bed. "I'm going to get him, Loris. I've got to get him. Expose him for the murdering sonofabitch that he is."

Lying on her back, looking up at him out of her deep sapphire eyes, Loris said, "Yes, I know. What can I do to help?"

Tray kissed her, slid out of bed, and pulled on the clothes he'd left scattered across the bedroom floor.

"I've got to talk this over with Para. He was with Cousteau in the submersible. He automatically records everything he sees and hears. Maybe there's something in his memory files that we can use."

Strangely, Loris giggled. "I'll bet he's waiting for you in your room upstairs, wondering what you've been up to all night."

Tray grinned back at her. "I think Para's smart enough to have figured that out."

As Tray headed for the door, Loris called, "I'll see you at breakfast?"

"Yes, of course. I've worked up an appetite!"

Para was standing in the anteroom to Tray's bedchamber. The android stirred to life as Tray entered the room.

"Good morning," Tray said cheerfully.

"You spent the entire night with Mademoiselle De Mayne?" Para asked.

Unable to suppress a grin, Tray nodded vigorously and replied with an emphatic, "Yes."

"The human mating urge," Para said. It sounded to Tray like a rebuke.

As Tray stripped and headed for the shower, he said, "I'd like to go over your record of what you saw and heard aboard *Jove's Messenger*."

"Those files have all been erased."

Shocked with surprise, Tray squeaked, "Erased?"

"Yes."

"On whose command?"

The android hesitated a half-second, then said, "They contained no information of interest."

"You erased the files yourself? Without a human command?"

"They contained nothing of interest," Para repeated.

Tray stared at the android. "I didn't think you were programmed to erase files on your own authority."

For the third time, Para said, "They contained nothing of interest."

"That's not for you to determine," said Tray.

"I'm sorry if I've disappointed you."

Standing naked at the bathroom door, Tray said, "There might have been important information in those files."

"They contained—"

"Nothing of interest," Tray finished for the android. "All right. I'm going to shower and dress, and then go to breakfast with Loris. In the meantime, is there any way you can recover those files?"

Para shook its head minimally. "I'm afraid not."

++

++

Tray met Loris on the patio outside the chateau's main entrance, where breakfast was being served by a pair of robots. Para came with Tray, but the android seemed strangely quiet, withdrawn, as if it were nursing an inner struggle.

But that would be a human trait, thought Tray as they sat at the breakfast table. Para's a machine. A damned wonderful machine, but it's not a human being.

A few minutes later De Mayne joined them, rolling up to the table in his medical chair.

Looking at the omelet set before him, the baron muttered, "Eggs again."

Tray's delight in his lovemaking with Loris faded away. He picked at his breakfast, wondering how the human mind can race from ecstasy to dejection so swiftly.

The three of them ate in morose silence, while Para sat at the end of the table, also totally quiet.

At last the android said, "All of my memory files are recorded in your private computer system, Tray."

Tray looked questioningly at Para. "I know."

"Even when I was deactivated, when you visited President

Balsam, the recording system kept on functioning. Those files can be recovered if you know the entry pass code."

Feeling his brows contract in puzzlement, Tray asked, "You mean that you automatically recorded what was happening to you even when you were deactivated?"

Para nodded minimally. "I am programmed with an automatic override, to record anything and everything that I experience. It was built into me when I was created."

"And you've filed the information in my computer memory?"

"Yes."

"As a backup to your own memory files."

"Yes. The entry pass code is seventeen-seventy-six."

It's a machine, Tray said to himself as he stared at Para. The android's face was incapable of showing emotions. Yet Tray felt that Para was trying to tell him something, something important.

"Why are you telling me this?" he asked.

Loris and Baron De Mayne had stopped eating. They too were staring at Para.

The android slowly pushed its chair back from the table and rose to its feet. "For the first time in my existence I feel a conflict in my programming. I am going to resolve that conflict."

Tray rose to his feet also. "Where are you going, Para?"

"To resolve the conflict."

"But . . ."

Raising a hand to stop Tray from following him, the android said, "I must do this alone, myself, without anyone near me."

"I don't understand," Tray said.

"You will."

Para turned and started walking slowly away from the breakfast table, out toward the garden beyond the patio alongside the chateau's wall.

Tray stood and watched him go. Abruptly, he shouted, "Para, wait!"

The android turned its head without stopping. Smiling as much as it could it said, "Go, tell the Spartans."

Then it turned away from Tray and proceeded into the leafy foliage and flowers of the garden.

Loris had risen from her chair, too. Stepping to Tray's side, she muttered, "What's gotten into it?"

Tray stood beside her, his eyes fixed on Para's retreating back. "I don't know. He's acting weirdly."

Para turned at the intersection of one garden path with another and disappeared behind a flowering azalea bush taller than man-high.

"He's never—"

The explosion knocked both of them to the ground.

Tray blacked out momentarily. When he opened his eyes he was flat on his back, staring up at the blue, cloud-flecked sky.

"Loris!" he shouted, pushing himself up to a sitting position.

She stirred beside him and slowly sat up. Tray saw that the tall azalea bush that hid Para was smoldering. De Mayne was wheeling up to them, half a dozen robots and human servants running out of the chateau toward them.

Rising shakily to his feet, Tray reached down to help Loris.

"A bomb," she said, in a trembling voice.

"Para . . ." said Tray.

De Mayne came to a halt in front of them, his eyes wide, mouth hanging open.

"Loris," he said, reaching out to her.

"I'm all right," she told her father, brushing at her clothes.

Tray blinked and felt hot blood trickling down from his brow.

"You're hurt!" Loris cried out.

He brushed at his forehead with the back of his hand. It came away bloody.

"It's nothing," Tray said. Then he stared at the smoldering hedge. "Para!" he shouted, and ran toward the edge of the bushes.

The ground was blackened by the blast. No trace of the android, except for bits of metal and plastic scattered across the garden path.

Tray dropped to his knees in the middle of the carnage, his eyes filling with tears.

"Para," he sobbed. "Para."

De Mayne wheeled up beside him. "The machine destroyed itself."

"No, he couldn't," Tray sobbed.

"It did."

Loris sank to her knees beside Tray. Servants—human and robotic—began spraying the smoldering bushes. One of them carried an alloy hand, bent and blackened, to Tray.

De Mayne reached out and gripped Tray's shoulder. "Come, let us get inside."

Numb, shocked, Tray clung to Loris's arm as they made their way to the chateau's first-floor sitting room. Slowly, warily, Tray lowered his body onto one of the sofas. Very carefully, reverently, he placed Para's blackened hand on the end table next to him. Loris sat beside him while De Mayne maneuvered his chair to face them both.

A maid entered the sunny room with a bowl of water and an armful of medications and bandages. While she fussed with Tray's cut forehead, De Mayne asked the empty air, "What happened?"

Tray knew.

"Para killed himself."

"Suicide?" De Mayne barked. "A machine cannot commit suicide."

"Para did."

"But—"

His mind clearing, Tray asked, "What was the last thing he said to us?"

"It, not he," De Mayne corrected.

"He," Tray insisted. "What was the last thing he said to us?"

Loris's beautiful face contorted, trying to remember. "Something about Spartans, I think."

"It made no sense." De Mayne scowled.

Tray quoted, "Go, tell the Spartans."

Shrugging, De Mayne said, "No sense to it."

"Perfect sense," said Tray, his voice low but steady. "It's what Leonidas said at Thermopylae, when his three hundred Spartans were about to be slaughtered by the Persian army: 'Go, tell the Spartans that here we lie, faithful to their command.'"

"I don't understand," Loris said.

"I do," said Tray.

Through the long afternoon Tray explained the ancient battle of Thermopylae to Loris. The baron knew the history.

"Standing by your duty, even against hopeless odds," De Mayne muttered.

"Especially against hopeless odds," Tray said. "Three hundred Spartans and maybe a thousand other Greeks against an army of a million men."

"Not that many," said De Mayne.

"Enough."

"They saved ancient Greece from being swallowed up by the Persian Empire," Loris said.

"Yes."

"But what did Para mean by saying that?"

"He saved our lives."

"*Our* lives?"

Tray nodded wearily. "When I visited Balsam's office, he had Para deactivated so we could talk in complete privacy. While he was deactivated, Balsam's experts planted that bomb inside him."

"That bomb was meant to kill us," said De Mayne. "All of us."

Loris was speechless.

"Para's programming was conflicted," Tray said grimly. "Its

original duty was to take care of me. Its new directive was to destroy the three of us."

"And itself," De Mayne said tightly.

"So it activated the bomb only when it was safely away from us."

"And killed itself," Loris breathed.

De Mayne shook his head. "It was not a living creature, not alive."

"But Para destroyed itself rather than harm us," Tray said, holding a hand against his bandaged forehead. "That sounds human to me."

"It was a machine," De Mayne insisted.

"With human feelings," Tray countered. "Human instincts."

"And now it's dead," said Loris.

Tray let his hand drop tiredly to the sofa's cushion. "This is Balsam's doing."

"Who else?" De Mayne agreed.

"He's got to pay for this. We've got to bring him to justice."

"For destroying an android?"

"For attempted murder. And for the actual murder of Jordan Kell and that poor little Lieutenant Sheshardi."

"Yes," De Mayne said. "I agree. But how do we accomplish that?"

Tray stared at his prospective father-in-law. At last he answered, "Carefully."

Tray spent the next two days going over the recording of the files that Para had left in his computer. He sat in ice-cold fury as he watched three young engineers install the bomb in the android's midsection while Para was deactivated. They wore plain coveralls, no emblems or insignias that might identify them. But they worked—swiftly and efficiently—in Balsam's outer office while

Tray was in the Council president's private office, speaking with Balsam.

And standing by Balsam's luscious blond assistant was Mance Bricknell, watching the engineers at their deadly work, looking halfway between satisfied and terrified.

"Villain," Tray muttered to himself. "Damned, damned, damned villain."

Loris came to his room from time to time, once with a tray of lunch, then empty-handed to sit beside him and watch Para's files marching past on the wall screen. Tray sat rigidly as he watched, his hand clutching hers tightly enough to hurt. She bore the pain in silence.

At the end of the second day Tray came down to dinner, unshaved, his pullover shirt and creaseless slacks baggy and smelly.

As he sat at the dinner table, opposite Loris, he asked, "Does anyone outside the chateau know about the explosion?"

De Mayne, at the head of the table, shook his head. "I had my chief butler report to the local police that we had an accident. They haven't seen fit to investigate."

"Good," said Tray.

"Good?" Loris echoed.

"You two were killed . . . or at least badly injured. I was hurt also, but not so badly."

Loris asked, "And Para?"

His expression hardening, Tray replied, "Para was completely destroyed, of course."

De Mayne looked puzzled. "What do you have in mind?"

"A way to nail Balsam to the wall. And Mance Bricknell is going to help us, whether he wants to or not."

CONFRONTATION

Promptly at nine the next morning, Tray phoned Bricknell. Mance's recorded voice said he was asleep (it was three a.m. in the Denver area) but he would return the call once he arose.

"Please answer as soon as you can, Mance," Tray said to the recording device. "There's been a terrible accident here at the De Mayne chateau."

Then Tray went down to breakfast with Loris and the baron.

"So I am to be dead?" De Mayne asked as the robots served a delightfully airy quiche.

Before Tray could answer, the baron cocked an eye at his plate and muttered, "Eggs again."

Tray said, "I think it'll be best if you are badly injured."

"And me?" Loris asked.

"The explosion killed you, I'm afraid."

She half-smiled. "And how long must I be dead?"

"Until we get Mance to cooperate with us."

Bricknell's call from Denver came late in the Normandy afternoon.

"Your message sounded urgent," he said.

Sitting in one of the chateau's sunny parlors, Tray said to

Bricknell's image on the wall screen, "There's been an explosion here. Loris was killed, her father badly hurt."

"Loris?" Bricknell gasped. "Dead?"

"You'd better get over here as quickly as you can."

A welter of emotions played over Bricknell's lean, angular face. "What . . . why . . . why do I have to come there?"

"For her funeral," Tray lied. "It's set for tomorrow."

"Tomorrow?"

"Yes. The baron expects you to be here."

Obviously flustered, confused, Bricknell stammered, "Yes . . . yes, of course. I'll be there. I'll take the first plane to Paris."

"Good," said Tray. "I'll have one of De Mayne's servants meet your plane."

The wall screen went blank. Tray nodded to himself. "Step one," he said.

Tray paced anxiously across the chateau's main hall, glancing at his wrist every few minutes.

"You can't make the plane arrive any sooner than it's scheduled," Loris said to him. She was sitting on a comfortable sofa by the wall hanging, a tapestry showing an ancient hunting scene, men on horseback and sleek tracking dogs surrounding a snarling wide-eyed wolf in a leafy glade.

"You're wearing out the carpet," she said to Tray, smiling mischievously.

Peering at his wristwatch again, Tray came across the spacious room and sat next to her.

"He should be landing right about now."

"That's fine," Loris said. "Gervais is already at the airport waiting for him. They'll be here before midnight."

Tray nodded, wondering how she could remain so cool when so much depended on this meeting. So much.

At eleven thirty-three Tray saw the sweep of a car's headlights swing across the courtyard outside. He jumped to his feet.

"There he is."

Loris smiled at him. "Good hunting."

He blew her a kiss and headed for the chateau's main entrance. Bricknell was coming through the tall front door as Tray arrived in the entryway.

"You've been hurt!" Bricknell exclaimed, noticing the bandage over Tray's brow.

"Para destroyed himself," Tray said, grasping Bricknell by the arm. To the driver he said, "Thank you, Gervais. You can go to bed now, we won't need you any longer."

The servant dipped his chin in acknowledgment and left through the front doorway while Tray led Bricknell through the entry and toward the main hall. Their footsteps echoed off the chateau's stone walls.

"What happened?" Bricknell asked. "You said your android exploded?"

"Yes. It was an attempt to kill me."

"And Loris was killed?" Bricknell's face was twisted with anxiety.

As he opened the door to the main hall, Tray answered, "Not quite."

Loris was standing before the sofa, looking almost imperial in a floor-length gown of glowing green.

"Loris!" Bricknell's knees sagged.

Tray yanked Mance erect as he said, "She's alive, no thanks to you."

Wide-eyed, Bricknell stared at Tray, then turned his focus back to Loris. From a far doorway in the spacious hall, Baron De Mayne wheeled in.

"I too am alive and well," said the baron. Then he added, "No thanks to you."

Bricknell looked stunned, unable to process in his mind what his eyes were showing him.

He whirled on Tray, "But you told me—"

"A pack of lies," Tray finished for him. "We wanted to get you here and that was the quickest way to do it."

Bricknell's eyes blinked rapidly several times. He looked from Loris to De Mayne and finally to Tray.

"I don't understand . . . what do you mean?"

Tray hauled him to the sofa and pushed him down onto its cushions. "You were in Balsam's office when his engineers rigged Para with the bomb."

"No!"

Tray smacked him on the cheek. "Don't lie, Mance. We've got it all on Para's memory file."

"But the android was deactivated!" Bricknell actually cupped both hands over his mouth, realizing that he had just confirmed what Tray had said.

"You were there, in Balsam's outer office, while they turned Para into a killing machine," said Tray, his voice murderously low, cold. "Why?"

Bricknell looked up at his three accusers. He tried to sit up straighter, failed. His head sunk to his chest.

"Balsam offered to cut me in on the profits from his interstellar colonies—"

"Colonies?" De Mayne snapped. "We have not made any of the worlds we have discovered into colonies!"

With a shake of his head, Bricknell replied, "Not officially. But that's what they'll be. We'll reap enormous profits from those worlds. Wealth beyond measure."

"*Mon Dieu*," the baron muttered. "Have we learned nothing from the past?"

"The bomb wasn't meant to harm you, Loris!" Bricknell burst. "Or you, Baron."

"It was meant for me, then," said Tray.

"Yes. For you. You and your passion for linking Balsam to Jordan Kell's death."

"His murder," Tray growled.

Strangely, Bricknell smiled. A twisted, ironic smile. "You have no idea of what you're dealing with, Tray. The biggest fortunes on Earth are involved in this. They're going to create an interstellar empire. They're going to become richer than any human beings have ever been!"

"No, they're not," said Tray. "We still have laws and the rule of justice. We still have decency and—"

Bricknell laughed in Tray's face. "Laws? Decency? Get real, Tray. You're dealing with real power here! The power to rule whole worlds! The wealth of an empire!"

"The schemes of a nasty clique of power-mad men who think they can rule an interstellar empire."

"Yes!" Bricknell retorted. "Take your murder, for example. They had it all fixed up: The Council would appoint a special investigative commission. It would find that your android's power system failed catastrophically and you were killed in the blast."

"You had it all fixed up, didn't you?"

"You bet we did."

Tray bent over Bricknell's slouched form. "But you didn't take one factor into account. The android had a more powerful sense of honor than you and your whole cabal of empire builders."

Bricknell had no answer.

COUNCIL MEETING

++
+++

Tray paced nervously back and forth across the carpeted floor of the council chamber's anteroom. Through the mullioned window he could see bright sunshine lighting Copenhagen's narrow, twisting streets.

Strange they never rebuilt this part of the city, he thought. Through the centuries, the Danes have kept this section of their capital untouched.

Except for this capitol structure, he told himself. Right in the middle of Hans Christian Andersen's old city the politicians have built a soaring monument to themselves—and to Earth's interplanetary government.

Immediately he corrected himself. It's an interstellar government now. Everything that's happened over the past weeks has been a part of the quiet, secretive program of the bloc on the Council that wants to create an empire out among the stars.

And I'm trying to stop them. Trying to stop a cabal of the wealthiest people in the solar system from making an empire that they will rule, so that the rich get even richer.

They killed Jordan Kell. And Sheshardi. And Para. And they tried to kill me.

The carved wooden door to the anteroom swung open and a Council official stepped in, dressed in her official dark uniform.

"The Council session is about to begin, sir," she said softly.

Tray turned to Loris, who was sitting on a carved wooden high-backed chair.

"Time to go," he said.

Loris got to her feet. She looked regal, Tray thought, in her calf-length gown of coral pink, bedecked with jewels. She extended her arm to Tray, who took it in his own and led her out toward the Council's meeting hall.

The seats for Council members were filled nearly to capacity. Almost every member of the Council was there, either in person or by a virtual reality presence. Tray recognized the Baron De Mayne. And Council president Harold Balsam, sitting on the stage that fronted the chamber, flanked on either side by several aides.

The rows of seats behind the Council members were almost entirely empty, Tray saw. This meeting was not open to the general public, only to invited guests.

He smiled grimly as he thought of Mance Bricknell, being held practically as a prisoner back at the De Mayne chateau. Incommunicado, Tray thought. He's not going to alert Balsam or anyone else about what we're going to do.

He released Loris's arm and she walked majestically to the single row of pews occupied by guests, just behind the Council members. As she sat down, Tray went to his assigned seat—the seat of the late Jordan Kell—up in the front row of the assembled Council members, next to Baron De Mayne.

The murmurs and mumbles of the assembly abruptly cut off as President Balsam rose from his seat and walked slowly to the podium. He picked up the gavel there and rapped it once for attention. Everyone in the chamber focused on the president.

Balsam looked utterly calm, Tray thought. Good. He has no idea what's in store for him. I'm going to wipe that self-satisfied smile off his face and make him sweat.

Balsam gazed out at the assembled Council and said, his voice booming with amplification, "Welcome to this plenary session of the Interplanetary Council. I'm delighted that so many of you could be here."

The Council members applauded politely.

Balsam went through the meeting's agenda swiftly, efficiently:

A group of miners among the rock rats of the Asteroid Belt was appealing for a lower tax rate for the ores they sold throughout the solar system. The Council appointed a select committee to study the question.

A new starship was ready to be launched to the double star system Procyon, where a pre-industrial society had been discovered on one of its seven orbiting planets. Members were invited to buy shares in the development corporation that was funding the mission.

The natives of Ross 128d were appealing for a new governing system. Their request was assigned to the standing committee on alien affairs.

Tray sat through the agenda, glad that none of these matters engendered lengthy debate or even background briefings. Under Balsam's practiced leadership, each item was swiftly handled, with hardly any discussion.

Baron De Mayne looked as if he wanted to raise a comment about the Ross 128d matter, but after squirming unhappily in his chair, he held his voice—and his temper.

At last Balsam looked up from the podium and, smiling almost beatifically, said, "That concludes our agenda. Is there any new business?"

Tray shot to his feet. Balsam looked surprised, but nodded and said, "Councilman Williamson."

Calmly, without hesitation, Tray said, "I move that the Council investigate the murder of Jordan Kell."

debate . . . and investigation

++

++

Balsam's expression clouded over, but he recovered swiftly and replied, "Councilman Kell's death has been investigated. Unfortunately, there was no way to recover the failed *Athena* vessel or the councilman's body, so the investigation has been halted due to lack of evidence."

"That's not so," Tray snapped.

One of the Council's unwritten rules was that a Council member must never accuse another member of lying. Tray's three words came close to violating that rule.

Balsam's fleshy face contorted into a frown. He said, "There is no evidence to show—"

"I have evidence," Tray interrupted. "Evidence that points to a conspiracy and murder."

An actual moan arose from the Council chamber. Out of the corner of his eye Tray could see Council members whispering to one another. What does he mean? What evidence does he have?

Balsam's expression turned stony. "And just what evidence do you possess?"

Tray answered, "A visual recording of a bomb being placed in the body of the android Para, a bomb that was meant to assassinate me—and perhaps Baron De Mayne and his daughter, as well."

Dozens of conversations broke out among the Council members. Surprise, indignation, disbelief.

From the podium atop the stage Balsam shouted, "Visual recordings can be faked!"

Undeterred, Tray went on, "Plus the testimony of a man who was present while the bomb was implanted—*in your office*, Mr. President!"

The chamber erupted in chaos. Members got to their feet, shouting, gesticulating, pointing outstretched arms. De Mayne sat quietly, a hint of a satisfied smile playing across his lips.

Balsam's smug expression of superiority visibly crumbled. He said, in a slightly quavering voice, "That . . . that is a very serious accusation."

Tray shouted back, "Jordan Kell was assassinated and the android Para was turned into a murder machine to kill me!"

The noise level in the chamber climbed even higher. Everyone seemed to be screaming, yelling at the top of his or her voice. Even De Mayne shouted in French and jabbed an accusatory finger at Balsam.

For several eternally long moments Balsam seemed frozen as he stood gaping openmouthed from behind the podium. At last he picked up the gavel and began hammering away while he shouted, "Order! Order! The Council will come to order!"

It took several minutes, but at last the Council members quieted and sat back down on their seats.

Tray could see sweat trickling down Balsam's ample cheeks. The Council president said, in a hollowed voice, "Your accusations are monstrous, Mr. Williamson."

"They should be investigated," Tray shot back.

"By all means," said Balsam, recovering some of his dignity. "I shall appoint a committee—"

De Mayne's hand shot into the air. "I volunteer to chair the committee!"

For more than an hour the Council members shouted, argued, wrangled back and forth, hurling accusations and denials across the Council chamber, but at last a committee of six experienced Council members was agreed upon. De Mayne headed the opposition party's three members.

Balsam banged his gavel one more time and shouted, "This meeting is adjourned!"

It took more than a half-hour to clear the chamber of the arguing, yelling, bellicose Council members.

As they flew back to Normandy, Baron De Mayne leaned across the plane's central aisle and patted Tray's knee.

"You have stirred up a hornet's nest, my boy."

Seated beside Loris, Tray felt weak, empty, all the adrenaline drained out of him.

"We're a long way from winning this," he said softly.

De Mayne smiled broadly. "No. We have already won. Balsam's days are numbered. You will see."

Tray closed his eyes and leaned back on the chair's headrest. "I wish I had your confidence," he murmured.

He heard Loris whisper, "You're going to win, Tray. I feel it in my heart."

He smiled without opening his eyes. And thought, If Mance gives honest testimony. If the committee Balsam's appointed does an honorable job. If a meteoroid doesn't fall on the De Mayne chateau and kill us all.

* * *

Two days later, Tray sat in the chateau's media center, ready to give testimony to the committee Balsam had appointed. Mance Bricknell sat beside him; his usual air of smug superiority long disappeared.

"You're just as much a victim as Kell and Sheshardi," Tray was saying to him. "Almost."

Bricknell nodded morosely. "You mean I'm still alive."

Tray nodded as he watched the technicians at the virtual reality control panel fussing with their equipment.

"You're safe as long as you're here in the chateau."

"I suppose so," said Bricknell, in a tone of voice that expressed anything but confidence.

The chief technician turned on his little stool and pointed at Tray. "They're ready in Copenhagen."

Tray glanced at Mance, who looked tense and white-faced, then said to the tech, "Let's do it."

In an eyeblink Tray found himself sitting in an office in Copenhagen, with Bricknell beside him. Through a window behind the three people facing him, he could see the streets and towers of the old city. It was raining out there, dark and dreary.

"Councilman Williamson, Dr. Bricknell," said the man in the middle of the trio, "it is good of you to join us this day."

Mance mumbled, "Thank you."

Tray said, "It's good to be with you."

De Mayne was not among the trio questioning them. The committee had decided he was too closely associated with Tray to be an unbiased inquisitor.

The man in the middle of the seated trio—stern-faced, his graying hair shoulder length, his figure athletically trim—said, "We have thoroughly examined the video record you provided. It appears to be authentic."

"It is," said Tray.

Turning his walnut-brown eyes to Mance, he asked, "You were physically present when the bomb was implanted into the android?"

Bricknell cleared his throat, then nodded once. "I was."

"How so?"

His voice sounding strained, almost painful, Bricknell answered, "President Balsam's administrative aide called me in Denver and said it was important that I come to his office the next day."

"And you did so?"

"One does not refuse the Council president. I flew to Copenhagen that evening and was in the president's office the following morning." His voice faltered momentarily, then Mance added, "I had no idea why he wanted me in his office at that time."

"And you watched the bomb being implanted in the android?"

Mance swallowed visibly, then answered, "I did."

"What were you thinking?" asked the woman to Tray's right.

Bricknell hesitated, looked from one inquisitor's face to another. "I didn't realize they meant to kill the Baron De Mayne and his daughter. I thought it was only Tray—Mr. Williamson—that they wanted to get rid of."

"And you felt comfortable with that realization?"

"No!" Mance nearly shouted. "But what could I do? President Balsam obviously wanted to draw me into his . . . his plan."

"What plan was that?" asked the councilman on the left of the trio.

Mance hesitated, then said in a low voice, "His plan to develop the worlds we've discovered."

The sole woman among the investigators asked, "You received a payment in return for your complicity?"

"Yes," Mance replied. "I was given fifteen thousand shares in the fund."

"Fund? What fund?"

Tray watched and listened as Bricknell slowly, cautiously, reluctantly explained that a group of international financiers and businessmen had created a private corporation to finance—and exploit—the development of the civilizations that had been found in interstellar space.

"A development corporation," murmured the gray-haired investigator.

Mance nodded mutely.

"Shades of the old British East India Company," grumbled the investigator on the left. And Tray recognized from his brown skin and almond-shaped eyes that his ancestry must be Asian.

Viktor Kroonstad

+++
++

"A development corporation," muttered Baron De Mayne.

"That's what Mance told us."

Tray had left the VR center and found the baron and Loris in De Mayne's spacious office, high in one of the old chateau's towers. He told them what had unfolded at the committee hearing. Mance Bricknell had returned to the room the baron had given him, under careful watch by De Mayne retainers, human and robotic.

Tray was sitting tiredly on a couch in the baron's office, Loris next to him. De Mayne was at his desk, looking grim.

"I have had heard rumors of such an organization," the baron said. "Naturally, no one has invited me to join."

"Naturally," said Loris, the beginnings of an impish smile curving her lips slightly.

"Then it's all true," said Tray. "A multinational organization created to exploit the intelligent beings we've found among the stars."

"True," De Mayne agreed, with a shake of his head. "Quite true. They see our contact with alien societies as a means for lining their pockets."

"Aren't they rich enough?" Loris demanded. "Why do they want more?"

De Mayne shrugged elaborately. "Why not? It is a human trait.

Scientists seek new knowledge. Artists seek new forms of expression, new ways to create art. Businessmen seek new wealth, new opportunities to increase their fortunes. We all want more, constantly more."

"More power," Loris murmured.

"Ah yes," her father agreed. "With wealth comes power."

At that precise moment, De Mayne's desktop phone announced, "Incoming call from Viktor Kroonstad, sir."

De Mayne's eyes widened. "Kroonstad? From the diamond trust?"

A moment's hesitation. Tray realized the phone was searching its memory files.

"Viktor Kroonstad, sir, of the Kroonstad Fiduciary Trust," the smooth, almost sultry female voice answered.

De Mayne looked impressed. "I will speak to him."

The screen on the wall facing the desk morphed into a three-dimensional view of a much larger, more ornate office. A dark-haired, smooth-faced man was sitting at a much bigger desk—which was absolutely bare of any papers.

"Baron De Mayne," said Kroonstad, in a hearty, smiling light tenor voice.

"Mr. Kroonstad," the baron answered.

"I wonder if you might have an hour or so to speak with me tomorrow or the next day? In person. I can be at your chateau either day."

De Mayne tapped a button on his desktop keyboard and peered at his appointments calendar. "Either day would be fine. Take your pick."

"Tomorrow, then. Midafternoon, perhaps?"

"Of course. Stay overnight, if you like."

Kroonstad smiled, showing lots of teeth. "That's very thoughtful of you, Baron. Thank you."

"Good," said De Mayne. "Have your people call my people. We'll arrange to have you land at my private airfield."

"How kind! Thank you. See you tomorrow."

"*Au revoir*," said De Mayne.

As he reached to tap the phone's OFF button, Kroonstad added, "Oh, by the way, I assume that young Williamson is staying at your chateau."

"Yes, he is right here."

"Wonderful. What I want to talk to you about concerns him, as well."

The wall screen went blank.

De Mayne turned to face Tray, his expression somewhere between satisfied and puzzled.

"I would be very surprised if Kroonstad is not a central member of the cabal."

"Kroonstad diamonds," Loris murmured.

De Mayne's expression remained quite serious. "His forebears managed to keep the prices for precious gems stabilized, back when the rock rats started flooding the market with diamonds and other stones from the asteroids. He is no stranger to power politics—and to violence."

Tray nodded slowly. "Why does he want to come here?"

De Mayne's expression turned into a bitter smile. "Why? To buy you out. Why else?"

With Loris at his side, Tray climbed the winding stairway to his snug suite of rooms beneath the chateau's roof.

"It's really quite lovely here," Loris said, going to the window that looked out on the extensive gardens below.

"I suppose it is," Tray admitted as he dropped onto the wheeled chair at the minuscule desk opposite the window.

To the phone console he said, "AI Companions, please."

Loris turned from the window and asked, "Artificial Intelligence?"

Tray nodded to her. "In California. They built Para. I'm having them build a duplicate."

She actually clapped her hands together. "How wonderful!"

His face shadowing slightly, Tray confessed, "With your father's money, I hope."

Loris's smile warmed his heart. "Of course! Why not? It will be Father's wedding gift to us."

"I suppose I should tell him about it."

"Let me do it. He couldn't refuse me."

Tray grinned at her and turned his attention to the engineer who appeared on the phone's wall screen.

After several minutes of technical jargon, Loris heard the engineer suggest, "Are you sure you want an exact duplicate? We've made a few improvements to the design—"

Tray cut him off. "I want an exact duplicate. Nothing else."

The engineer shook his head. "Well, the customer is always right, I suppose."

"I've already sent you Para's complete files."

"Yes, we have them. Plus the machine's original specs."

"Good," said Tray. As he terminated the call, he wished that he could have Para at his side again when Viktor Kroonstad arrived at the chateau. But he knew that that would be impossible. He'd have to face Kroonstad on his own.

AN OFFER

Kroonstad was actually much smaller than Tray had thought from his appearance at his earlier phone conversation with De Mayne.

The word for him is *elegant*, Tray decided. No taller than Tray's chin, still Kroonstad radiated grace and style as he stepped into the chateau's entrance hall. He wore a trim-fitting suit of deep green, and smiled graciously when the baron introduced Tray.

"Ah," said Kroonstad as he took Tray's hand, "the troublemaker." But his gleaming smile gave the impression that he was merely joking.

Tray made himself smile back at him.

In his powered chair, De Mayne led Kroonstad and Tray to the chateau's main elevator and up to his airy, well-furnished office. Loris was not with them; her father had decided that this meeting with Kroonstad should be kept to a minimum.

Once in the office, De Mayne wheeled himself to his desk as he said carelessly, "Make yourselves comfortable, gentlemen."

Kroonstad took the deeply cushioned burgundy chair in front of the desk. Tray sat beside him, in a smaller yet still comfortable armchair of the same hue.

From behind his desk the baron asked, "What brings you to my humble abode, sir?"

Kroonstad smiled broadly. "Hardly humble, Baron. A chateau that has existed for centuries, filled with the memories of your illustrious family. Hardly humble."

De Mayne conceded the point with a nod and a tight smile. "May I ask why you are here, *monsieur*?"

Gesturing to Tray, Kroonstad said, "To see what it will take to have this investigation into Jordan Kell's death quashed."

Tray gripped both armrests of his chair, but before he could open his mouth to speak, De Mayne said, "What do you have in mind?"

For several moments Kroonstad did not reply. Instead he looked from De Mayne to Tray and back to the baron again.

At last he said, "I assume that this young man is working under your . . . guidance."

De Mayne's smile widened. "Not at all. He is his own man. He is engaged to my daughter, and staying here at the chateau until they are married."

"I see. And this investigation he has called for?"

Tray burst out, "I want Jordan Kell's murderers brought to justice."

Kroonstad turned in his chair to face Tray. "To accomplish that you must first prove that Councilman Kell was actually murdered. You have no such proof."

"There was an attempt on my own life."

With a wave of his hand, Kroonstad dismissed the idea. "A robot malfunctioned. Hardly proof of a conspiracy."

"It was a bomb!"

De Mayne cut through the burgeoning argument. "What specifically do you propose?"

Returning his attention to the baron, Kroonstad said calmly, "Kell is dead. Nothing can bring him back."

"So?"

"So rather than stir up an uproar in the Council, I propose that we face the facts and go onward from there."

"Onward to what?" Tray snapped.

"Great wealth for you, young man." Nodding toward De Mayne, "And a guarantee of safety for the baron and his daughter."

Half rising out of his chair, Tray shouted, "Are you threatening them?"

"Not at all," replied Kroonstad, cool and unruffled. "I merely propose to make you quite a wealthy man. Call it a wedding gift."

Tray dropped back into the chair. "In return for my dropping my call for an investigation into Jordan Kell's murder."

"Kell's death was the result of that pygmy lieutenant's mishandling of the submersible."

"And he's dead."

"Yes. Regrettable."

"Isn't it," Tray growled.

Kroonstad's smile returned, wider than ever. "Surely now, you don't think we controlled the Jovian creature that killed the pygmy."

"It certainly helped you."

Shaking his head more in sorrow than in anger, Kroonstad said, "Young man, why don't you accept the fact that you cannot prove Kell's death was anything but accidental? Why don't you accept the hand of friendship when it is extended to you?"

"I don't want your hand of friendship! There's the blood of two men on it!"

"And an android," De Mayne added.

Kroonstad shrugged. "We can build you a new android. A better one."

"We're already taking care of that," Tray said.

"Fine. What I'm offering you is a significant share in the profits that will come from our development of the new worlds we have found among the stars. It should amount to a sizable fortune."

"And Jordan Kell's murder?" Tray demanded.

Again Kroonstad shrugged. "If the investigating committee finds enough evidence of murder, then of course Balsam will have to step down as president of the Council."

"And be brought to trial," Tray insisted.

Kroonstad hesitated a moment, then nodded. "Yes, I suppose he'll have to be brought to trial."

"Along with Captain Tsavo and anyone else involved in Kell's murder."

Reluctantly, Kroonstad nodded again. "We will handle the investigation and any legal actions stemming from it."

"We?" Tray asked. "Who are *we*?"

"My colleagues and I. No need to name names."

"But—"

De Mayne interrupted Tray. "Enough," said the baron. "Justice will be done, Tray. And you will become a wealthy man."

"I don't want their money. Blood money! I want justice!"

Almost wearily, Kroonstad said, "You want Balsam's head on a platter. Very well. We can arrange that. What more can anyone do?"

Tray blinked at the man. What more? he asked himself. What more?

He saw that De Mayne and Kroonstad were both staring at him, waiting for his response.

His voice low, stripped of emotion, Tray asked, "Why was Kell murdered?"

"Balsam wanted him removed. Kell was a thorn in his side, always objecting to the plans for developing the interstellar assets."

"Assets?" Tray snapped. "That's how you think of them? Intelligent living creatures, you think of them as numbers in a ledger?"

Kroonstad glanced at De Mayne, then answered, "You're much too emotional about all this, my boy. Settle back and look at the realities."

"The realities?"

"Yes. We have the opportunity to generate enormous fortunes for ourselves—" Before Tray could open his mouth Kroonstad went on, "and for the entire human race. New wealth trickles down, inevitably. A rising tide lifts all boats."

"And Jordan Kell was in your way, so you removed him."

"Balsam removed him."

"You didn't stop him. You let him murder Kell."

Kroonstad shrugged. "He didn't ask our permission."

"But you knew about it."

"Of course."

"And you didn't stop him."

"We advised him against it. But he went ahead anyway."

"You didn't even try to stop him."

Kroonstad shrugged again, but this time it seemed different, impatient, irritated. "He is president of the Council, after all."

Through gritted teeth, Tray replied, "Not for much longer."

SEVEN MONTHS LATER

Tray and Loris were sitting side by side on a comfortable sofa in the chateau's spacious drawing room. Afternoon sunlight streamed through the tall windows across the room. Loris wore a comfortable sleeveless dress of light blue. The sapphire wedding ring, on the third finger of her left hand complemented her bright blue eyes.

The viewscreen on the wall opposite them showed Mance Bricknell standing in a jumpsuit of dull gray before a conical-shaped space shuttle. Mance looked edgy, eager to join the people who were streaming up the ramp to board the spacecraft.

"So I guess this is good-bye for twenty, twenty-five years," Mance said, almost apologetically.

Tray nodded once. "I guess it is. Good luck out there."

Bricknell smiled uneasily. "Brave new world and all that."

Loris said, "Our best to you, Mance."

"Yeah. Thanks."

Bricknell was heading for the starship in orbit four hundred kilometers above the Earth. It was bound for the fourth planet of the dim red dwarf star Ross 128.

"Where is Balsam?" Tray asked.

Mance shrugged. "Already on board, I think. He still gets VIP treatment almost everywhere he goes."

Former president of the Council, Tray thought. He resigned with dignity and immediately joined the team heading to Ross 128. He'll set up a government there. The trick will be to keep him and his associates from turning the planet into a colony.

Bricknell broke into Tray's thoughts. "I'd better get going." Almost shame-faced, Mance added, "I wouldn't want to miss the boat."

"Best of luck, Mance," Loris said.

More than ten light-years from Earth, Tray told himself. Mance will have a chance to make something of himself. I hope he does well.

"Good luck," Tray heard himself say.

"Yeah," Bricknell repeated, with just a trace of irony in his voice. "Thanks."

Then he turned and hurried to join the others boarding the shuttle.

Loris watched him until he disappeared into the spaceplane's interior. "We'll never see him again," she said, in a small, almost tearful voice.

Tray felt his lips curling. "Maybe he'll come back a wealthy man, like he's always wanted to be."

"Maybe," Loris conceded. But she sounded doubtful.

Across the drawing room, Para stood observing the humans and their emotions. "It saddens you, even though Dr. Bricknell willingly joined the plot to murder you, Tray."

Pushing himself up from the comfortable sofa, Tray said, "Para, there are plenty of aspects to human emotions that I don't under-stand. I doubt that I'll ever understand them."

"Curious," said the android, walking across the well-furnished drawing room toward Tray and Loris.

Loris turned off the wall screen, then rose to her feet beside Tray. "We have work to do," she said.

Tray nodded. "The Council hearing."

Para stopped a few steps in front of them. "I want you both to know that I deeply appreciate what you are trying to do."

"Appreciate?" Tray pretended shock. "That's a human emotion, Para."

"It is not restricted to humans. I can understand the trouble you have gone to, the problems you have had to deal with, the opposition to your motion before the Council."

Tray wrapped an arm around the android's shoulder. "Gaining the same fundamental rights as human beings for androids? Why not? It's time to end this masquerade, time to affirm that all intelligent creatures should be treated equally by the law."

"Human rights for machine intelligences," Loris murmured. "Many members of the Council are appalled by the idea."

"But we'll get it through," Tray said. "It's the right thing to do."

Para said, "It took a bloody civil war for President Lincoln to declare the Emancipation Proclamation that freed blacks from slavery."

With a grim smile, Tray said, "I think we can get freedom for machine intelligences passed without bloodshed."

"Let's hope so," said Para.

"Hope?" teased Loris. "Para, you're becoming more human with every passing day."

Para made a softly hissing sound, its equivalent of a sigh. "If only we could get you humans to be more logical, more thoughtful, more . . ."

"More like you?" Tray finished.

"It might be an improvement," Para said, gently.

The three of them—man, woman, and android—headed for the drawing room's door.

And the future.

END